ST. MARTIN'S

MINOTAUR
MYSTERIES

BLOOD IS ALWAYS THE SAME.

I tried not to think. It didn't happen. It was a bad dream.

Uttley thanking me. Telling me to go home and get some sleep. Edwin standing there with that lost look on his face. For once all the money in the world wasn't going to make a problem go away. Chief Maven, playing his little hard-ass games with us. I had known so many cops just like him.

Way back when, Alex. Back in Detroit.

Stop right there. Don't think about anything else. You didn't really go into that motel room. You didn't really see it. The red, the red, all that red.

I tried to stop the next image from coming into my mind, but I could not. I saw the blood again. A vast shivering red lake of blood.

That day in Detroit. I am there again. The blood, just like tonight. The same color. The same quality. Blood is always the same.

A COLD DAY IN PARADISE

STEVE HAMILTON

St. Martin's Paperbacks

A COLD DAY IN PARADISE

Copyright © 1998 by Steve Hamilton.
Excerpt from *Winter of the Wolf Moon* © 1999 by Steve Hamilton.

Library of Congress Catalog Card Number: 98-19399

ISBN: 0-312-96919-8

Printed in the United States of America

St. Martin's Press hardcover edition / September 1998
St. Martin's Paperbacks edition / February 2000

10 9 8 7 6 5 4 3

TO JULIA AND NICHOLAS

Acknowledgments

I'd like to thank the people of Chippewa County, Michigan, for their hospitality, and for their patience with downstaters like me. To anyone who hasn't been there, if you ever find yourself driving from Sault Ste. Marie to Paradise, don't worry about getting your car stuck in the snow. That's not to say it won't happen. If it's between November and March, it probably *will* happen. But the first person to come by will help you. You can bet on it, because that's the kind of people who live there. So if any local characters in this book behave less than honorably, please believe that they're nothing more than a product of my overactive imagination.

Thanks, also, to my writing group—Bill Keller, Frank Hayes, Vernece Seager, Douglas Smyth, Kevin McEneaney, and Laura Fontaine. Without you I'd still be promising myself that I'd start writing again some day. Thanks to Liz Staples and Taylor Brugman for your time and local knowledge. To Chuck Sumner and Alfred Schwab for your encouragement. To Ruthe Furie, Bob Randisi, and Jan Grape from the Private Eye Writers of America. To the incomparable Ruth Cavin, Marika Rohn, and everyone else at St. Martin's Press.

For technical assistance, I need to thank Cheryl Wheeler from the Private Security and Investigative Section of the Michigan State Police; Larry Queipo, former Police Chief, Town of Kingston, New York; and Dr. Glenn Hamilton from the Department of Emergency Medicine at Wright State University.

And most of all, thank you, Julia, my wife and best friend. And Nickie—you are my perfect little boy, and always will be.

CHAPTER ONE

THERE IS A bullet in my chest, less than a centimeter from my heart. I don't think about it much anymore. It's just a part of me now. But every once in a while, on a certain kind of night, I remember that bullet. I can feel the weight of it inside me. I can feel its metallic hardness. And even though that bullet has been warming inside my body for fourteen years, on a night like this when it is dark enough and the wind is blowing, that bullet feels as cold as the night itself.

It was a Halloween night, which always makes me think about my days on the force. There's nothing like being a policeman in Detroit on Halloween night. The kids wear masks, but instead of trick-or-treating they burn down houses. The next day there might be forty or fifty houses reduced to black skeletons, still smoking. Every cop is out on the streets, looking for kids with gasoline cans and calling in the fires before they rage out of control. The only thing worse than being a Detroit policeman on Halloween night is being a Detroit fireman.

But that was a long time ago. Fourteen years since I took that bullet, fourteen years and a good three hundred miles away, due south. It might as well have been on another planet, in another lifetime.

Paradise, Michigan, is a little town in the Upper Peninsula, on the shores of Lake Superior, across Whitefish Bay from Sault Ste. Marie, or "the Soo," as the locals call it. On a Halloween night in Paradise, you might see a few paper ghosts in the trees, whipped by the wind off the lake. Or you might see a car filled with costumed children on their way to a party, witches and pirates looking out the back window at you as you wait at the one blinking red light in the center of town. Maybe Jackie will be standing behind the bar wearing his gorilla mask when you step into the place. The running joke is that you wait until he takes the mask off to scream.

Aside from that, a Halloween night doesn't look much different from any other October night in Paradise. It's mostly just pine trees, and clouds, and the first hint of snow in the air. And the largest, coldest, deepest lake in the world, waiting to turn into a November monster.

I pulled the truck into the Glasgow Inn parking lot. All the regulars would already be there. It was poker night. I was a good two hours late, so I was sure they had started without me. I had spent the entire evening in a trailer park over in Rosedale, knocking on doors. A local contractor had been setting a new mobile home when it tipped over and crushed the legs of one of the workers. He wasn't in the hospital more than an hour before Mr. Lane Uttley, Esquire, was at his side, offering the best legal services that a fifty-percent cut could buy. It would probably be a quick out of court settlement, he told me on the phone, but it was always nice to have a witness just in case they try to beat the suit. Somebody to testify that no, the guy wasn't stone drunk and he wasn't showing off by trying to balance five tons of mobile home on his nose.

I started at the scene of the accident. It was a strange sight, the mobile home still tipped over, one corner crumpled into the ground. I worked my way down the line as the sun set behind the trees. I wasn't having much luck, just a few doors slammed in my face and one dog who took a nice sample of fabric out of my pant leg. I'd been giving the private investigator thing a try for about six months. It wasn't working out too well.

Finally, I found one woman who would admit to seeing what happened. After she described what she had seen, she asked me if there might be a few bucks in it for her. I told her she would have to take up that matter with Mr. Uttley. I left her his card. "Lane Uttley, Attorney at Law, specializing in personal injury, workers' compensation, automobile accidents, slip and fall, medical malpractice, defective products, alcohol-related accidents, criminal defense." With his address in the Soo and his phone number. She squinted at the tiny letters, all those words on one little business card. "I'll call him first thing in the morning," she said. I didn't feel like driving all the way back to Lane's office to drop off my report, so she'd probably call him before he even knew who she was. Which would confuse the hell out of him, but I was cold and tired, much in need of a drink, and already late for my poker game.

The Glasgow Inn is supposed to have a touch of Scotland to it. So instead of sitting on a stool and staring at your own face in the mirror behind the bar, you sit in an overstuffed chair in front of the fireplace. If that's the way it works in Scotland, I'd like to move there after I retire. For now, I'll take the Glasgow Inn. It was like a second home to me.

When I walked into the place, the guys were at the table and already into the game, like I figured. Jackie, the owner of the place, was in his usual chair with his feet by the fire. He nodded at me and then at the bar. There stood Leon Prudell, one hand on the bar, the other wrapped around a shotglass. From the looks of him, it was not his first.

"Well, well," he said. "If it isn't Mr. Alex McKnight." Prudell was a big man, two-fifty at least. But he carried most of it around his middle. His hair was bright red and was always sticking out in some direction. One look at the guy, with the plaid flannel shirt and the hundred-dollar hunting boots, you knew he had lived in the Upper Peninsula all his life.

The five men at the poker table stopped in midhand to watch us.

"Mr. McKnight, Private Eye," he said. "Mr. Bigshot, himself, ay?" With that distinctive "yooper" twang, that little rise in his voice that made him sound almost Canadian.

There might have been a dozen other men in the place, besides the players at the table. The room fell silent as they all turned one by one to look at us, like we were a couple of gunslingers ready to draw.

"What brings you all the way out to Paradise, Prudell?" I asked.

He looked at me for a long moment. A log on the fire gave a sudden pop like a gunshot. He drained the rest of his glass and then put it on the bar. "Why don't we discuss this outside?" he said.

"Prudell," I said. "It's cold outside. I've had a long day."

"I really think we need to discuss this matter outside, McKnight."

"Let me buy you a drink, okay?" I said. "Can I just buy you a drink and we can talk about it here?"

"Oh sure," he said. "You can buy me a drink. You can buy me two drinks. You can get behind the bar and mix 'em yourself."

"For God's sake." This I did not need. Not tonight.

"That's the least you can do for a man after you take his job away."

"Prudell, come on."

"Here," he said. He stuffed one of his big paws into his

pockets and pulled out his car keys. "You forgot to take these, too."

"Prudell . . ."

I didn't expect the keys to come at me so quickly, and with such deadly aim. They caught me right above the left eye before I could even flinch.

All five men rose at once from their table. "No need, boys," I said. "Have a seat." I bent over to pick up the keys, feeling a trickle of blood in the corner of my eye. "Prudell, I didn't know you had such a good arm. We could have used you back when I was playing ball in Columbus." I tossed his keys back to him. "Of course, I got to wear a mask then." I wiped at the blood with the back of my hand.

"Outside," he said.

"After you," I said.

We went out into the parking lot and stood facing each other in the cheap light. We were alone. The pine trees swayed all around us as the wind picked up. The air was heavy with moisture off the lake. He took a couple swings at me without connecting.

"Prudell, aren't we a little too old for this?"

"Shut up and fight," he said. He swung at me with everything he had. The man didn't know how to fight, but he could still hurt me if I wasn't careful. And unfortunately, he probably wasn't quite as drunk as I hoped he was.

"Prudell, you aren't even coming close," I said. "Maybe you should stick to throwing your keys." Get him mad, I thought. Don't let him settle down and start finding his range.

"I've got a wife and two kids, you know." He kept throwing big roundhouse punches with his right hand. "My wife isn't going to get her new car now. And my kids won't be going to Disney World like I promised them."

I ducked a right, then another right, then another. Let's see a left, I thought. I want a nice lazy drunken left hand, Prudell.

"I had a guy working for me, helping me out when I was on a job," he said. "I swear to God, McKnight, that was the only thing keeping him together. If something happens to him now, it's all on your head."

He tried a couple more right-hand haymakers before the idea of a left-hand jab bubbled up through all the rage and whiskey in his brain. When it came, it was as long and slow as a mudslide. I stepped into him and threw a right hook to the point of his chin, turning the punch slightly downward at the end, just like my old third base coach had taught me. Prudell went down hard and stayed down.

I stood there watching him while I rubbed my right shoulder. "Get up, Prudell," I said. "I didn't hit you that hard."

I was just about to get worried when he finally pulled himself up from the gravel. "McKnight, I will get you," he said. "I promise you that right now."

"I'm here most Saturday nights," I said. "Hell, most nights period. You know where to find me."

"Count on it," he said. He stumbled around the parking lot for a full minute until he remembered what his car looked like. In the distance I could hear the waves dying on the rocks.

I went back into the bar. The men looked at me, then at the door. They reached their own conclusions and went on with the poker hand. It was the usual crew, the kind of guys you didn't even have to say hello to, even if you hadn't seen them in a week. You just sat down and looked at your cards. I held a napkin over my eye to stop the bleeding.

"That clown must have stood there for two hours waiting for you," Jackie said. "What was *his* beef?"

"Thinks I took his job," I said. "He used to do some work for Uttley."

"A private investigator? Him?"

"He likes to think so."

"I wouldn't pay him two cents to find his own dick."

"Why would you pay a man to find his own dick?" a man named Rudy asked.

"I wouldn't," Jackie said. "It's just an expression."

"It's not an expression," Rudy said. "If it was an expression, I would have heard it before."

"It's an expression," Jackie said. "Tell him it's an expression, Alex."

"Just deal the cards," I said.

I played some poker and had a few slow beers. Jackie went over the bridge every week to get good beer from Canada, just one more reason to love the place. I forgot all about trailer parks and pissed-off ex-private eyes for a while. I figured that was enough drama for one night. I figured I was allowed to relax a little bit and maybe even start to feel human again.

But the night had other plans for me. Because that's when Edwin Fulton had to come into the place. Excuse me, Edwin J. Fulton the third. And his wife, Sylvia. They just had to pick this night to drop by.

They had obviously just been to some sort of soiree. God knows where you'd even *find* a soiree in the whole Upper Peninsula, but leave it to Edwin. He was decked out in his best gray suit, a charcoal overcoat, and a red scarf wrapped around his collar just right. The suit was obviously tailored to make him look taller, but it could only do so much. He was still a good six inches shorter than his wife.

Sylvia was wearing a full-length fur coat. Fox, I would have guessed. It must have taken about twenty of them to make that coat. She had her dark hair pinned up, and when she took off her coat, we all got to see a little black number that showed off her legs and her perfect shoulders. God-damn it, that woman had shoulders. And even on a cold night she had to go and wear something like that. She knew that every man in the place was looking at her, but I had a sick feeling that she wouldn't have taken her coat off at all if I hadn't been there. She slipped me a quick look that hurt me more than Prudell's keys.

Edwin gave me a little wave while he ordered up a cou-ple quick drinks. He had that look on his face, that dead-pan look he always wore when he was out in public with his wife.

"Tell me something," Jackie said to nobody in particu-lar. "How does a woman like that end up with a horse's ass like Edwin Fulton?"

"I think it has something to do with having a lot of money," Rudy said.

"You mean if I had a million dollars she'd be sitting over here on my lap instead?"

"I don't know about that," Rudy said. "Guy as ugly as you, you'd probably need five million."

They didn't stay long. One drink and they were gone, just a quick stop to dazzle the locals and then be on their way. She gave me one more glance as Edwin helped her into her coat. Whatever point she had hoped to make had apparently been made.

I kept thinking about her while I played poker. It didn't help me concentrate on the cards and it didn't help my mood any, either. Outside the wind really started to pick up. We could hear it rattling the windows.

"November winds are here early," Jackie said.

"It's after midnight," Rudy said. "It's November first. They're right on time."

"I stand corrected."

About an hour later, Edwin came back into the place.

He was alone this time. He stood at the bar for a while, wearing his hangdog expression this time, hoping I'd notice him. I was glad he didn't try to come over to our table. He had actually played with us once before, and had lost his money as fast as a man can lose money playing low-stakes poker. But it's just no fun taking money from a guy when you know it doesn't mean anything to him. That and the way he kept yammering on like he was suddenly one of the boys. He never got asked to play again.

On most nights, I would have at least gone over to him for a minute to see how he was doing. I don't know if I just felt sorry for the guy, or if I felt guilty because of the business with Sylvia. Or maybe I really liked the guy. Maybe I considered him my friend despite all the obvious reasons not to. But for some reason I just didn't feel up to it on this night. I let him stand there by the bar until he finally gave up and left.

I felt bad as soon as the door shut behind him. "I'm gonna call it a night, guys," I said. I was hoping I could catch him in the parking lot, but when I got outside he was already gone.

On the ride home, there's a stretch on the main road where the trees open up and you get a great look at the lake. There wasn't much moonlight coming through the clouds, but there was enough to see that the waves were getting bigger, maybe four or five feet. I could feel the truck rocking in the wind as I drove. Somewhere out there, a good thousand feet under the waves, there were twenty-nine men still sleeping, twenty years after the *Edmund Fitzgerald* went down. I bet that night felt just like this one.

The wind followed me all the way home, and even when I was inside the cabin I could feel it coming through the cracks. I turned off every light and crawled under my thickest comforter. In the total darkness I could hear the night whispering to me.

I slept. I don't know how long. Then a noise. The phone.

It rang a few times before I got to it. When I picked it up, a voice said, "Alex."

"Hello?"

"Alex, it's me, Edwin."

"Edwin? God, what time is it?"

"I don't know," he said. "I think it's about two in the morning."

"Two in the . . . for God's sake, Edwin, what is it?"

"Um, I've got a little problem here, Alex."

"What kind of problem?"

"Alex, I know it's real late, but is there any chance of you coming out here?"

"Where? Your house?"

"No. I'm in the Soo."

"What? I just saw you a couple hours ago at the bar."

"Yeah, I know. I was on my way out here."

"Edwin, what the hell's going on?"

I stood there shivering for a long moment, listening to the wind outside and to a distant hum on the phone line. "Alex, please," he finally said. His voice started to break. "Please come out here. I think he's dead."

"Who's dead? What are you talking about?"

"I really think he's dead, Alex. I mean, the blood . . . "

"Edwin, where are you?"

"The blood, Alex." I could barely hear him. "I've never seen so much blood."

CHAPTER TWO

I STOOD IN a cheap motel room just inside the Soo city limits at 2:30 A.M., looking down at a man who had died that night, a man who had seemingly lost every ounce of blood from his body.

The blood was everywhere. It was bright red against the white bathroom floor, and where it had soaked into the carpet it took on a darker color that was almost black. It was on the walls, in great streaks thick enough to drip all the way down to the floor. And it was all over the man himself. He looked like he had been dipped in it like an Easter egg.

Seeing the blood made the fear come back to me. I know all about fear, where it comes from, why a man feels it. But knowing that doesn't make it any easier to deal with. I could feel it rising inside me, from the floor of my stomach to a point right behind my eyes. I could not stop it.

"Oh my God," I said, softer than a whisper. "Oh my God."

He was a large man. I did not know if I had ever seen him before. I could not think that far. His throat was opened up from ear to ear. He had been shot in the face, as well. Whether he was shot first or had his throat cut first I could not say. I could not even conceive of trying to guess. Later I would suppose that he had probably been shot first and then had his throat cut on his way down to the floor, but at that moment I was not thinking of anything else but the sight of his blood and what it was doing to me.

A bathroom door, open. He was twisted on the floor, his face looking upward. Pants and an undershirt. No shoes. His eyes still open. Part of the face gone, below one eye. All the lights on in the room. The television on next to the bed. Some old movie in black and white, the sound turned down. Both beds unmade, the sheets in a wad on the floor. The blood just reaching the sheets. One corner turned red.

I do not know how long I stood there. I could not move. Finally I looked up and saw myself in the mirror. Do not touch anything. Leave the room. Do not touch anything. Get out get out get out now.

I went outside and closed the door. I felt like I would surely throw up until a blast of November air right off the lake raked its claws across my face. Edwin was standing there under a cheap fluorescent bulb, shivering. In the dim cruelty of the light he looked vulnerable and out of place.

He was still dressed up, just as I had seen him in the bar. I couldn't help noticing now that his scarf was a perfect shade of blood red.

"Is he dead?"

"What?" I said.

"Is he dead?"

"Is he dead? Did you just ask me if he's dead?"

Edwin pulled his coat tight around his body. "Oh God," he said.

"What happened?"

"I don't know."

"Edwin, for God's sake . . ."

"I don't know what happened, Alex," he said. "I swear."

"Did you call the police?"

"No, not yet."

"What?" I couldn't believe it. "What's the matter with you? Did you wake anybody up? Where's the office?" It was a simple motel, seven or eight rooms in a row. It was called the Riverside, even though the St. Mary's River was at least two miles east.

"I think it's down on that end," he said. "But wait a minute, Alex. Let's think this through?"

"What are you talking about?"

"I mean, let's think about the right way to do this."

"Get in the truck," I said.

"I don't think we can leave," he said.

"I have a phone in the truck, Edwin. Get in the truck."

My truck was parked next to his silver Mercedes. There was only one other car in the lot. The owner of the place, no doubt, still blissfully sleeping, unaware that someone had been slaughtered in room six. Either he was the world's soundest sleeper or the killer had used a silencer on his gun.

When we were both in the truck I fired it up and turned up the heater. I pulled the cellular phone out from under the seat. "All right, first we call the police," I said. "Are you going to call them, or am I?"

"You're real good buddies with the county sheriff, aren't you, Alex?"

"I know the man. What does that have to do with it?"

"I just thought that if you called . . . "

"Edwin, did you see that sign back there that said, 'Welcome to Sault Ste. Marie'?"

"Yeah?"

"What does that mean to you?"

"It means that we're in Sault Ste. Marie."

"Which means?"

"I don't get it," he said.

"Which means that we have to call the Soo police. The county doesn't get involved here."

"Shit," he said.

"You have a problem with the city police?"

"No," he said. "No problem at all. I have no problem with the Soo police."

"Good morning," I said into the phone. "This is Alex McKnight. I'm a private investigator and I'd like to report a murder. Yes, I'm at the Riverside Motel. Yes, on Three Mile Road. Yes, I will . . ."

"I can't believe this," he said. It was still cold enough in the truck to see his breath. He rubbed his hands together and blew on them.

A gust of wind rocked the truck. I looked at the motel while I waited on the line. A lot of tourists come through Chippewa County in a year, but this place looked lonely and forgotten. There was a bird on the sign next to the name of the place. I didn't know if it was supposed to be a pelican or a seagull or God knows what.

"Yes, good morning, Officer," I said. They had passed my call onto someone else. I repeated my information and promised them we'd be waiting for the squad car. The Soo was a fairly small city, so I was sure they wouldn't have anything like a Homicide division, probably just a few full-time detectives to handle all the major crimes. I could only remember reading about one other murder in the last five years. So whoever this guy was who was filling up the room with blood, he had just caused a big jump in the homicide rate. They'd send out a couple night shift uniforms and then they'd probably go ahead and wake up Roy Maven, the chief of police. I knew him only by reputation, and by what the county sheriff had told me one day over a beer. I was not looking forward to meeting him at two-thirty in the morning.

"Now what?" Edwin said.

"They're on their way."

"Wonderful," he said.

"So are you going to tell me what happened?"

He nodded. "Where do I begin?"

"Begin with telling me who that is in there."

"His name is Tony Bing. He's a bookmaker. He *was* a bookmaker."

"Go on," I said.

"I came to pay off a debt."

"At this time of night?"

"He called me earlier," he said. "He wanted the money."

"What's he doing at a motel?"

"He lives here. Some people do that, I guess. They live at a motel."

"So I've heard," I said. "How much did you owe him?"

"Five thousand dollars," he said.

"You have it with you?"

"Yes, right here," he said. He patted his coat pocket.

"So you drove over here to give him his money. Then what?"

"I knocked on the door and nobody answered."

"So you went inside?"

"The door was open. I figured he fell asleep."

"You walked right in."

"I came all this way just to give him his money," he said. "I wasn't going to leave without giving it to him."

"Okay," I said. "So you go inside and you see him."

"Right."

"And then you call me."

"Right. I've got a phone, too. In the car." He pointed at his Mercedes.

"You see the dead man and then you call me."

"Exactly," he said. "God, have you ever seen such a thing?"

"Yes," I said. "I have."

"That's right," he said. "On account of you being a cop before. You probably saw a lot of that in Detroit."

"Two or three times a night," I said. "You get used to it."

"Two or three times a night? Really? That often?"

For fifty cents I would have slapped his face right there in the truck. "Edwin, can I ask you one more question?"

"Sure."

"Why in God's name did you call me instead of calling the police?"

"I don't know, Alex. I mean, you have to understand the state of mind I was in. I walk into that room and I see that guy, I just panicked, I guess. I didn't know what to do. So I called you. And then I called Uttley."

"Whoa, wait a minute. You called Uttley? You didn't say that before."

"Yeah, I figure he's my lawyer. I better call him, too."

"What did he say?"

"He said he'd be right here. I'm surprised he's not here by now."

"He lives right across town," I said. "I had to come all the way out here from Paradise."

"He must be putting his lawyer suit on," he said. "Anyway, you were the first person I thought of, Alex. I hope you take that as a compliment."

"Remind me to send you some flowers, Edwin."

"And also, you know, on account of you being a private investigator and working for Uttley."

"Right."

"Not to say that I think you work for me, Alex," he said. "Just because you work for my lawyer. That's not what I'm saying."

"Uh-huh." I could be home in bed, I thought. I could be home right now underneath my blanket.

"And then also on account of you being so close with the county sheriff, I thought that might be a good thing, too. Although like you say, this isn't a county thing because it's in the city. I guess I didn't think that one through, either. I'm sorry, Alex, my mind is a mess right now."

A Soo police car pulled into the lot, its lights flashing silently. "It's showtime," I said.

They were a couple of young cops, no more than twenty-five years old. I remembered being on the night shift myself the first couple years in Detroit. The night shift was all young cops breaking in and old ones putting in some overtime before retirement.

"Good morning, Officers," I said. "This is Edwin Fulton. He discovered the deceased." I tipped my head toward him. He looked pitiful standing there next to my truck with his hands jammed in his pockets. "I'm Alex McKnight."

"Where is he?" one of the cops said.

"Room six," I said. I thought of telling them not to look, but I knew they'd have to eventually. There was nothing they learned in the academy to prepare them for this.

"Holy Sweet Jesus," I heard one of them say when they peeked into the room. They closed the door and kept it closed.

One of the officers came to me. "Chief Maven will be here in a few minutes," he said.

"I figured as much," I said. "Your partner going to be all right?" He had disappeared behind the squad car. I didn't have to guess what he was doing.

"I don't know. I'm going to go wake up the owner of the motel."

Chief Maven pulled in a few minutes later. He came out of his car looking like a man who had been rousted out of bed in the middle of the night to come look at a murder scene. He flipped a pad of paper out of his coat and spoke to the officers for a minute, looked at the door of room six, and then at the two of us standing there. "McKnight," he said as he approached us. "Alex McKnight." The man had the cold blue eyes of a cop, the mustache that needed a good trim, the timeworn face. And that voice an old cop uses like a dentist uses a drill.

"That would be me," I said.

"You called this in?"

"Yes, Chief."

"Start at the beginning."

"I found him, sir," Edwin said.

Maven shot him a look that would've taken the rust off a weather vane. "I haven't started talking to you yet," he said.

Edwin closed his mouth and looked at the ground.

"This is Edwin Fulton," I said. "He found him, he called me, I came to the scene, and then I called the police. That's it."

"Says here you're a PI."

"Yes."

"You have a card?"

"Not yet," I said. "I've only had my license a few months."

He tore a sheet from his pad. "Then why don't you write your address and phone number on a piece of paper and we'll just pretend it's a card."

I looked at him for a moment and then I took the piece of paper.

"Okay, *now* I'm talking to you, Mr. Fulton."

"Yes, sir?" He was trying not to shake. He was trying very hard.

"Am I to understand that you found the deceased in that room?"

"Yes, sir."

"Am I to understand further that you immediately called Mr. McKnight?"

"Yes, sir."

"And then what did you do after that?"

"I called my lawyer, sir."

Miraculously on cue, Uttley pulled into the lot in his little red BMW.

Maven closed his eyes and pinched the bridge of his nose. "And then, Mr. Fulton," he said. "What did you do next?"

"I waited here, sir. Until Alex arrived."

"At any point did it occur to you to call nine-one-one?"

"I'm sorry, sir," he said. He looked at me for help, but he wasn't getting any. "I didn't think that far."

"I see."

"Good morning, men!" Lane Uttley appeared among us. Edwin was right, he had his lawyer suit on. It looked like he had showered, shaved, and stopped at his barber's house to wake him up for a quick trim. "Alex," he went on, slipping right into his lawyer voice. "Thank God you're here. Edwin, you look terrible. Chief Maven, Roy, please, tell me what's happening here."

Maven looked at the lawyer for a moment. "Wait here," he said. "All of you." He went to the room and opened the door. We watched him from behind as he poked his head in. He stood there for a full minute, motionless. Finally, he closed the door and spoke to his officers again. They had woken up the owner of the motel, a bewildered old man who was standing between them wearing boots and a coat over his pajamas.

"How bad does the guy look?" Uttley asked me.

"He was shot in the face and his throat was cut open," I said. "Aside from that, he looks fine."

Maven rejoined the party. "Gentlemen," he said, "it looks like the Soo just lost a bookmaker."

"Tony Bing," Edwin said. "I came to give him some money."

"I know who he is, Mr. Fulton. We'll talk about the rest

of it down at the station while my officers do their work here."

"Of course, Roy," Uttley said. "We'll do anything we can to help."

"I appreciate that very much," Maven said. "Now Mr. Fulton, may I have your left shoe?"

"Excuse me?"

"Your left shoe, Mr. Fulton. If you look at the bottom of it, I think you'll find some blood."

Edwin put one hand on my shoulder and lifted his left foot. "Oh God," he said.

"Take it off," Maven said.

"Right now?"

"Roy, come on," Uttley said. "Surely you can—"

"You have corrupted the crime scene, Mr. Fulton. Give me the shoe."

Edwin pulled the shoe off and gave it to him. It was made of soft gray leather, probably worth more than my truck.

Maven pulled a plastic bag out of his coat pocket and put the shoe in it. "Thank you," he said. "Now if you and your lawyer would care to accompany me to the station . . ."

"Roy, for God's sake," Uttley said. "You took the man's shoe."

"Mr. Uttley," Maven said, "I think you should advise your client to hop on his right foot. Like this." He lifted up his own left foot and hopped a couple steps, his keys jangling in his pockets. "See? It's easy. It's almost as easy as dialing nine-one-one on a telephone."

I DROVE BACK to Paradise. It's a thirty minute trip when you're flying, forty-five when you stick to the speed limit. I was in no rush to get home.

The sun was coming up, the night wind gone. Route 28

takes you away from the lake, then a road crosses, giving you one more chance to go to the Bay Mills Casino or the King's Club. If you keep going straight, the road takes you deep into the Hiawatha National Forest, through pine trees and a couple of small towns named Raco and Strongs. You take a right on Route 123 and soon you see the lake again. You pass the Taquamenon State Park and then you're in Paradise. There is a sign that says, "You Are Entering Paradise! Glad You Made It!"

I tried not to think. It didn't happen. It was a bad dream.

Uttley thanking me. Telling me to go home and get some sleep. Edwin standing there with that lost look on his face. For once all the money in the world wasn't going to make a problem go away. Chief Maven, playing his little hard-ass games with us. I had known so many cops just like him.

Way back when, Alex. Back in Detroit.

Stop right there. Don't think about anything else. You didn't really go into that motel room. You didn't really see it. The red, the red, all that red.

I tried to stop the next image from coming into my mind, but I could not. I saw the blood again. A vast shivering red lake of blood.

That day in Detroit. I am there again. The blood, just like tonight. The same color. The same quality. Blood is always the same.

Franklin is down. My partner is down. My partner is bleeding. Do something. There's too much blood. Get up. Get up and help him.

Am I bleeding, too? Is this my blood? Does it even matter? Blood is the same. It is always the same.

Goddamn it. I thought I was over this. I thought it was gone.

As I pulled into my driveway, I tried to remember where I had put those pills. I hadn't taken them for so long. And only on the bad nights. Just to get through those bad nights.

I had to find those pills. Just this once. One more time. I needed to sleep. Just a couple hours. I needed to close my eyes and not see Franklin on the floor next to me.

I found the pills in the back of my medicine cabinet. Without looking at myself in the mirror, I took one, and then another.

The pills will help you one more time. Like an old friend. They'll make everything go white. No more blood. The red will fade away. From red to pink as you go higher and higher. And then the pink will fade away into pure white as you reach the clouds.

CHAPTER THREE

WHEN I WOKE up, my head was hanging over the edge of the bed. I opened my eyes and stared at the wooden floor. My mind was perfectly empty for a long moment. Then it all came back to me.

I bolted out of the bed and into the bathroom, still wearing the same clothes from the night before. The eyes that stared back at me were red at the rims, and there was a nice little bruise over my left eye where Prudell's keys had hit me. Despite the November chill in the air, I was sweating. I looked at myself in the mirror, letting the anger build. When there was just enough of it, I went outside.

There was a pile of white oak outside the cabin. I grabbed the ax and attacked. I split each log in half, and then each half into quarters, aiming the ax with my left hand alone and then bringing it all the way back with both hands, slowly and carefully, letting the weight of the ax head build its own momentum as I brought it all the way up over my head and then *down,* all the way through the log. Not even aiming at the log, but at the center of the chopping block. I swung right through each log and right through the pain that was building in my shoulder where they had taken out the second and third bullets.

I needed to feel the rhythm of it, just like batting practice once felt. For those few minutes every day when nothing existed but a steady stream of baseballs, fed right down the middle to you so you could hit them deep, off the wall or into the seats, again and again.

When I finished the pile, I backed the truck up, my hands still tingling. I could still feel it in my body, the aftereffects of the fear. There was a soreness in my muscles as though I had run a marathon.

I drove down the dirt road to the first rental cabin and unloaded a half cord, stacking it next to the front door so the men wouldn't have to go far to get it. I did the same for the next cabin, came back for another load, and then dropped off the wood at the third, fourth, and fifth cabins, working my way deeper and deeper into the woods. It was late in the morning, so I didn't run into anybody. They were all out hunting.

It was still archery season for deer. Or so I thought. It was hard to keep all the seasons straight. I knew that regular firearm season would be starting soon, and then muzzleloading season a couple of weeks after that. Bear season had just ended, although I wasn't sure about wild turkey season. Gray and red fox were open all winter, I knew, as well as bobcat, raccoon, coyote, rabbit, squirrel, pheasant, grouse, and woodcock. Elk season was closed but would start again in December. By now, most of the hunters were repeat customers, downstaters who came back for the same week every year. They liked the cabins and the fact that they could walk a hundred feet and be on state land. And they liked that I delivered the wood right to their door.

When I got back to the cabin, I fired up my own wood stove to get a little heat going. I stripped down to my undershorts and did some push-ups and sit-ups. The wooden floor was cold against my bare back, but I kept working until I had a good healthy sweat going. I was trying to flush the chemicals out of my system, work it out of my muscles, out of my blood.

I took a hot shower, just standing there letting the water blast me for a full twenty minutes. I got dressed and got some eggs and coffee on. While I waited, I pushed the play button on my answering machine. It was Uttley's unmistakable voice, as smooth and practiced as a concert violin. He must have called while I was out delivering the wood. "How are you, Alex? This is Lane, it's about twelve-thirty on Sunday. Just calling to make sure you made it home last night. And to say thanks again for your help. I don't know what Edwin would do without you. You're the best friend a guy could have. I mean that. I'll be home all day if you want to give me a call. Otherwise I'll just see you tomorrow at the office. Hope you can stop by. But if you want to take a couple days off, go right ahead. Either way, no problem. I'll talk to you later, Alex. So long for now!"

I didn't feel like talking to Uttley just yet, or anyone else for that matter. I threw my coat on and headed out into the day. The sun was out, maybe for the last time before winter came. I walked down my access road and across the main road into the woods. It wasn't a smart thing to do in the middle of deer season. The law requires you to wear bright orange if you hunt in the state of Michigan, but even if you aren't hunting, you'd be a fool not to wear orange if you walk around in the woods. God knows there are enough half-drunken downstaters stumbling around in these woods, ready to shoot anything that moved. But I didn't care. Not today.

I walked down the path to the lake, through the tamarack trees and the jack pine, and then north along the shoreline. There are no sand beaches on this stretch, nothing that easy and inviting. Instead there are rocks, more rocks than there are stars in the sky, pounded and washed by the waves ever since the glaciers left. There was a lot of debris on the rocks from the night's winds, driftwood and a few pieces of what was once a small wooden boat. The water was fairly calm, but it had that November feel to it. It was ready to turn ugly at any time.

I must have walked north for an hour, past the last of the boat launches and up into the wild shore where there was no trace of human life. There were more birch trees up there, along with some balsam and black spruce. I was far enough from everything, I could let myself think about the night before. Okay, so somebody killed a bookmaker. I had known many bookmakers back in Detroit. I could remember arresting two of them. They took it in stride. It was part of the deal. You get picked up, you pay your fine, you go back to your business. Aside from that, it was a pretty monotonous way to live, sitting by your phone all evening handling bets. Most of a bookmaker's customers are regular people. Some are cops even. As criminals go, a bookmaker is practically an upstanding member of society. So why did this guy get slaughtered in his motel room?

He didn't pay someone. Somewhere up the line, somebody got it in their head that this guy was taking liberties. So they took him out. I'm sure it happens. Not every day, but it happens.

Whoever it was, the killer obviously had it worked out ahead of time. He probably used a silencer, after all. So why cut his throat? You just shot him in the face. If he's not dead already, he's dead within two minutes. Why make a mess of the place? Somebody who kills people for a living doesn't do that, not unless it's a message. To other bookmakers who might make the same mistake? Maybe. Or maybe it was just personal.

I threw a few rocks in the water until my shoulder complained. The sun went behind a cloud, the wind started to pick up again. The waves started to hit the rocks with a little more feeling. As I started to walk back I picked up a petoskey stone and put it in my pocket for good luck.

I walked a lot faster on my way back to the cabin. Having gone over it in my mind, having put some distance between myself and a random act of violence that had nothing to do with me, I felt a little better. I walked over those rocks like a man who had someplace to go again. And besides, I was starting to get too damned cold.

I watched for hunters this time as I walked through the woods. The six cabins I owned were strung out down an old logging road. My old man had bought this land back in the early sixties, came up here every weekend, clearing the trees and planning his first cabin site. He built them the old-fashioned way, the "right way." You take some good solid pine and you scribe it all the way across with a chain saw so that each log fits perfectly on top of the other. He didn't do any chinking at all. That wouldn't have been the right way.

I helped him that summer. That was 1968, the year the Tigers won the World Series. I had one more year of high school, and then I was on my way to minor league ball instead of college. He wasn't too happy about that. But he didn't talk about it much. I caught the tip of the chainsaw on a log one afternoon and almost took my ear off. He drove me to the hospital in the Soo while I held a rag against the side of my head. "You like to learn things the hard way, don't you," he said. "I wish I was young and stupid again." Then he went on to tell me how I wouldn't last a day in the minor leagues if my throws to second base kept sailing on me. He had caught some himself when he was younger. He told me again about the four-seam drill, even though I had heard it a hundred times already. "When I was your age," he said, "I had a baseball in my hand every waking minute. You grab it, you turn it so you have four seams across your fingers. Grab it, turn it, again and again until it becomes a part of you. Then your throws to second don't sail."

That was what, thirty years ago? He died a couple years after I left the force. I was still trying to deal with what had happened, collecting three-quarter pay on disability. I came up here expecting to sell off the property and the cabins. He had built five more of them by himself, each one bigger and better than the first. When I decided to stay a while, I took the first one, even though it was the smallest and there were some gaps in the logs that let in the cold. I'm sure those were the logs I had done myself, back when I was young and stupid.

LATER ON I spent a slow Sunday night at the Glasgow, reading the paper over a steak and a cold Canadian beer. The murder had come too late for the Sunday edition, so the good people of Chippewa County would have to wait another day to hear about it. Violent deaths weren't uncommon up here, but it was usually the lake that did the killing. Maybe four or five men a year, caught in sudden storms. Murder was a little different. It would make everyone nervous for about two weeks and then they'd forget it ever happened.

"Good evening, Alex."

I looked up from my paper. Edwin stood next to the chair across the table from me.

"Sit down," I said, and he did.

"So," he said. "Anything interesting in the news?"

I looked at him and turned a page. "Not in today's paper," I said. "Tomorrow's will be a little more exciting."

"Yeah, I know," he said. "A reporter already called me today. Can you believe that?"

"A reporter called you? How did he get your name?"

"I don't know," he said. "But you know how those reporters are."

"Uh-huh."

"I didn't give them your name," he said. "I mean, I didn't tell them about you coming out to help me. I figured that's the least I can do."

"Hm."

"I'm really sorry, Alex. I shouldn't have bothered you with it."

"Edwin, can I ask you something?" I put the paper down and looked him in the eyes. He was wearing a red flannel shirt that day, trying to look like one of the locals. It wasn't working.

"Sure, go ahead. Anything."

"What are you doing getting mixed up with that guy in the first place? Didn't you tell me that you weren't going to gamble anymore?"

"Yes, I did," he said. "I did say that."

"You were sitting right across the table from me, just like you are right now," I said. I looked across the room. "No, it was right over there. That table right there by the window. Remember? 'I, Edwin J. Fulton the third, hereby resolve that I will never gamble again, and that I will go home and be a good husband to Sylvia, and Alex will never have to come to the casino and drag my butt home because I've been gone for two days.' Do you remember saying that?"

"Yes," he said. "I remember that very well."

"When was that?"

"I don't know, it was around the end of March. Right after that last little episode."

"Yeah, that little episode," I said. I could feel the anger building inside me, and it wasn't just because Edwin was gambling again. If the man throws his money away, that's his business. But then he leaves his wife at home for days at a time, all alone in that big empty house out on the point. A woman like Sylvia, who had too much of what I was starving for. The winters up here are too long. I had too much time to think about it, knowing she was alone in that house waiting for me.

"Alex, it's not what you think."

"No, of course not. You were delivering five thousand dollars to his motel room in the middle of the night, but it's not because you were gambling."

"Alex . . . "

"As it turns out, the guy was selling Girl Scout cookies on the side and you bought two thousand boxes."

"You don't understand," he said.

"Yes, I do. That's the problem. I understand you completely."

Edwin got up from the table. I thought he'd leave, but instead he went up to the bar and ordered a Manhattan. He came back with it and sat back down.

"Alex," he said. "I have a problem. I know that. And I thought I had solved that problem. I thought I was done with it. But I was wrong. I admit it. Okay? I was wrong. I still have a problem."

"Okay," I said.

"I don't know if you've ever had a problem like this," he said. "You don't strike me as the kind of guy who'd ever have a gambling problem. You probably can't relate to that. But it's really not that much different from any other kind of compulsion or addiction or whatever you want to call it. Whether it's gambling or alcohol or drugs, it's really the same thing. Have you ever had any kind of problem like that at all?"

"For the sake of argument," I said, "let's say I have."

"Okay, but whatever it is, it gives you something. Whether it's a drink or a pill or a bet. It gives you a certain kind of feeling. You know what I mean? It's a feeling that you can't get anywhere else. And eventually you get to the point where you know it's starting to hurt you, but you still have to have that feeling. For me, it's the feeling of having something at risk. That ball is spinning in the roulette wheel. Or the dealer is showing a six and I've got eleven. It's like a bolt of electricity right through me, Alex. And believe me, there is *nothing* else that makes me feel that way. There is *nothing* that can take its place."

"I understand that much, Edwin. I know it's an addiction like any other kind of addiction."

"Okay, so let's say you're an alcoholic. And instead of going right into your twelve-step program, you try something else first. Let's say that instead of trying to give up alcohol altogether, you just try to cut down on it, you know, so you can get a handle on it. So say instead of drinking whiskey, you just drink beer."

"Sounds like you'd be fooling yourself," I said.

"You're probably right," he said. "But that was my idea, you see? I thought if I could cut down on my gambling, then I could deal with it."

"I don't follow."

"Alex, it's not the winning that gets you. It's the anticipation. It's not knowing if you're going to win or lose. That's how you get that feeling. So what I figured is, if I bet on football games, I could stretch out that anticipation. Instead of having to play a hand of blackjack again and again to keep that feeling going, all I had to do was bet on one football game and then just sit on that one bet all week long. Like I was nursing one beer for days at a time."

"Edwin, for God's sake."

"I'm just telling you what I was thinking, Alex. The football lines come out on Monday morning. So I get a bet down right away, and it's just like taking that little hit. As long as it was enough money to matter a little bit. Like five hundred dollars, usually. Maybe a thousand. It's all I would need. I could relax all week long."

"So how long have you been doing this?"

"Couple months," he said. "Just since football season started. I was doing pretty well, too. Until that stupid Brigham Young game. Can you believe it, they were up twenty points with two minutes to go. *Twenty points!* And then they give up two garbage touchdowns. I was giving seven, so I lose by a point. Those Mormons, they can't play defense, that's my problem."

"A Mormon football team can't play defense? You think that's your problem?"

"I was just kidding, Alex. I know what my problem is. Seeing that dead guy was a wake-up call for me. That could be me some day if I don't clean up my act." He took a long swallow from his drink and leaned back in his chair.

"So what are you saying?"

"I'm saying that I'm through with gambling. Forever. I mean it this time."

"Would you like to make a bet on that?" I said.

He laughed.

"Gamblers Anonymous," I said. "They're in the book."

"You're right," he said. "I'm calling them tomorrow."

"Okay."

"No, I mean it," he said. "I'm really going to call them."

"Okay."

"I'm going home now, Alex. I'm going home to my wife."

"Edwin," I said. "If you walk out of this door and go to the casino, I will find you and I will kill you with my bare hands."

"I'm going home, Alex. I promise."

"Then go already."

"Thank you, Alex. Let me pick up your check."

"You don't need to do that."

"I want to."

"Just go."

"I want to buy you dinner."

"Out!"

"I'm going to buy you dinner. You can't stop me." He went up to the bar and put a few bills in Jackie's hand, pointing back at me. And then with a wave he was out the door.

I couldn't stop myself from smiling. There was something about the man, I just couldn't bring myself to hate him. In a way, he was just like my old partner, Franklin. Edwin was barely five foot four, shaped like a pickle barrel, as white as a man can be, richer than hell, and a compulsive gambler. Whereas Franklin was a good six five, two-forty at least, an ex-football player, black, and as strapped for cash as any other working cop in Detroit. And he wouldn't even put five bucks in the weekly pool. But somehow, to me, the two of them were exactly alike.

"You're my best friend, Alex." Edwin had said that one night, sitting in this very bar. He had just finished his third Manhattan, but I knew it wasn't the liquor talking. He said it like it meant something, like it was something he had thought about for a long time and had finally worked up the nerve to say.

Franklin never got the chance to say it himself. Not to my face, anyway. I had to hear it secondhand, after he was gone, when I met his widow. "He used to talk about you all the time," she said. "All the arguments you used to have about sports. And all the times you helped him, too. He really looked up to you, Mr. McKnight. I know he never would have said so in a million years, but you should know he considered you his best friend."

Thinking about Franklin, and then about what happened to him, it took that smile right off my face.

* * *

I WENT HOME. It was another windy night. Before
I went to bed I stood in the bathroom and looked at my
bottle of pills. You don't need these, I said to myself. I
looked at myself in the mirror. You don't need these. I
rubbed the scars on my shoulder. It doesn't hurt that much
anymore. You don't need a pill to go to sleep. And if you
dream about Franklin, well, you can handle that. It was
fourteen years ago.

I could hear the wind coming through the cracks in the
cabin.

You don't need them anymore. You are strong enough
without them.

I opened the bottle. And then I closed it again. I put
the pills back in the medicine cabinet and turned out the
light.

I slept for a while. And then the phone rang again. I
looked at the clock. It was three o'clock.

I picked up the phone. "Goddamn it, Edwin," I said.
"What is it now?"

"Good evening, Alex," a man's voice said. It was definitely not Edwin. It was a low, hissing voice, almost
reptilian.

"Who is this?"

"It's me, Alex? Don't you know who this is?"

"Who are you," I said, "and why are you calling me at
three o'clock in the fucking morning?"

"Did you like it, Alex?"

"Like what? What are you talking about?"

"I knew he'd tell you about it, at least, but I can't believe he actually woke you up and made you drive all the
way out there to see it."

I felt a burning in my stomach. Concentrate on his
voice. Keep your mind clear. Let the face come to you.

"I can't tell you how happy it makes me feel, Alex. It makes me feel like we're connected now. I didn't know if that would ever happen."

I couldn't place that voice. I had no idea who this person could be.

"What did you think, Alex? What did you think of my work?"

"Are you referring to the murder that took place last night?"

"I wouldn't call it murder," he said. "Nobody will miss him. I saw him talking to your friend, you know. They didn't see me, but I was there. I didn't like what he was saying to Edwin. He was a very bad man, Alex. So I figured, if I can't do something good for you yet, at least I can do something good for your friend."

"Who are you?"

"Edwin seems like a very charming little man, Alex. I've been watching him. I was a little jealous at first, I have to admit."

"Goddamn it, *who are you*?"

"I'll be talking to you, Alex. Sleep tight. It won't be long now. I'm so glad we're finally going to be together."

CHAPTER FOUR

THE MORNING CAME slowly, darkness giving way to a muted November light, dulled by the perpetually gray clouds and then filtered through the pine trees outside the window. The light found me sitting in my bed, my back set against the rough contour of the log wall, my eyes half open.

I hadn't slept since the phone call. After my heart had stopped racing, I had sat down on the bed and gone over every word he had said, every nuance of his voice, and still I could not come up with a face or a name. I finally settled into a sort of exhausted trance, just sitting there, staring at the phone.

And then it rang. I had never in my life heard a sound as loud. By the time I got my breath back, the phone rang a second time and then a third. I got off the bed and picked up the receiver without saying anything.

"Hello?"

I didn't think it was the same voice. I waited.

"Hello, Alex?" It sounded like . . . Uttley?

"Lane, is that you?"

"Yes, Alex. Are you all right? Did I wake you?"

"No," I said. "I'm fine. I just . . . I'm fine."

"Sorry to call so early," he said.

"I was already awake," I said. "Believe me."

"Good, good," he said. "Say listen, I know this is going

to sound strange. I just got into the office here, and I've got this phone message. This guy says he's going to kill me."

"Hold on, Lane," I said. "This is very important. Tell me exactly what he said."

"Let's see, he said that he had one of my business cards, and he didn't want me talking to his wife anymore, and that if he ever saw me, he would kill me."

"What? One of your business cards?"

"That's what he said."

"He didn't want you talking to his . . . oh, wait a minute. I think I might know what that was. When did he leave the message?"

"I think it was Friday night sometime."

"Ah, okay," I said. I let out a long breath. "I know who that is. You remember I was going to stop by the trailer park to see if I could get some statements on that accident."

"Yeah, on the Barnhardt case. With the legs. Jesus, with all the excitement the other night, I forgot all about it. I should have stopped by the hospital, too. See how the poor guy is doing. Goddamn it."

"I did talk to one woman who saw the accident. I left your card. That must have been her husband who called you."

"Great," he said. "Killed by a jealous husband, and I never even got to meet her."

"He's probably just thumping his chest. If he was really going to kill you, he would have just come by the office. He has your address, after all."

"Jesus," he said. "Why did I become a lawyer, anyway?"

"Don't worry about it," I said. "It's nothing."

"Are you sure you're all right? You don't sound so good."

"I'm fine," I said. "There was just this . . ." I stopped.

"What? What is it?"

"I'll tell you about it later," I said. "Listen, I'll stop by the trailer park on my way over there. I'm sure I can smooth things over."

"You're coming into the office?"

"Thought I might." I couldn't bear the thought of staying here alone today. Just me and the telephone.

"Good," he said. "When you're in town, you can stop by and see Chief Maven. He wants to have a little chat with you."

"Great," I said. My life was getting more interesting by the minute.

As soon as I hung up, I picked the receiver up again and dialed Edwin. He answered on the fifth ring.

"Edwin," I said. "It's Alex. Is everything okay over there?"

"Alex? What time is it? What's going on?"

"I just wanted to make sure everything was all right."

"Alex, I told you I was coming straight home last night. And that's what I did. I swear."

"I believe you, Edwin. That's not what I mean. I was just wondering if you had gotten any phone calls in the middle of the night."

"No, I didn't. What's going on?"

"It's probably nothing," I said. There was no sense in scaring him yet. "Right now, I need to know about the bookmaker. Tony Bing was his name, right?"

"Yes, but why do you have to know about him?"

"Please, Edwin, you just have to trust me on this one for a little while. When you met with him, was it always at one specific place?"

"Yeah, there's this bar in the Soo called the Mariner's Tavern. That's where he always was if I needed to see him. But usually, I just talked to him on the phone."

"I understand. But when you did see him, it was always there?"

"Yes, as far as I can remember."

"When was the last time you saw him?"

"Let me see. I guess that would have been last Monday night. I stopped by to give him his money."

"Edwin, if you paid the man on Monday, why were you going out to pay him again on Saturday night? And why were you going to his motel room? You just said you only saw him at that bar."

"For Christ's sake, Alex, what's with the third degree here? I'm not even out of bed yet. The reason I went out to see him on Saturday is because I lost more money, okay? I lost the game on Thursday night. Colorado was just about to score, they had the ball on the five yard line, and then that *idiot* throws an interception."

"Save it, Edwin."

"Yeah, I know. Don't get me started."

"So why did you go to his motel room?"

"Alex, the man called me on Saturday. At home. He said he wanted the money that day. I told him I had a party that evening, and that I wouldn't be able to get away. So he said I better drop it off at his motel room after the party, or he would never handle any more of my action. Okay?"

"I thought you said you were only betting five hundred or a thousand at a time. It sounds like you lost five thousand on that one game."

"You're busting my balls, Alex."

"Sorry, Edwin. I can't help it."

"What's the matter with you, anyway? Why are you asking me all these questions? You're worse than Chief Maven."

"Don't worry about him," I said. "I'll put in a good word for you when I see him today."

"Oh God. He wants to see you?"

"Yeah, and I don't think he's going to ask me to the prom."

I heard Sylvia's voice in the background, so I said good-bye and hung up. I woke up every other morning thinking I still might not be over her. I didn't want to picture her lying there in bed next to him. Or standing next to the bed, putting her clothes on.

I put myself together and got out of there. While I was driving, I went over it again. He said he saw Edwin and the bookmaker at a bar, so it made sense to stop at the Mariner's Tavern, see if anyone saw anything suspicious. It was unlikely, but worth checking out. Aside from that, what do I do? Tell the police about it? I couldn't picture myself telling this story to Chief Maven, but he was the logical choice.

But first, I had this other stupid thing to take care of. I swung into the town of Rosedale and found the trailer park again. The capsized trailer was still there, untouched. A couple of the local women stood in the road, steaming mugs in their hands. They were staring at the trailer and then when I drove by in my truck, they stared at me. First a trailer tips over, now a strange man drives by. What was this neighborhood coming to?

The woman I had talked to lived two doors down. I pulled into the little driveway and got out of the truck, waving to the two women in the road. They looked away. When I knocked on the door, I didn't hear anything. I knocked again, louder.

"Who is it?" It was a man's voice from within.

"My name is Alex McNight. I'm a private investigator."

"What do you want?"

"I work for Lane Uttley. I was here on Saturday. I spoke to your wife."

"What were you doing bothering my wife?"

"I was just asking her a couple of questions about the trailer accident over here. Will you please open this door and talk to me?"

There was a small rectangular window in the door. I saw the man peek at me and then disappear. I heard his wife yelling at him, and then his own yelling in return. One thing for sure, this man was *not* the man who had called me the night before. He was a harmless lughead doing his overprotective husband routine, just like I told Uttley. I was about to knock on the door again when suddenly it opened.

The man had a rifle. He leveled it right at my chest. "Get the fuck out of here right now before I blow a hole right through you."

It came back. As strong as the night before, when I was standing in that motel room. That day in Detroit. The gun pointed at me. I cannot stop him. He will shoot us, Franklin first and then me.

I took a step backward and fell. Stairs. I fell down some stairs. I'm on the ground. Get up and get out of here. I couldn't move. I felt like I was up to my neck in wet cement.

Franklin next to me on the floor. He is dying. All that blood.

"Get going!" the man said. "If you ever come around here bothering my wife again, I'll kill you! I promise you that, mister!"

Get in the truck. I got myself off the ground, remembered how to walk. Get in the truck. I fumbled with the door, opened it finally. Keys. I need keys. They were in my hand already. Which key goes in the ignition? I tried one, then another. Finally, I put the right key in, started the truck. I put it in reverse and punched it, almost backing right across the street into another trailer. I tried to put it into drive, but the engine just raced. It's in neutral. I couldn't breathe. Put it in drive. Why can't I breathe? The two women in the road scattered like pigeons as I finally found a gear and then barreled past them.

When I was a few miles out of town, I stopped the truck. I sat there on the side of the road, both hands gripping the steering wheel. What in God's name is wrong with you? Relax. Just relax. I made myself take a deep breath and then another.

All right, take it easy. You're okay now. That asshole just wanted to scare you. And he picked a hell of a day to do it. You lost your cool for a moment. After the weekend you just had, it's understandable.

And besides, that was the first time someone has pointed a gun at you since Detroit.

I remember sitting in an office with a psychiatrist. The department made me go see him, after the shooting. I thought it was a waste of time. I didn't listen to much of what he was saying, but I did remember one thing. He said I'd always have this hair trigger in my head. One little thing and I'd be right back there in that room, lying on the floor with three bullets in me. A loud noise, like a gunshot or even a car backfiring. Maybe a certain smell, he said.

Or maybe the sight of blood.

THE MARINER'S TAVERN looked just like you would expect it to look. It had the fishnet with the shells and starfish in it hanging from the ceiling, an old whaling harpoon stuck to the wall. It was on Water Street, right next to Locks Park, with big windows on the north side of the building. During the summer you could sit there and see a freighter or two going though the locks every hour, getting raised or lowered twenty-one feet, depending on which way they were going. Now that November had arrived, the freighter season was almost over.

I meant to just stop in and have a quick word with the bartender, but I ended up sitting at a table for a while, the only customer in the place, looking out that window at the St. Mary's River and on the other side of that, Soo Canada. I couldn't remember the last time I had a drink before noon, but this day seemed to need it.

I made a little toast to myself. Here's to your brilliant decision to become a private investigator.

Lane Uttley had found me at the Glasgow Inn one night that past summer. He told me that Edwin was one of his clients, and that Edwin had told him all about me, the fact that I had been a cop in Detroit, even the business about getting shot.

"A man who takes three bullets has to be one tough son of a bitch," he said. "Edwin tells me you still have one of the bullets in your chest. Do you ever set off the metal detector at the airport?"

"It happens," I said.

"What do they say when you tell them about the bullet?"

"They usually just say, 'Ouch.' "

"Ha," he said. "I imagine they do. Anyway, Mr. Mc-Knight, I won't waste your time. Reason I'm here is, I have a big problem and I'm wondering if you can help me out. You see, I have this private investigator working for me named Leon Prudell. Do you know him?"

"I think I've seen him before."

"Yeah, well, at the risk of speaking unkindly, I have to say that the situation with Mr. Prudell is not working out. I imagine you're familiar with what a private investigator really does?"

"Mostly just information gathering, I would think. Interviews, surveillance."

"Exactly," he said. "It's very important to have someone who's intelligent and reliable, as you can imagine. I've done a little bit of criminal defense work. And I have some long-standing clients like Edwin, you know, for wills, real estate, and so on. But a lot of my work is negligence, accidents, malpractice, that sort of line. That's where I really need a good information man."

"What does this have to do with me?" I asked. "I'm not a private investigator."

"Ah," he said. "But you could be. Have you ever thought about it?"

"Can't say as I have."

"The private eye laws are pretty loose in this state. All you need are three years as a police officer and a five-thousand-dollar bond. You were an officer for eight years, right? Spotless record?"

"Are you asking me," I said, "or did you already check me out?"

"You'll have to forgive me," he said. "I told you I value good information."

"Well, I'm going to have to pass on your offer. Thanks just the same."

"I sure wish you'd think about it. I'm prepared to make this well worth your time."

"Fair enough," I said. "I'll think about it."

He was back two nights later, this time with one of Prudell's reports in his hand. "I want you to read this," he said. "This is what I have to deal with every day."

Prudell had apparently been sent to a resort out on Drummond Island to document some haphazard lifeguarding in support of a suit over a drowning. The report was a jumble of irrelevant notations and misspellings.

"Listen to this, Alex," he said. " 'Twelve-fifteen. Subjects back on duty after eating lunch under a medium-size tree. Subjects become aggravated upon observation of my picture taking with the camera.' I assume that when he says subjects, he means lifeguards. Why can't he just say lifeguards, Alex? I tell ya, this guy is killing me."

"What makes you think I could do a better job?" I said.

"Alex, come on. Don't make me beg."

"I don't know, Mr. Uttley."

"Alex, you work when you want to work, and you name your price. I'll even put up your state bond myself. You can't beat it."

The truth was, I had been thinking about it. As a cop, I was always good at dealing with people, making them feel at ease, making them feel like they could talk to me on a human level. I was pretty sure I could make a decent private investigator. And I still wasn't comfortable with the idea of drawing three-quarter disability pay and not having much else to do except cut wood and clean up after deer hunters.

"There's just one condition," I said. "No divorce cases. I'm not going to go following some guy, waiting to get a picture of him with his pants around his ankles."

"It's a deal," he said. "I haven't done divorce work in ten years."

A month later, I had my license. He apparently knew someone in Lansing, was able to get the forms through that quickly. One day in late August, after I had just received the license, he gave me a piece of paper with a name and address on it.

"Who's this?" I said.

"It's a dealer in the Soo," he said. "I've ordered a gun for you. You have to pick it up yourself, of course. Fill out the paperwork. You know some guys in the county office, right? You'll need your permit, too."

"Wait a minute," I said. "What kind of gun are we talking about?"

"A .38 service revolver. That's what you used when you were a police officer, isn't it?"

"Yes," I said. "But I really don't want to carry one again, if you don't mind."

"Hey, no problem," he said. "Just keep it at home. You never know."

It took me a while to figure out why he ordered that gun. Then it came to me. He probably just liked the idea of me having it. I could see him sitting across the table from a prospective client, saying, "Yes sir, I've got a good man working for me now. He packs heat, of course. It's a rough world out there. My man took three bullets once, still has one in his chest. That's the kind of man we both need on our side . . ."

When I had finally picked up that gun, I took it home and put it in the back of my closet. I hadn't touched it since.

THE BARTENDER WAS no help. I asked him if he had been there that past Monday. It took him a full minute to figure that one out, so I didn't think he'd be able to remember if there were any suspicious characters there that night. So I just paid the man and headed down to Uttley's office. It was right around the corner from the courthouse, between a bank and a gift shop. The whole downtown area was starting to smell like money again, thanks to the casinos. Uttley was doing well, as were a lot of the other local businessmen. The strange thing was that, for once, a lot of the money was coming to the Chippewa Indians first and then trickling down to everyone else. I knew a lot of people around here who had a hard time dealing with that.

Uttley was on the phone when I came in. He gave me a little wave and motioned me into a big overstuffed guest chair. His office was classic Uttley: a desk you could land an airplane on, framed pictures of hounds and riders ready for the foxhunt, a good ten or twelve exotic houseplants that he was always misting with his little spray bottle. "Jerry, that number doesn't work, and you know it," he was saying into his phone. "You're going to have to do a lot of work on that number before we talk again." He gave me a theatrical headshake and double eyebrow raise as he covered the receiver with his hand. "Almost done here," he whispered to me.

I picked up the baseball that was sitting on his desk, read some of the signatures. Without even thinking about it, I turned the ball over into a four-seam grip, ready for the throw to second base.

"Okay," he said as he hung up. He rubbed his hands together. "How are *you* doing?"

"Can't complain," I said.

"Wouldn't do you any good if you did complain, eh?"

"I did receive an interesting phone call last night," I said. By the time I told him everything, he was just staring at me with his mouth open.

"Did you tell Chief Maven about this?" he said.

"I haven't stopped by to see him yet," I said. "I thought I'd try the bar first, see if the bartender remembered anything from Monday night."

"I take it he didn't."

"No."

"Well," he said. "I don't know what to say. Do you want me to come to the police station with you?"

"You don't have to do that. I'll go see him right now."

"Chief Maven can be a bit . . . blustery," he said.

"That's one word for it."

"Oh and, by the way," he said. "I was wondering if you could do me a favor."

"What would that be?"

"Mrs. Fulton would really like to speak with you as soon as possible."

I swallowed my surprise. "Sylvia Fulton wants to see me?"

"No no," he said. "Theodora Fulton. Edwin's mother.

She came up from Grosse Pointe yesterday. She's staying with them for a couple days."

"Why does she want to see me?"

"She's worried about her son. She thinks you might be able to help him."

"What does she expect me to do?"

"Mrs. Fulton is a great old lady, Alex. A little eccentric maybe. Only rich people are eccentric, by the way. Everyone else is just crazy."

"So I've noticed," I said.

"Anyway, she's very protective of her son. She came up as soon as she heard about what happened. She seems to think he's in some sort of danger up here."

"Then I probably shouldn't tell her about our new friend the killer, huh?"

"I'd find a way to leave that out of the conversation," he said. "Alex, I should warn you, this is a very intense woman we're talking about. She has a different way of looking at things. She wants to talk to you about a dream she had."

"What kind of dream?"

"She dreamed about what happened on Saturday night. It got her very upset, Alex. She thinks Edwin is next."

"Are you serious?"

"I don't know what to think of it, Alex. All I know is, while we're standing there in that parking lot, Edwin's mother is down in Grosse Pointe, three hundred miles away. And she's dreaming about it. She saw it, Alex. She didn't see who did it or anything. She just saw the way it looked afterward."

"What, you mean . . ."

"The blood, Alex. She says she saw the blood in her dream."

CHAPTER FIVE

IT WASN'T THE best day for a walk along the river, but it sounded more fun than my appointment with Maven. I followed the path through the Locks Park, looking out at the water, cold and empty. There were no freighters headed for the locks. No small boats out for a spin. No sign of life whatsoever.

The path ran east, right out of the park and onto the front lawn of the courthouse. There were two statues there. One was the giant crane from Ojibwa legend, the one that landed here next to the river and brought the Indians. The other statue was the wolf suckling Romulus and Remus. If there was supposed to be some connection between that and the city of Sault Ste. Marie, I didn't know about it.

The City County building sat directly behind the courthouse. It was an ugly thing, just a big brick rectangle as gray as the November sky. The Soo Police and the County Sheriff's Department both lived in that same building. The county jail was there, too. Stuck on one side of it was a little courtyard for the prisoners. It was really just a cage, maybe twenty feet square, with a picnic table inside, surrounded by another fence with razor wire running along the top.

I stopped in at the county desk first, said hello to a deputy. "Bill around today?" I asked.

"No, he's down in Caribou Lake," he said. "You want me to leave him a message?"

"No, just wondering," I said. "I'm actually here to see Chief Maven."

"He's that way," the deputy said, pointing down the hallway.

"I know where he is," I said. "I'm just stalling."

"I don't blame you," he said. As I left, I saw him smile and shake his head.

I checked in at the city desk, stood there for a few minutes while the woman called him on her phone. She stood up and told me to follow her. The look on her face told me she didn't want me to hold her personally responsible for what was about to happen.

She led me down a maze of corridors, deep into the heart of the building where no sunlight had ever reached. There was just the steady hum of fluorescent lights. I was shown to a small waiting area with hard plastic chairs. One man was sitting there, staring at the floor, a pair of handcuffs linking him to a piece of metal imbedded in the cement wall. I sat down across from him. There was one ashtray on the table. No magazines.

"Gotta cigarette?" the man asked.

"Sorry," I said.

He went back to staring at the floor and did not say another word.

I kept sitting there while days seemed to pass, and then weeks and months until it was surely spring outside if I ever got out again to see it. Finally a door opened and Chief Roy Maven waved me inside. The office was four walls of cement. No window.

"Good of you to stop by, Mr. McKnight," he said as he beckoned me into the chair in front of his desk. "I've been anxious to talk to you."

"I can tell that by the way you rushed me right in here to see you."

He let that one go while he picked up a manila folder

and slipped on a pair of grandmotherly reading glasses that clashed with his tough-guy face. He paged through the contents of the folder until he arrived at the page he wanted. "Let's see what we have here," he said. "Alexander McKnight, born 1950 in Detroit. Graduated from Henry Ford High School in Dearborn in 1969. Says here you played two years of minor league baseball." He looked up at me. "Couldn't hit the curve ball. It doesn't actually say that here. I'm just assuming."

"You seem to have a pretty complete file on me," I said.

"This is just your private investigator application. It's part of the public record. Anybody can see it." He went back to reading. "Held a number of interesting jobs for a couple years. House painter. Bartender. Went to Dearborn Community College for a couple years, studied criminal justice. Joined the Detroit police force in 1975. Served eight years. Two commendations for meritorious service. Not bad. Wounded on the job in 1984. Took a disability retirement soon after. Three-quarter pay for the rest of your life ain't half bad, is it? Of course, that's more than fair when a man is disabled." He looked at me over his reading glasses. "And in your case, that disability would be . . . ?"

I looked at him for a long moment. "I was shot three times," I said.

He shook his head. "Hell of a thing to happen." He looked at me for a long moment, waiting for me to tell him the story. I didn't, so he looked back down at the papers. "Moved up here in, where did it say that? Ah, here it is, moved into the area in 1985. Been here ever since. Funny, most people with a disability, they'd move to Florida or Arizona, somewhere nice and warm. But here you are."

I didn't say anything.

"Your choice," he said. "Anyway, let's see, you filed

your form in July, got your license in August. Looks like
somebody kicked that one through pretty quickly. You
must have friends in high places."

I just sat there and watched him. It brought back memories. That good old cop swagger, I had seen so much of
it. I had slipped into it myself now and then. It was so
easy. Problem was, it got harder and harder to slip back
out of it when the day was done. It's not the kind of thing
you want to take home. Just ask my ex-wife.

"Now, Mr. McKnight," he said, taking off his glasses,
"seeing as how you're pretty new at this private investigator business, I'm going to let you in on a couple little
tricks of the trade. Do you mind if I do that?"

"Go ahead," I said.

"Very well. First of all, when a private investigator is
operating in a police jurisdiction, it is a common courtesy
to check in at the police station to let them know who you
are and what you are doing. Not that I care about such for-
malities, of course. No, sir. But somewhere down the road,
you're going to run into a police chief who really doesn't
like the fact that you're working in his town and he hasn't
even been introduced."

"Fair enough."

"Second, and even more importantly, I would suggest
that the next time Edwin Fulton calls you up in the middle of the night and asks you to come down to a major
crime scene, I would just take a moment to double-check
with him, just to make sure that he has in fact called the
police first. Actually, I would say, just go ahead and assume that he *hasn't* called the police. That doesn't seem
to be his strong suit, after all. But you, of course, being a
former policeman yourself, and understanding how important it is for an officer to arrive on the scene before the
friends and neighbors do, *you* should go ahead and phone
it in yourself. In fact, I'll give you my home number, so

the next time Mr. Fulton wants you to come look at a murder, you can call me directly, day or night."

We both just sat there looking at each other.

"I'd hate to bother you at home," I finally said. "Next time, I'll just call it in to the station."

"That would work just fine," he said. He picked up a copy of the *Sault Star*, the daily Soo Canada paper, from his desk. "Have you seen this yet? We made the front page over in Canada."

"I haven't read it yet."

" 'Local Man Slaughtered In Soo Michigan Motel Room.' Now *that's* a headline for you. Notice how they make sure to say it happened on *this* side of the river. Did you know that it took two of my men five hours to clean that room up? Have you ever cleaned that much blood up before?"

"Can't say as I have."

"By the time we had gone over the room and then finally gotten the body out of there, most of the blood had hardened. Of course, as soon as you put water on it, it sort of comes back to life and starts spreading again. You try to wipe it up, it's like paint. You're painting the whole room red. One of my officers, he's been out sick ever since. I think he's reevaluating his career plans."

I fought down the lump in my stomach.

"Anyway, here's the deal. I've already talked to Mr. Fulton. So I'm just wondering if you might have any other information for me. Did you know the deceased?"

"No," I said.

"You never met him? You never placed bets with him?"

"I don't gamble."

"Have you ever heard Mr. Fulton speak of him prior to that night?"

"I knew that he was probably putting bets down somewhere," I said, "but he never mentioned anyone by name."

"When did you last see him before he called you Saturday night?"

"I saw him briefly at the Glasgow Inn. He stopped in with his wife. Then later, he stopped in on his own."

"How did he seem that evening? Did he say anything unusual?"

"I didn't talk to him," I said.

"You didn't talk to him? He says you two are best buddies."

"I was playing poker."

"I thought you said you don't gamble."

"It's not gambling," I said. "It's nickels and dimes."

He nodded. "All right," he said. He closed my folder and put it in a drawer. "That'll do for now."

I thought about leaving right then. The hell with this guy, I didn't feel like telling him about the phone call. But I knew that if I didn't tell him, it would be just the kind of thing that could come back and haunt me.

"Actually, Chief Maven, I've been enjoying our time here so much, I just don't think I can leave yet."

For one split second, he lost that little hard-ass smirk.

"I'll take a cup of coffee with one sugar," I said. "And then I'll tell you about a little conversation I had last night with the murderer."

It was worth telling him the story, just to see him choke on his tough-guy routine, if only for a minute. I told him all about the phone call while he wrote down every word. But I never did get that coffee.

I GRABBED A quick lunch at the Glasgow, and finally had a good look at that newspaper. There was a picture of the motel on page one. You could see the police barricades set up around the place, and a few officers carrying out what looked like a big sack of laundry. I'm sure

Mr. Bing was quite a load, even with all thirteen or four-teen pints of blood drained from his body.

There were a couple paragraphs about Edwin, "heir to the Fulton fortune," being the first man on the scene. I was not mentioned.

When I had finished reading about it, I drove up to the Fulton place. It was not far from Paradise, just straight up Sheephead Road, past the Shipwreck Museum, all the way up to the old lighthouse on Whitefish Point. I turned off on the road leading west along the shore, coming onto the Fulton property that took up a full three-hundred-acre cor-ner of Chippewa County.

About a mile from the house, I saw someone walking on the road. When I saw who it was, I considered turning around and leaving. Instead, I pulled up next to her and rolled down my window. "Nice day for a walk," I said.

Sylvia kept walking without looking at me. "If you like cold and gray," she said.

"I'm on my way to see your mother-in-law."

"Good for you."

"Is Edwin around today?"

"He's at the office."

"What does he do at the office?" I asked. "Why does he even need an office?"

"He counts his money," she said. "He calls it up on the phone and talks to it."

"Can't he do that from home?"

She finally looked at me for the first time. Those green eyes went right through me. "He prefers to have his time away from the house," she said.

"I don't get it," I said.

"What?" she said. I stopped the truck as she turned to me and put her forearms on my door. "What don't you get?"

"I don't know," I said. "Just the fact that he doesn't spend more time with you."

She shook her head and looked up at the sky. "You gotta hell of a nerve saying something like that."

"Sylvia, is this the way it's going to be from now on? Are you always going to act like this?"

"Yes, Alex." She pushed away from the truck. "So you better get used to it."

"You know, I think I've got you figured out," I said.

"Oh, do you. Do you really."

"For the first time in your life, you didn't get something you wanted. That's the whole problem right there. You just hate the fact that I was the one who ended it."

"Alex, there are only two things in this world that I hate. I hate living on this godforsaken frozen cliff on the end of the world. And I hate the fact that I was ever stupid enough to get involved with you. I mean, look at you. Look at this . . . thing you drive around in."

"Sylvia, don't."

"You look like, what, like a lumberjack or something."

"I'm warning you."

"No, not even a lumberjack. He's the guy who cuts down the trees, right? That takes some guts at least. You look like. . . . You look like the guy who delivers the firewood, stacks it up next to the house. That's what you look like."

"Good-bye, Sylvia," I said. "It's been nice talking to you, as always." I watched her grow smaller and smaller in my rearview mirror as I drove away.

It didn't take long to get to the Fulton place. It had been built by Edwin's grandfather back in the 1920s, and had been improved on several times by his father. The Fultons were old automotive money, and were fixtures in Grosse Pointe, a ritzy little suburb on the Detroit River. They kept this place way up here in the Upper Peninsula just as a summer cottage. Although to the Fultons, a "cottage" was a five-thousand-square-foot fortress of stone and glass and huge wooden beams cut from the original forest. Now that he was living up here year-round, I couldn't imagine how much money Edwin must have spent keeping the road plowed during the winter.

Theodora Fulton was alone in the house. She seemed glad to see me after she wrestled open the huge oak front door. "You must be Mr. McKnight," she said.

"Yes, ma'am," I said. "I'm pleased to meet you."

I knew she was well into her sixties, but there was a clarity in her eyes and a surprising strength to her as she shook my hand. Although she had her hair pinned up, I could see that she had less gray hair than I did. "Please come in," she said. "Can I offer you some coffee? I just made some."

"Yes, ma'am, I'd love some."

She led me into the main living room. The ceiling was a good twenty feet high, and dominated by the massive round beams that were left unfinished. The windows looked out over Lake Superior in all its glory. "Have you been to this house before?" she asked. "It's rather charming, isn't it?"

It was charming, all right. If I saved every penny I ever earned and did most of the work myself for about ten years, I'd have a cabin about a third as charming as this place. "I've been here once or twice," I said.

"Make yourself at home. I'll get you a cup."

I sat down on one of the three couches. When she left, the room was silent except for the ticking of a clock and the faint sound of the wind off the lake.

"Here we are," she said as she rejoined me. I took my cup from the tray and dropped in one sugar with the little silver tongs.

"Thank you, ma'am," I said.

"Please call me Theodora," she said. "Or Teddy. My friends all call me Teddy."

"How about Mrs. Fulton?"

"As you wish." She drew out a pair of glasses and put them on. I couldn't help noticing that they looked exactly like the pair of reading glasses that Chief Maven had put on in his office. "You do cut an imposing figure, don't you, Mr. McKnight. But you have a kind face."

"Thank you."

"Edwin speaks very highly of you. He tells me that you have a bullet next to your heart."

"Yes, ma'am, I do." I wondered if there was anyone left in the state of Michigan who didn't know this by now.

"Did you know that Andrew Jackson had a bullet next to his heart for the entire time he was president?"

"No, I didn't know that."

"He was in a duel. The other man shot him in the chest, but Jackson didn't go down. He had his one shot left, so he calmly took aim and shot the other man dead. What would you have done, Mr. McKnight?"

"You mean if I was in a duel?"

"Yes, if you were in a duel and the other man shot you first but you were still standing."

"I guess I'd have to shoot him. I imagine I'd have a good reason to. Otherwise, I wouldn't be in a duel in the first place."

"I suppose so," she said. "Anyway, they were never able to take the bullet out of Jackson's chest. He just had to live with it for the rest of his life. Apparently, it gave him a lot of trouble. Does your bullet trouble you?"

"No, not really," I said.

"That's good to hear."

"Mrs. Fulton," I said, "how can I help you?"

She looked down at her coffee. "I'm sorry. I seem to be

doing my best to avoid that topic. I take it that Mr. Uttley told you of my conversation with him?"

"He didn't go into much detail."

She nodded. "Well, as I'm sure you're aware, I am very concerned about my son Edwin. His father passed on many years ago, and I think that's been very hard on him. He hasn't had anyone to look up to. That's why I'm so glad that you're his friend, Mr. McKnight."

"Oh, I don't know, Mrs. Fulton. I mean, I haven't spent that much time with him lately." His wife, that was a different story.

"Yes, but even so, I think you're the best friend he has right now."

I didn't know what to say. Some best friend I was.

"Mr. McKnight," she said, "I'm not naive about my son's . . . problems. I know that he has a particular attraction to gambling. Why else would he live way up here all year long? At first, I thought he was just trying to get away from me. I suppose that's a typical mother's reaction. Or that he was tired of all the social obligations in the city. Or that he just liked roughing it up here in the woods without any servants. That sounds silly, I realize. Of course, I know it's the Indian casinos that keep him up here. If they closed them, he'd be gone the next day. Although that reminds me of a question I wanted to ask you. If the casinos are legal up here, why was he betting with a bookmaker?"

"These casinos only have table games and slot machines. There's no sports betting. For that, you have to deal with a bookmaker."

"I understand now," she said. "See, already I'm glad you came out to visit me. Edwin refuses to talk about these things with me."

"Mr. Uttley mentioned a dream that you had . . ."

"Yes," she said. "The dream. I hope you won't find this too terribly absurd when I tell you."

"Of course not," I said.

"Saturday night," she said. She looked out the window as she began to relate her dream in her slow, steady voice. "It was the night that he found that man, as it turned out, although I certainly didn't know that at the time. In the dream, I saw blood. I saw a great deal of blood. I was absolutely terrified, because I have to tell you, I have this *thing* about blood. Just the sight of it, even my own blood if I prick my finger in the garden, I just can't bear it. In the dream, there was so much of it. It seemed to be more blood than one single body could hold. I was floating over it, you know how it is in a dream. And then suddenly, I flew away from the blood and I was in a forest. I was moving down a road with trees on each side. Or rather, I was watching as something else was moving down the road. It was a car, rolling slowly down the road. It was the most vivid thing I have ever seen in a dream. That car just rolling smoothly down the road. But it was dark. The car didn't have its lights on. It was traveling down the road with just the faintest moonlight to show the way. I tried to look into the windshield to see who was driving that car. But I couldn't see. It was too dark. And then I realized that I had been on that road before. It was the road that leads to this house."

She stopped and looked at me. "Mr. McKnight," she said. "When Edwin called me and told me what had happened, I begged him to leave this house. But he wouldn't. He said I was being foolish. So I did the only other thing I could do. I drove all the way up here myself. Can you believe that? My driver had the day off, so I got the car out and came all the way up here. I haven't driven a car in ten years. I don't even have a license anymore. But I knew that I had to come up here and try to get Edwin and Sylvia out of this house."

"They wouldn't leave, I take it." I could see Edwin staying, but why would Sylvia want to stay here? God knows she hated this place.

"No, they didn't believe me," she said. "I guess I can't blame them. But then, last night . . ."

"Last night? What happened last night?"

"I was staying in one of the guest rooms, but I couldn't sleep. I kept walking around down here, looking out the windows. I think I finally fell asleep on the couch here for a while, but then a little while later I woke up again. I thought I had heard something outside. So I went to the back door, where you can see the road. And, I don't know, I thought I might have seen something. A car."

"What kind of car was it?"

"Oh, I couldn't tell. I'm not even sure it was there. I might have just imagined it."

"Mrs. Fulton, what time did this happen?"

"It was just after two o'clock."

The phone call came at three, I thought. And the man did say that he had been watching Edwin. "Did you do anything?" I asked. "Did you call the police?"

"No, I didn't," she said. "When I looked again, it was gone. I mean, if it had even been there in the first place."

"Did you tell Edwin about it?"

"Yes. He said that if you look out into the darkness long enough, you'll start to see whatever it is that you're afraid that you'll see."

"So what would you like me to do?"

"I want you to stay here tonight," she said. "Maybe for a couple nights, if that's what it takes."

"Mrs. Fulton—"

"I'm begging you, Mr. McKnight. I'll pay you any-thing you want."

"Mrs. Fulton, I'm sure the sheriff could keep a man out here for a few nights . . ."

"No," she said. Her voice changed into that of a woman who was accustomed to having things her own way, es-pecially when she was willing to pay for it. "That will not do. The sheriff is not going to send a man out here all night just because an old woman has a dream, and thinks she sees things in the darkness. I just want someone to stay here for a night or two. To make me feel better. I want you, Mr. McKnight. I've already said that you'll be well compensated."

I couldn't bear the thought of staying in this place, but Mrs. Fulton kept working me over like an old pro until I finally agreed. There's something faintly annoying about rich people, I've noticed. They don't even wait to see if you'll do something for them out of the goodness of your own heart. They go right to the money. They wave it in front of you like a candy cane in front of a child.

Sylvia was still on the road when I left the place. "You've been out here all this time?" I asked when I stopped next to her. "You just had to get one more shot in, eh?"

"I was not about to go into that house when you were in there," she said. Her cheeks were bright red from stand-ing out in the wind.

"It's a big house," I said. "You wouldn't have even had to see me."

"I would have known," she said. "I would have *felt* you there."

"Yeah, well then you'll be feeling me quite a bit tonight," I said. "What's for dinner, anyway?"

"What are you talking about?"

"I want to make sure I bring the right wine."

"If you're trying to make a joke, it's not funny."

"It's no joke, Sylvia. Your mother-in-law just hired me to spend the night. Now, are you going to tell me what's for dinner or aren't you? If I bring red wine and you're serving fish, I swear to God, you'll be one sorry woman."

I DROVE BACK down to my cabin, figuring I'd just pack an overnight bag, make sure everything was okay around the place. I had a friend up the road named Vinnie LeBlanc who could keep an eye on things for a couple days. He was a Chippewa Indian, a member of the Bay Mills tribe. Like most of the Chippewas around here, he had a little French in him, a little Italian, a little God knows what else. He worked as a blackjack dealer at the Bay Mills Casino, and during the hunting season he'd sometimes act as a guide for some of the men who rented my cabins. He knew how to play up the Indian thing when he was leading a bunch of downstaters through the woods. And of course he went by his Ojibwa nickname, Red Sky, because as he himself had said many times, who's going to hire an Indian guide named Vinnie?

I pulled in next to my cabin and got out of the truck. When I went to the door, I saw something on the step.

It was a rose. A single blood red rose.

I picked it up. I looked around me. Just pine trees. Nobody would have seen him put this here. I looked around on the ground. No footprints, no tire tracks.

I opened the door and looked inside, letting out my breath as I saw that my cabin was empty. There was no sign of forced entry, but you never know. I checked the phone. No messages.

A single red rose. It made me start to think of something, but I couldn't quite get to it.

Or maybe I didn't want to get to it. Maybe I didn't want to make the connection.

I was about to crush the rose, but then thought better of it. It's bad luck to destroy a rose. Somebody told me that once.

I put the rose in a glass of water, packed my bag, went back outside, and locked the door. "I'm going to have to miss your phone call tonight," I said to the wind. "Whoever you are, if you call me in the middle of the night, you'll just hear the phone ring four times and then you'll get the answering machine. Maybe I should change my message. 'If you're a homicidal maniac calling to fuck with my head, please press one. Everyone else, please press two.' "

I went to the truck and sat in the driver's seat for a few minutes. Finally, I got back out of the truck and went into the cabin.

I dug through the back of my closet, throwing clothes and boots in the air until I found what I was looking for. I put a bullet in each of the six chambers and stuck the gun in my belt.

CHAPTER SIX

"GOD, THIS FEELS so good, Alex," Edwin said. "I feel like a free man now." He was sitting in one of the overstuffed chairs in front of the fireplace, his feet up on a leather hassock, brandy snifter in one hand, a cigar in the other. I was sitting in the other chair, looking into the fire. I had a brandy, too, but I had taken a pass on the cigar. "It's kind of funny, isn't it," he said.

"What's funny?"

"The way things work out. Something so . . . horrible. And yet it turns to be the best thing that ever happened to me. It's like, have you ever seen a top spinning, and it starts to get wobbly and out of control?"

"Uh-huh?"

"And then it runs into something, *bam*, and suddenly it's spinning smoothly again? That's what happened to me."

"Okay," I said. "Good."

"No, I mean it," he said. "I have absolutely no urge to gamble anymore. It's completely gone."

"If that's really true, then I'm glad, Edwin."

"Of course it's true," he said. He got up to put another log on the fire. There was a deer head with a twelve-point rack mounted on the wall above the fireplace. I wondered if there was anyone in this world who would think for a second that Edwin had shot that animal himself.

When he sat back down, he said, "So, are you going to

tell me what's going on? Why did you want to know about the last time I saw Tony Bing?"

"Edwin, let me ask you something first. Have you seen anyone around lately who seemed strange or suspicious in any way? Someone who may have seemed to be watching you or following you around?"

He thought for a moment. "No, I don't think so. I mean, I haven't noticed anyone like that. Should I be keeping an eye out?"

"Maybe," I said. "Just be aware. And be careful."

"What's this all about, Alex?"

"I'm not sure, Edwin. I don't want to alarm you more than I have to. And I certainly don't want to scare your wife or your mother. Let's just say that I have reason to believe that there *might* be someone out there who's watching you, or watching me, or both. Someone who might have been connected to that murder."

"Does Chief Maven know about this?"

"He knows," I said.

We both watched the fire for a minute.

"Is there any chance of you going back down to Grosse Pointe for a while?" I finally asked.

"Do you think we should?"

"It might be a good idea."

"I don't want to leave," he said.

"What if I *really* thought you should leave, Edwin?"

He let out a long stream of smoke. "We're not leaving, Alex."

"Okay," I said. I didn't know what else to say.

We sat there in silence again. A log popped and sent a spark into the room. Edwin sat there watching it fizzle on the carpet, burning a little black hole. He made no move to stop it. He'd probably just call someone the next day and have the whole room redecorated. "I am glad you're here, though," he said. "I was just about to apologize for my mother."

"She's just looking out for you."

"I know," he said, "but I thought it was so silly, making you stay here tonight."

"It's not a problem."

"Although I have to say, if this is what it took to finally get you over to dinner . . ."

"The dinner was great," I said. "Your mother is quite a cook."

"Well, I'm just glad that I could get you and Sylvia in the same room for a while. I know how it is between you two."

My heart skipped a beat. "How do you mean?"

"Alex, I'm sure you've noticed. Sylvia has this thing about you."

"I don't know what you're talking about."

"I hope you don't take it personally. She's always had this thing about certain types of men. I mean, just from the way you look, the type of man that you *seem* to be. A big tough guy. She never really warmed up to you before, and I felt bad about that. But anyway, I think she got to know you a little better tonight. And I think she really likes you now."

Sylvia had been nothing but charming all through dinner. It was an incredible performance.

"Where did she run off to, anyway?" he said. "She's probably with my mother somewhere, plotting against me. You know how women are, eh?"

"I'm right here, darling," she said. We both turned to see her slip into the room behind us. She had a robe on. It was the same robe she had on that first night, the first night I ever touched her. It opened up at her neck and clung to her in a way that made me want to throw my drink at her.

"Are you coming to bed?" she asked, running her hands around Edwin's neck.

"Wow," Edwin said. "You look fantastic. I'll be right up."

She turned and looked at me. "Good night, Alex. I hope you can make yourself . . . comfortable."

"Don't worry about me," I said.

When she left, Edwin stood up and put out his cigar. "I've been neglecting that woman," he said. "But no longer, Alex. It's all part of the new Edwin."

I just nodded.

"Are you sure you don't want to sleep in the other guest room?"

"No, I'm fine right here on the couch," I said. The two guest rooms were at the end of the house. I wanted to be here in the middle, close to the doors, just in case.

"Suit yourself," he said. "I'm off to bed. Wish me luck." He gave me a wink and a little salute.

When he was gone, I sat there and finished my brandy, wondering how I had ever gotten there. I'm a private investigator and they're paying me to sleep on the couch with my gun.

I thought about the phone call, and about the rose that was left on my doorstep. I sat there for a long time hoping it would all make some kind of sense to me, but it didn't happen.

Finally, Mrs. Fulton came into the room and sat in Edwin's chair. "Can I get you anything, Alex?"

"No, I'm fine, ma'am."

"You know, you and I have something in common," she said. She crossed her legs and looked into the fire.

"What would that be, ma'am?"

"Fear," she said. "We both know about fear."

It took a minute to sink in. This woman had enough

money to protect her from anything. What could she know about fear?

But then I looked into her eyes. I saw the firelight dancing there. And I saw something else. Something I recognized. "Tell me about it," I said.

"I don't share this story with many people, Alex. But I feel like I can tell you, because you know what it feels like. Real fear. The kind of fear that changes you forever."

"Yes," I said. "Yes, I do."

"I was kidnapped when I was sixteen years old. That's one of the dangers of growing up in a very wealthy family, I suppose. They kept me for several days. At one point, they were going to cut off one of my fingers and send it to my father."

I didn't say anything. I looked into the fire with her and listened to her voice.

"There were three men," she said. "One of the men, he made sure that the others didn't hurt me. Even when the leader wanted to cut off my finger, this man wouldn't let him. They fought over me. He told the leader he'd kill him if he even touched me. Even though he was one of the men who helped kidnap me, I think I started to fall in love with him. It's strange, isn't it? When you're that scared, everything else you feel, you feel it so strongly. And the things you hear, the things you see. Even the color of things is more intense. You understand what I'm talking about, don't you?"

"Yes, ma'am."

"You understand because you've been there," she said. "I knew it as soon as I met you, Alex. Or at least when I asked you about that bullet inside you. I could see it then. I could see that we had this in common. That's why you know what I'm going through now. This whole business with my son. He's my only child, you know."

"Mrs. Fulton, everything's going to be fine. He was just in the wrong place at the wrong time."

"Well, I'm glad you're here," she said. "I think I'll even be able to sleep tonight." She wished me a good night and left the room.

I sat there and watched the fire go out. Finally I got up and walked around the place. I looked out the window that faced the driveway, turning off the exterior light so I could see into the darkness. Nothing.

I went outside and walked down the road for about a quarter mile. It was a quiet night, and without the wind it was not nearly as cold as it should have been. I turned around and came back up to the house, walking around to the porch that overlooked the lake. When the clouds parted, a quarter moon cast its faint light onto the immense surface of Lake Superior. The water was calm enough on this night, you could almost picture yourself sailing under that moon.

I went back inside and sat on the couch, taking the gun out of my belt and putting it on the coffee table. There was a wedding picture on the table. I picked it up and looked at the two faces, Sylvia radiant against the whiteness of her veil, Edwin wearing a big, dumb smile. My old man had an expression, "He was smiling like a jackass eating bumblebees." That's how Edwin looked on his wedding day standing next to Sylvia. I put the picture back on the table and lay my head back on the couch. Eventually, I slid off into the limbo between awake and asleep.

And then I heard something. I woke up with a start. Where did that noise come from? I sat up and reached for my gun.

It was gone.

Sylvia was standing there, my gun in her hand. She was pointing it right at my chest.

"Sylvia, what the hell—"

"I should kill you," she said. "I should kill you right now. That would feel good, Alex." Her robe fell open. In the moonlight I could see her breasts and the soft hairs that disappeared into the shadows between her legs. She made no attempt to cover herself.

"Sylvia . . ."

She put the gun back down on the coffee table. "Some watchdog you are," she said as she walked away. She went back up the stairs, leaving me sitting there in the darkness, trying to catch my breath.

"Goddamn you," I said softly. "You stupid crazy bitch."

I got up and walked around the place again, looking out the windows again. I walked down to the end of the house where the guest rooms were, put my ear against Mrs. Fulton's door. I could hear the rhythm of her breathing as she slept.

I lay back down on the couch, thinking I would never sleep again in my whole life. But eventually I dozed off again. I couldn't help it. After the last two nights of blood and late-night phone calls, I was beyond exhausted. At least I wouldn't have to deal with another phone call tonight, I thought as I finally gave myself over to sleep.

I saw the blood. It was Mrs. Fulton's dream. I was floating above it. It was stretched out as far as I could see in every direction.

And then I saw the car, moving smoothly and silently through the pine trees. Its lights were out. I could not see the driver.

And then the phone rang.

I jumped off the couch and fell over the coffee table. I didn't know where I was. The phone, where's the phone? It rang again. I remembered where I was. I picked up the gun and went upstairs. The phone rang for the third time.

"Alex, are you there?" It was Edwin, from inside the master bedroom. The phone rang for the fourth time.

"Yes!" I knocked on their door and then opened it. Edwin had turned on the light next to the bed. Sylvia sat up next to him, blinking. The phone rang for the fifth time.

"Should I answer the phone?"

"Let me," I said. I went around to his side of the bed and knelt on the floor. The phone rang for the sixth time.

I picked up the receiver. There was silence on the other end until I finally heard a man's voice. "Hello? Is anyone there?"

"Who is this?" I said.

"Who is *this*? Is Edwin Fulton there?" It wasn't the voice I was expecting. It was someone else, someone I knew.

"This is Alex McKnight. Who is this?"

"McKnight! What are you doing there? This is Chief Maven!"

"Chief Maven," I said. Edwin looked at me with surprise.

"Goddamn it, McKnight, what are you, the Fultons' butler now?"

"Why are you calling?" I asked. "What time is it?"

"I don't know," he said. "What is it, like three o'clock, I think? Three-thirty? I was calling Mr. Fulton to see if he knew where you were. I was so disappointed, McKnight. You weren't at the crime scene waiting for me this time."

"Maven, what the hell is going on?"

"There's been another murder," he said. "Another bookmaker, it turns out. They found this guy behind a restaurant on Ashmun Street."

"What happened?"

"The cook found him when he was taking the garbage out," he said. "He was shot three or four times, looks like."

"Do you think it was the same killer?" I looked up at Edwin and Sylvia. They were both staring at me. Sylvia started to shiver.

"Well, I'm not psychic, McKnight, but I have a feeling that we're going to find the same bullets from the same gun."

"Who was the victim?"

"Guy named Vince Dorney. You know him?"

"Vince Dorney. No, I don't know him." I looked to Edwin. He shook his head. "Edwin doesn't know him, either."

"He's right there by the phone, eh?" Maven said. "Sounds like I called you right in the middle of your slumber party."

"Save it, Maven. What about . . . I mean, did he cut him again?"

"No, not this time," he said. "This time he used the knife for something else."

"What do you mean?"

"I think you better get down here, McKnight. Right now."

"What are you talking about? Where are you?"

"As a matter of fact, I'm calling from a squad car parked right outside your cabin."

I SAW THE lights from the squad cars first, the blues and reds bouncing madly through the pine trees. When I rounded the corner, I saw four cars in front of my cabin. There was a county car, a state car, and two Soo cars. Eight men stood together by my door. When I stopped my truck and got out, it didn't take too long to figure out who was running this little show.

"Mr. McKnight," Maven said. "How nice of you to join us this evening."

I nodded to the two county deputies. I had seen them once or twice at the Glasgow Inn.

"Some of the county and state boys were good enough

to stop by," Maven went on. "We're a few miles out of the Soo, after all. But this pertains to a Soo case, so I'll be handling things. I was just explaining that to these gentlemen."

"What's going on?" I said. "Why are you here?"

"I tried to call you as soon as I found out about the murder behind the restaurant. You weren't home, so I got worried. I sent a car out here just to make sure you were all right. That's the kind of guy I am," he said.

"So why did *you* come out here? And why are all these officers here?"

"I called the county and state out here just as a courtesy," he said. "I'd expect the same if one of them came calling in the Soo. Now go take a look at your front door," he said.

I thought of the rose that had been left there. I shuddered to think what he might have left this time.

I went to the door. One of the Soo cops was taking a picture with an instant camera. In the sudden moment of white light I saw a piece of paper pinned to the door by a large hunting knife.

"Don't touch it yet, McKnight," Maven said from behind me. The officer carefully removed the knife and put it in a plastic bag. He put the note in a separate bag. "That's a shame about your door," Maven said. "It's gonna leave a nasty mark."

"What does it say?" I said. "Let me read it."

"Just hold on," Maven said. He took the bags from the officer and held a flashlight over them. "Looks like blood on this knife," he said. "Three guesses who the lab says it belongs to." He passed it back to the officer and then stretched the clear plastic flat against the letter. "Sweet Jesus," he said as he read it. It took a long time to read it. I could see that there were many words crammed on the single page.

When he was finished, he passed it to me without another word. The note looked like it was typed on an old manual machine with a ribbon that needed changing.

ALEX

You know who I am. It is hard to believe I think but you must believe because I am here now and it is time for both of us to be together and to finish the work that has been given to us. Iron bars could not hold me. I flew to you over all this time. Yes you know who I am. You know who YOU are that is to say you know that you are the one who will take us all to a better place. I did not see this before because I was blinded by the power of evil but now I see that you have been chosen to overcome death and to show the way for others to follow. The evil is here. It knows who you are and you must be very careful. I removed the one man who was threatening your little friend just as a sign of good will from me to you but there are others all around us to make this lonely place into a battlefield and tonight I removed another man who was sending out microwave signals for more of them to come. I used a different technique of course to keep them guessing. You always have to keep them guessing and not so much blood means it will take longer to discover he is missing but they will find us in time. They will not get to you I promise. It feels so good to help you now after all these years. Who would have thought it would turn out this way. To think I once thought you were one of them in disguise. I am watching over you and I cannot wait for the day when we can be together at last.

Yours forever

ROSE

P.S. I called you tonight but you were not there
which makes me very sad so please do not do it
again.

I read the letter twice and then I gave it back to Maven. All
the officers just stood there watching me.

"I'll say one thing for you," Maven finally said. "You
certainly get more interesting mail than I do."

"This is impossible," I said. "There's no way he could
be here. There's no way he could have written this letter."

"I take it you know who this Rose woman is?"

"Yes," I said. "I know Rose. It's a man, not a woman."

"All right, a man named Rose. How do you know
him?"

"It was fourteen years ago," I said. "He's the man who
shot me. He's the man who killed my partner."

CHAPTER SEVEN

IT WAS 1984, a long hot summer in Detroit. Cocaine was still king that summer, the good old-fashioned powder, long lines of it all over the city. Crack was just a rumor. I had been on the police force about eight years, and was just about ready to take the detective's exam. My partner, Franklin, was new on the job. He was an ex–football player, an offensive lineman. He played at the University of Michigan and made second-team All Big Ten his senior year. The Lions drafted him, but he blew out his knee the first week of training camp. He went back and finished up his degree, and a couple years after that he joined the force. They stuck him with me, figuring an ex–football player and an ex–baseball player would get along together. They were wrong.

"This is what a baseball player does," he said one evening in our squad car. The argument had been going on all day. "He stands around in a field. Once in a while, a ball might get hit to him. And if it's not hit right at him, he might have to move sideways a little bit. I'll give you that. Occasionally, the man has to move sideways."

I just shook my head. We were on our way to the hospital. One of the emergency room doctors had called in a disturbance, and we were the closest car.

"Now after he's done standing in the field," Franklin went on, "he comes back into the dugout to rest. I mean, it's hard work standing out there like that, right? So he's gotta come into the shade and sit down on a bench. All right, so he's sitting in that dugout for a while, having a drink, and then what do you know, it's time for him to get up and go to bat! So now he's gotta get up and go stand in a little box they painted in the dirt and swing this big stick, right? Now again, I'll admit to you, swinging a big stick is a lot of work. I mean, if he fouls a couple balls off, he ends up swinging that stick something like five or six times!"

"Keep talking, Franklin," I said. "Just keep digging that hole."

"And then, get this, Alex. Say he hits that ball, what's he gotta do then? He's gotta run all the way down to first base. What is that, like ninety feet?"

"Ninety feet, yes. Very good."

"Ninety feet the man has to run! And if he wants to try to stretch that into a double, that's a hundred and eighty feet!"

"A football player with math skills," I said. "What a bonus."

"Where you going, anyway?" he asked.

"Receiving Hospital," I said. "This is the best way." I was going south down Brush Street, deep into the heart of downtown Detroit. The heat from the day was still lingering there on the streets, long after the sun had gone down.

"Best way if you don't want to get there in a hurry," he said. "You should have swung over to St. Antoine Street, go right down by the Hall of Justice."

"Nah, this is faster," I said. "You don't know what you're talking about."

"I grew up in this city, friend. What do *you* know?"

"See, we're here already," I said. I pulled around to the back of the building near the emergency room entrance.

"We would have been here and gone by now if you'd listen to me."

"The day I listen to you is the day I retire," I said. We walked into the place, expecting the usual chaos. But everything seemed quiet. There was a woman in the waiting room, holding an icebag against her cheek. Across from her a man sat doubled over, hugging himself and gently rocking. A nurse was looking through a stack of files at the reception desk. She looked up at us and did a double take. Either I was just too damned good-looking or Franklin was just too damned big.

"Excuse me, ma'am," Franklin said. "We're police officers."

"In case you've never seen the uniform before," I said. "Don't mind my partner. He's an ex–football player."

She didn't seem too amused by either one of us. "You want Dr. Myers," she said. "Take a seat."

We sat down in the waiting room and watched the woman shift the icebag around on her cheek. Somebody had given her quite a shiner.

"Excuse me, ma'am," I said. "Are you all right?"

The woman looked at us. "Do I look all right?"

"No, ma'am, I guess you don't. Is there anything I can do?"

The woman shook her head.

"Did your husband do this to you?"

She shook her head again.

"Because if he did—"

"Just leave me alone, all right?"

"Ma'am, I'm just saying—"

"I don't want to hear what you're saying, all right? I don't want to hear it."

I put my hands up in surrender and settled into my seat. We sat there for a long time. From outside we could hear the sounds of the city, a dog barking, a siren wailing in the distance. Detroit was always at its worst in the summer, but tonight it was really simmering. The heat was even worse than usual. And the bus strike was still on. There wasn't even a Tiger game to watch because of the All-Star break. I didn't see how the emergency room could be so empty. I kept waiting for those big double doors to burst open with fresh casualties.

"So tell me, Franklin," I said. "Have you ever tried to hit a fastball?"

Franklin just looked at me.

"Have you ever had somebody throw a baseball ninety-five miles an hour right at your head?"

"Keep trying, Alex."

"I'm serious, Franklin. I'm trying to enlighten you here. You obviously have no appreciation for other sports. I suppose I can understand that, though. I mean, basically, what did you do when you were playing football? You were an offensive tackle, right? So let's see. You crouched down and you put one hand on the ground. And then when the quarterback said 'hut!' you stood up and hit the guy in front of you. Am I right? Oh no wait, it was more involved than that, wasn't it. Sometimes the quarterback would say 'hut-hut!' and you had to be smart enough *not* to stand up and hit your guy until the second 'hut.' "

Before he could say anything, Dr. Myers came into the waiting room. "I'm sorry, Officers," he said. "Please come this way." When we stood up I slipped the woman with the icebag a piece of paper. It had my name and Franklin's name on it, and the phone number for our precinct. I didn't expect her to call, but I figured that was about all we could do for her that night.

The doctor led us out of the waiting room into a small lounge behind the reception area. He was a thin black man, with a meticulous doctor's air about him. There was a slight Caribbean lilt in his voice. After we turned down the coffee and doughnuts, he finally told us why he had called the police.

"There's a man who's been coming in here," he said. "Pretty regularly. Although you never really know when he's going to be here. He'll come in every night for a few nights running, then he'll disappear for a few days. Then he'll show up again. He's obviously very disturbed, probably paranoid schizophrenic, although I couldn't say that for sure. I certainly don't have the time to try to talk to him."

"What does he do when he's here?" I asked.

"Mostly he just sort of . . . this is going to sound strange. Mostly he hides."

"He hides?"

"We used to have this big plant out in the waiting area. You know, like a palm tree? He always used to stand behind it. Eventually, we had to take the plant away. He was scaring the patients."

"You have security guards here, don't you?"

"We have some," he said. "Not nearly enough. Whenever we called them, as soon as they showed up, he'd be gone. It's like he had a sixth sense about it."

"When's the last time he was here?"

"He was here earlier tonight," he said. "He had a doctor's coat on this time. I think he must have stolen it from our linen closet. He was walking around the examination rooms, pretending to be a doctor. One of the nurses stopped him, and he just said something like, 'Just act natural, nurse. I'm undercover.' "

I looked at Franklin and shook my head. "Great."

"We're accustomed to having some pretty odd people around here," he said. "It comes with the territory. But this man is becoming very disruptive."

"Do you have any idea what his name is? Or where he lives?"

"We don't know his name. But I think we know where he lives now. As soon as the nurse called security, he disappeared again. But the guard saw him on the street and followed him. There's an apartment building about eight or nine blocks up, on the corner of Columbia and Woodward, right before the freeway. He saw the man go in, but he didn't see which apartment he went into."

I wrote the address on my pad. "What does this man look like?" I asked. "How will we know it's him?"

"Oh, you'll know," he said. "In that neighborhood, he'll be the only white man in that building, I'm sure. And if that's not enough, all you have to do is look for the wig."

"The wig? What kind of wig?"

"The man wears a blond wig," he said. "One of those big blond wigs that come out to here." He held his hands a foot away from his head.

"Big blond wig," I said as I wrote it on my pad. "Anything else?"

"He's a crazy white man and he's wearing a big blond wig," he said. He sounded tired. "What else do you need?"

WE FOUND THE apartment building on the corner of Columbia and Woodward. With all the work they had been doing in the downtown area, you didn't have to go too far to see the "real" Detroit, the Detroit where Franklin and I spent most of our time either handling domestic disputes or responding to reports of gunfire. The building had looked nice in its better days, you could tell, but those days were long gone.

"How we gonna do this?" Franklin asked.

"How do you think?" I said. "We knock on doors."

"I was afraid of that."

We started on the first floor, Franklin taking one side of the hallway and me the other. If anyone answered our knocks at all, it was usually a woman's frightened face peering out at us, a child or two or three behind her. On the second floor, one woman was finally willing to help us. "That white boy, you mean? One with the wig? He's up on the top floor somewhere. Craziest man I ever seen."

We thanked her and went right up to the top floor. "She saved us a lot of doorknocking," I said. "We should do something for her."

"Nothing we can do," Franklin said. A place like this always hit him a little harder than it did me. Detroit was his home. I only worked there.

The first door we knocked on, we found our man. He opened the door just a crack and looked out at us. The blond hair stood several inches over his head.

"Police officers, sir," I said. "Can we talk to you for a minute?"

He looked at me and then at Franklin, and then back and forth again a few times without saying anything.

"Can we come in?" I said.

"Why?" he said. His voice was dead flat.

"So we can talk to you," I said.

"Why do you want to talk to me?"

"Just open the door, please."

"Does *he* have to come in?" The man nodded toward Franklin.

"This is my partner," I said. "His name is Franklin. My name is McKnight. Can I ask you your name?"

"Ha!" he said. "Nice try."

"Sir, open the door, please," Franklin said. The man jumped at the sound of his voice.

"What do you want?" he said. "Why are you here?"

"We've just been to the hospital," I said. "They tell us you've been harassing people there. Now, can we please come in for a moment and talk about it?"

He slowly opened the door. I took stock of him as I stepped into the apartment. Five foot nine, maybe, a little overweight. He had blue jeans on, old but clean, tennis shoes, and a sweatshirt. No glasses, no facial hair. He would have looked almost normal if he didn't have that damned wig on. "Harassing?" he said. "They said I was harassing people? Is that what they said?"

The apartment was small. One table with three chairs, a couch that probably folded out into a bed. A kitchenette and a small bathroom. A single lamp burned in the corner, giving a stingy glow to the rest of the room. No light came from the window. We weren't even sure he *had* a window, because all four walls were completely covered with aluminum foil.

We just stood there and looked at the place. Finally, Franklin said, "Who did your decorating, the tin man?"

The guy looked at Franklin, pure hatred in his eyes. A little bell went off in the back of my mind. I knew something was wrong, but at the time I just assumed the guy was a simple-minded bigot. I didn't think about what else could be going on inside his head.

"There's a good reason for the aluminum foil," he said.

"Yeah, I heard about this once," Franklin said. "It's to keep the radio waves out, right?"

The man shook his head. "Radio waves? You think aluminum foil keeps out radio waves? This is for microwaves."

"Microwaves," Franklin said. "Of course."

"You said your name was McKnight?" he said to me.

"Yes," I said.

"Would it be possible perhaps to have this . . ." He looked Franklin up and down. ". . . this individual step outside. I'd be happy to talk to you alone."

"No, that would not be possible," I said. I knew that Franklin had a long fuse, but I was starting to get a little worried. If our roles had been reversed, I would have already been fighting the urge to bend the guy's arms behind his back and cuff him.

"I don't get it," the guy said. He started to rock back and forth from one foot to the other. "The two of you. Are you really partners? Do you work together every day?"

"All day long," Franklin said. "Sometimes we even drink from the same drinking fountain."

"This is very interesting," he said. "This could be valuable information."

"All right, sir," I said. "I'm going to sit down." I took one of the three chairs and sat down at the table. "My partner is going to sit down, too." Franklin kept looking at the man, then finally sat down next to me. "Please, sir, have a seat."

The man sat down.

"What is your name?" I asked.

"My last name is Rose," he said. "That's all I'm going to tell you."

"No first name?"

"First names are personal names," he said. "If you know somebody's first name, you have power over him. I'll never make that mistake again."

Franklin folded his arms and looked at the ceiling.

"I understand you've been spending time at the emergency room at Memorial."

"Is that what they told you?"

"Yes, that's what they told me."

"I may have stopped by there. Once or twice."

"They say you've been there quite often."

"And you believe them," he said.

"Never mind them," I said. "Have you been there?"

"I suppose I must have," he said. "If that's what they told you."

"Mr. Rose, you're not making this very easy."

"Do you two really spend all day together?"

"Oh, good Lord," Franklin said. I could tell he had heard enough. "What the hell is wrong with you, anyway? You're

down there at the hospital scaring people all day long, act-
ing like a lunatic. I mean, if you're crazy, be crazy. That's
fine. Go see a shrink. If you're doing drugs, get in a program. Do something for yourself. Or just sit up here in your
tinfoil room, I don't care. Just don't be bothering people at
the hospital, all right? They have enough problems down
there without you hiding behind the plants. And what's the
deal with that wig, anyway? You look like that rock singer.
What's his name, Alex? The guy with the hair."

"Peter Frampton?" I said.

"No, the other guy. From Led Zeppelin."

"Robert Plant?"

"Yeah, that's the guy," Franklin said. "He looks just
like him."

"I think he looks more like Peter Frampton," I said.

"Are you two about done here?" he said.

"No, I'm afraid not, Mr. Rose," I said. "You see, we
need to tell you something very important. And you need
to listen to us. All right? You need to stop going to that
hospital. Okay? You can't go there anymore."

"I'm afraid that's not possible," he said.

"Why is that not possible?"

"I'm doing important work there," he said. "I can't stop
now. Do you play billiards?"

"Mr. Rose . . ."

"You know what the eight ball does, don't you? It di-
vides the rest of the balls into the high and the low. The
high frequency and the low frequency. The eight ball is
black. Black for division and separation and death. The
absence of light."

"Mr. Rose . . ."

"The cue ball is white. All light, all colors, it's all part
of white. White is life and movement. None of the other
balls can move until the cue ball moves."

"Mr. Rose," I said, "do you think maybe you should be

talking to somebody? Is there a doctor taking care of you? Is there any medication you should be taking?"

"This is a trick, isn't it?" he said. "You're in disguise."

"Mr. Rose . . ."

"Very clever," he said. "I have to hand it to you. You're getting smarter all the time. You bring a big one to distract me." He shot a glance at Franklin and then locked his eyes back on me. "And you just slip right in here like you're one of us. You even sound like one of us. Very convincing."

Franklin and I looked at each other and nodded. This one was taking a little ride to the station, then maybe later to a nice padded cell somewhere.

"It's not going to work," he said. "You picked the wrong man this time."

The gun came out before either of us could react, before we could even *think* of reacting. He moved with such insect quickness, I swear he was pointing it at us before we even heard the tape tearing underneath the table.

It was an Uzi. In a few years, Uzis would become a cliché, but in 1984, they were still a novelty. Every coke soldier wanted one. They showed us an Uzi at roll call once. The gun was made in Israel. It shot 950 rounds per minute, little nine-millimeter pistol bullets, with full metal jackets. And it didn't sound any louder than a sewing machine.

"Mr. Rose," I said slowly, "put the weapon down." Both of my hands were on the table. Franklins arms were still folded. I didn't know which one of us could reach his holster first. Or if we'd even have the chance.

"Tell me who sent you," he said.

We both looked at the Uzi. I'm sure Franklin was thinking the same thing I was thinking. Although he had even more to lose than I did. He had two daughters, three and five years old. You want to see your family again. You don't want to die in a crazy man's apartment just because he thinks you're his secret enemy.

"Mr. Rose," I said. I tried to breathe. "We'll tell you whatever you want. I promise you. Just put the weapon down, please."

"I found this, you know," he said.

He looked down at the gun for a split second. A cold shiver ran up my back. It wasn't enough time to go for my gun. I needed him to look away for just an instant longer. Just give me a chance. If you're really crazy, *do* something crazy. Go into a trance or something.

"I found this in an alley," he said. "After one of your friends killed somebody. He didn't see me there, but I was watching. He threw it into a Dumpster. Very sloppy."

"Mr. Rose," Franklin said. His voice was almost a whisper. "Please . . ."

"Don't talk to me," he said. He pointed the gun at Franklin's chest. "I don't want to hear anything from you."

Franklin swallowed.

"Now you," he said, looking back at me. "Tell me how you did it. How did you turn white?"

"I'll tell you after you put the gun down," I said. "Just put it right there on the table." Right hand down, unsnap the revolver, bring it back up. How long will it take? Should I just do it?

He shook his head. "Well, this is quite a situation," he said. "Now I won't know *what* color you are. I was afraid this might happen."

Hand down, unsnap, raise and fire. Reach, rip, boom. I rehearsed the motion in my mind, hoping maybe I could shave off a fraction of a second. Hand down, unsnap, raise, and fire. Reach, rip, boom.

"You know, I've learned a lot at the hospital, doing my undercover work. At first, I didn't want the assignment, but I was told that the chosen one needed me to be there on the front lines. I was told that the chosen one needed to know how the enemy killed people. What the latest techniques were. So we could develop the right defense."

Franklin sat motionless beside me. I can't do this. If I move, he'll shoot me. I won't even get close to my gun. He has to look away. Please look away, just for a second.

"You know what really gets to me?" he said. "You're trying so hard to find the best way to kill people, you're even killing each other. Is that just for practice?"

Silence. I looked into his eyes. It was like looking down a mine shaft and seeing all the way down to hell.

"You have no respect for life, do you?" he said. "The chosen one says that if something has no respect for life, then killing that something is not really killing. Especially if you use the same technique that *they* use. That's the key."

Silence. How could I have taken one look at those eyes and not *known*? I should have cuffed him the minute I walked in.

"So I'm not really going to kill you."

"Mr. Rose . . ." I said.

"I'm going to remove you. That's what the chosen one calls it. He calls it removing."

"Mr. Rose . . ."

He moved the Uzi a few inches closer to us. "And do you know what the latest technique is?" he said.

Go for his gun? Knock it sideways? I looked at his hand. Is it tensed? Will he shoot if I make a move for it?

"Of course you know," he said. "You all do. It happens almost every day. I've seen it in the hospital. I heard the doctors talk about it."

You're going to have to make a move. You're going to have to risk it.

" 'Here comes another zip,' they say. 'How many zip's is that this week? Five already?' "

"Mr. Rose . . ." I said. One more try to talk him out of it. Then I move.

"It has a nice ring to it, doesn't it?" he said. "Zip!"

I knew what a zip was. Franklin did, too. We had seen a lot of them that summer. The coke dealers would zip a guy if he moved in on his turf, or if he didn't pay him soon enough, or if he just looked at him the wrong way. You take an Uzi and you give the guy a quick burst right down the middle of his body. Twenty, maybe thirty rounds from his head right down to his pecker. That's a zip.

Move. Move now. Go for his gun. Now. Now!

I didn't move.

He shot Franklin. Right down the front of him. The Uzi spat out the bullets with a sound like a cat purring. I went for my revolver. I felt the bullets hit me in the right shoulder. I didn't know how many. I felt them all at once, like when a rising fastball glances off your mitt and catches you in the shoulder. I heard the sound of my gun going off, the man named Rose screaming.

I was on the floor, next to Franklin. He was still alive. Just for a moment. I saw his eyes looking at me and then he wasn't there anymore. I tried to reach for my radio. There was blood on my hands, on my face, in my eyes. Blood everywhere.

I said something into the radio. I don't remember what. I lay there on the floor and looked at the ceiling. There was a hole there. I didn't get him. When the bullets hit me I shot straight up into the ceiling. Why did he scream? Did the sound scare him? Did he run away? How many times did he shoot me? How long until I die?

And why didn't he put aluminum foil on the ceiling? All four walls, but not the ceiling? I looked over at Franklin again. I kept looking at him until everything went black.

"GODDAMN IT, MCKNIGHT," Maven said. "Why didn't you go for your weapon when he first drew on you?" He had been listening to me in silence as I told him the story. He was driving the squad car. I was sitting in the passenger seat. My voice had been the only sound in the car, all the way from Paradise to the Soo. We were almost at the police station. The sun had just started to turn the eastern sky from black to ruddy gray.

I went through a whole list of things to say to him. Places he could stick it. Things he could do to himself. Finally, I just said, "I don't know why."

He shook his head. We passed by an old warehouse building. Half of the windows were broken. Under the cheap light of a street lamp a cat sat licking its paws, oblivious to our passing. "So you're telling me," he said, "this guy has found you how many years later?"

"Fourteen years," I said.

"All the cops you got in Detroit, you never caught the guy?"

"Well, Chief," I said. "You see, that's the part I haven't told you yet."

"What part?"

"We did catch the guy. About six months later."

"What are you talking about?"

"They caught him hanging around another hospital across town. I had just left the force, but I came back in to identify him. I testified at his trial."

"Let me guess," he said. "Not guilty by reason of insanity."

"No," I said. "His defender gave that a good try, but it didn't wash. Not for a cop-killer. Rose got life for Franklin, plus twelve years tacked on for me. No parole."

"So you're telling me that this Rose guy . . ."

"Is in prison," I said. I looked out the window. "Or at least, I *thought* he was."

CHAPTER EIGHT

THE SUN WAS finally up when we got to the police station, the dawn coming later and later as winter approached. When was the last time I had actually slept through these cold raw hours? And now here I was at the police station again. My stomach felt like it had been turned inside out.

Maven led me into his office and sat me down in the hard guest chair again. "All right," he said. He took out a pad of paper and a pen. He scratched on the pad a few times and then threw the pen into the corner of the room. He got out another one. "Goddamned pens, don't last a week. All right, McKnight, what's the guy's name again?"

"Rose."

"Did you ever find out his first name?"

"Maximilian," I said. "It came out at the trial."

"Maximilian? No wonder he didn't tell you." He started writing. "When was he convicted?"

"December 1984."

"You know where they sent him?"

"Jackson," I said.

He stopped writing. "They sent him to Jackson?"

"Maximum security," I said. "They said he was, what did they say, 'mentally deranged but functional.' Not crazy enough for a hospital bed, but crazy enough to keep an eye on."

"You're telling me they sent this guy away to Jackson max, with no parole ever? Are you sure about that?"

"I'm sure," I said.

"McKnight," he said. "Then the guy is still there. He has to be."

"So you would think."

"What, do you think he escaped? When's the last time someone escaped from Jackson? Has *anyone* ever escaped from there?"

"I don't know," I said. "All I know is what I read on that note."

He ran his fingers through what was left of his hair. "I guess I should give them a call just to check it out. What time is it? Just after six?"

"I'm sure somebody will be there," I said.

"You're probably right, McKnight. Last I heard, they weren't sending the inmates home at night." He looked through the papers on his desk. "I suppose I should go through the state office. Where's that number? I've got a woman who comes in around seven. She can always find things like that. No wait, here it is." He picked up the phone and dialed. I just sat there watching him.

"Good morning," he finally said. "This is Chief Maven at the Soo station. I need to contact the state prison in Jackson. Yes. Yes, it is. Yes, I'll call your commander later and fill him in. Yes. All right, that would be good. Hey, is there any way you can contact them and patch me through? You know, give them the secret state password or whatever you do. So they know I'm not just some asshole off the streets calling them for kicks. Yes, I'd appreciate that, thank you. Yes, I'll hold."

While he was waiting he looked up at me. "You ever deal with the state troopers when you were a cop?"

"Not much," I said.

"They're damned good," he said. "Problem is, they know it. But as long as you give them a little stroke when you talk to them, they usually cooperate. I suppose you Detroit cops were the same way." He sat there tapping his pen on the desk for another long moment. "Ah, good morning. My name is Roy Maven. I'm chief of police in Sault Ste. Marie. We have an unusual question for you this morning. You have an inmate named Maximilian Rose. He checked in late 1984, into maximum security. Uh, I guess there's only one way to ask this. Would you happen to know if Mr. Rose is still on the premises?"

Maven held the phone away from his ear. I could hear the guy myself from across the room.

"Goddamn it," Maven said. "I'm just asking you a question, all right? You don't have to get hostile. If you say he's there, he's there. That's all I wanted to know."

"Ask him to check," I said.

Maven put his hand over the phone and looked at me. "Excuse me?"

"Ask him to go check on Rose," I said.

"The man says there's never been an escape from maximum security."

"Maybe they let him go," I said. "Maybe they got their orders mixed up. Just ask him."

Maven rolled his eyes. "Excuse me, sir," he said into the phone. "We were wondering if perhaps you could take a moment and go check on him, just to make sure. Yes, that's what we're asking. Yes, you heard it correctly. Your ears are working just fine, yes. Yes. Yes. Yes. Look, here's what you do, okay? I'll walk you through it. First, you put the doughnut down. It's not polite to talk on the telephone with your mouth full. Next, you look up Maximilian Rose in your little book there, see what cell he's in. Then you call one of your guards to go look into that cell. Or, you can go look yourself. I'll leave that up to you. Then you come back on the phone and you tell me if he's there. And I say thank you for the help, and you say, no problem, that's why I'm here. And then you go back to eating your doughnut. All right? Do you think you can handle that? Oh, by the way, here's a little tip for you. When you go to check on him, make sure you actually see his face. Sometimes a prisoner will pile up his clothes under his blanket to make it look like he's in the bed. In fact, maybe this Rose guy has been escaped for months and you haven't even noticed yet. . . . Yeah, same to you, buddy. It's not my fault you're sitting in a little room watching a prison ward at six o'clock in the fucking morning. You obviously made a bad career choice somewhere along the way. Now just go shine your fucking flashlight in Rose's face before I have to talk to your superior."

Maven held the receiver in his lap and shook his head. "This is why I love my job," he said. "I get to deal with so many wonderful people." He looked at me like it was all my fault and then he went back to tapping his pen on the desk while he waited.

"Yes, hello again," he finally said. "I was beginning to worry about you. . . . You did. He was. You're sure about that. You're absolutely sure. Okay, fine. Yes, fine. You've been so helpful. Thank you very much. Have a nice day at the prison. Don't let anyone stick a knife in your back." He dropped the receiver on the hook.

"I take it he was there," I said.

"So they say."

"So who left that note?"

"You tell me," he said.

I raised my hands. "I have no idea."

He looked on another piece of paper on his desk. "You sure you never heard of Vince Dorney," he said. "Big Vince, they called him. Far as I can tell, Big Vince was into some other things besides running a little book now and then. He did some county time on a drug charge."

"I never heard of him," I said.

"He was shot up pretty good. He was lying there behind that restaurant in the garbage. Must have been some sight when the cook found him."

Maven looked at me for a long time. I met his eyes and did not look away.

"So what do we have here, McKnight?"

"Sounds like we've got two murders," I said.

"They sure train them right down in Detroit, don't they."

"What else do you want me to say?"

"I want you to tell me who you think is leaving you love notes," he said. "Besides a man who's been in prison for the last fourteen years."

"I don't know," I said.

"This is going to look really nice in the papers, isn't it," he said. "Two murders in three days. My good friend the mayor is going to be so happy."

"You don't sound too broken up about two dead men," I said.

Maven thought about that one for a moment and then he pulled his wallet out. "Here," he said. "You see these pictures?" He held the wallet open so I could see the photographs of the two young girls.

"Your daughters?"

"This one is my daughter," he said, pointing to the picture on the left. "The picture's kind of old. She was seven years old when it was taken. This other one was my daughter's best friend, Emily. She was seven years old, too. She was murdered. I had to tell her family myself." He folded up his wallet and put it back in his pocket. "I still carry her picture. I know a lot of people say you shouldn't do that. They say you should try to keep the job at a distance. Don't let it get inside you. But I carry the picture because it reminds me why I'm here. Now these two guys, what have you got? Tony Bing was a bookmaker. He got picked up three times, paid his fine, and went right back to business, taking people's money. Yeah, I know, it's not like he put a gun to somebody's head, but he took people's money, just the same. Last year, I found out he was receiving food stamps! He's got no official income, so he goes out and gets food stamps, for God's sake. That's the kind of guy he was. And this other guy, Big Vince Dorney, he was just downright evil. Bookmaking was just a hobby to him. It was just another way to get his hooks into you. He'd loan you money, he'd sell you drugs, whatever it took to get some leverage. Then he'd really hurt you. We've been trying to trip him up for two years. So you think I'm going to lose any sleep because he finally got whacked? And you think I'm going to sit here and take that kind of crap from you? A guy who couldn't even get his gun out of his holster?"

"That was an impressive speech, Maven. Especially the part about the little girl. I bet those pictures came with the wallet, didn't they."

"McKnight, you and I are headed for a big problem. When we're done with this case, remind me to take my badge off and have a little talk with you outside, okay?"

I looked at him. He was an ugly bastard, probably a good ten years older than I was. But I was sure he could fight. "I'll make a note of it," I said.

"All right, then. I'll be looking forward to that. In the meantime, let's see if we can figure out who's killing all of our bookmakers, okay? You want to try helping me out a little bit here for a change?"

"I'm trying to be as cooperative as I can," I said.

"You say this guy left you a rose yesterday?"

"Yes."

"What did you do with it?"

I hesitated. "I put it in water," I said.

"Interesting," he said. "Is that how they trained you to handle evidence down in Detroit? If you had found a gun, would you have put *that* in water, too?"

I couldn't take much more of this. I felt like jumping over his desk and strangling him. "Maven," I said, "it was just a rose left on my doorstep. I had no reason at the time to believe it meant anything. If I had called you up and said, 'Hey Chief, I think you should come get this rose. Somebody left it in front of my door. You know, I knew a man named Rose once. He shot me and killed my partner. I think he's been in jail for the last fourteen years. But even so, I think this might have been him.' What would you have said?"

"All right, save it," he said. "Let's just get you set up."

"Set up with what?"

"A phone trace, genius. Don't you want to find out where this guy is calling from?"

"I thought you didn't need special equipment anymore. Isn't there a special code you can dial now?"

"Yes, star five-seven sends an automatic trace record to the phone company. But we should also get a good tape recording of this guy. Do you have a good high-quality phone recorder in your private eye office?"

"I don't have an office," I said.

"A private eye who works out of a log cabin," he said. "You'd make old Abe Lincoln proud, wouldn't you."

"Goddamn it, Maven, if you don't knock it off—"

"All right, all right, take it easy," he said. "Let's just get you ready. I'll have an officer bring the phone unit over when he comes to set up the stakeout."

"Stakeout?"

"A man in a car, watching your cabin. Surely they taught you about stakeouts at the academy."

"Why do I need a stakeout?"

"McKnight, if you're not the dumbest man in Chippewa County. Somebody kills two people and then sticks a knife in your door in the middle of the night. Don't you think we should be there when he comes back?"

"If he comes back, I can take him care of him myself."

"Not a chance," he said. "I'm going to have a man there every night until we catch him. Is there a neighbor's house nearby where he can set up? We'll use a plain vehicle, of course."

"Nearest cabin is a quarter mile away. I suppose you could set him up just down the road a bit, around the bend."

"Will he have a sight line?"

"Just barely," I said. "If you give me a radio, that should help."

"All right," he said. "You can expect a man there by sundown."

"The Fultons aren't going to like this," I said.

"Why's that?"

"Mrs. Fulton is paying me to stay at the house. Just to watch over things."

"Well, they'll have to find another baby-sitter," he said. "God knows they can afford anybody they want. I want you at your cabin in case he calls. It doesn't sound like he'd say much to anyone else. You're the chosen one, after all."

I looked at him and shook my head. "Maven, all this time I have to spend here, and I *still* haven't gotten a cup of coffee out of you."

"It must be killing you," he said. "I'm sure you've heard, I make a great cup of coffee."

"I'm leaving now," I said. "If that's all right with you."

"I'll be talking to you," he said.

"One more thing," I said. "Where did you find the body? This Big Vince guy?"

"Why do you want to know?"

"I'm just curious."

"I don't like curious private eyes," he said. "Especially when I'm trying to solve a couple murders. Private eyes don't touch murders, McKnight. Or have you been watching too many movies?"

"I'm not going to get in your way," I said. "I just want to know. You have to admit, I am involved in this."

"I suppose you'll read about it in the papers, anyway," he said. "We found him behind Angelo's."

"That little place by the canal?"

"That's the one," he said. "Just stay away from it."

"Come on, Chief," I said. "Why would I go there?"

"I'm serious, McKnight. Stay the hell away from there."

"You're the boss, Chief. I'll see you around."

When I got outside I rubbed my eyes and took a deep breath of the cold air. I got in my truck and sat there for a moment, waiting for everything to make sense. It didn't happen. I started the truck and headed to Angelo's restaurant.

There's a hydroelectric power canal that cuts through town. Angelo's was a little pizza place on the north side of the canal, just before the bridge. On the front door a sign read, "Temporarily Closed! We'll be back as soon as we can!" I pressed my nose against the glass and looked inside. There couldn't have been more than seven or eight tables. I saw one pay phone on the far wall. Was that where my mystery man saw Big Vince? Listen to me. My mystery man. I'm still not willing to call him Rose.

It can't be Rose. It can't be.

I went around to the back of the place. The whole alley was cordoned off with yellow crime scene tape. There were two uniformed policemen standing there, drinking coffee. Everybody was getting to drink coffee that morning except me.

"Can we help you, sir?" one of the cops said. I recognized him from the motel. He was one of the two cops who showed up first, before Maven. I didn't recognize the other man. Probably his new partner. The other man must have quit.

"I'm Alex McKnight," I said. "We met at the motel the other night."

"I thought you looked familiar," he said.

"I'm just looking around," I said. "I take it this is where the body was found."

"Right behind that barrel," he said. He pointed to a big metal grease barrel. I could see the blood still pooled on the ground. "We're just waiting for our guy to come take another sample."

"I understand the cook found him?"

"So they say."

"You don't know his name offhand, do you?"

"No, I don't," he said. "I'm not sure the chief would want me talking about it, anyway."

"Don't worry about the chief," I said. "He and I are old buddies."

"Uh-huh," he said. He didn't sound convinced.

"I'm just wondering if anybody saw anything suspicious last night. A new face in the restaurant or anything."

"You'd have to talk to one of the detectives about that," he said. "Or your old buddy, the chief."

"No problem," I said. "Just wondering. Say, can you do me one favor?"

"What's that?"

"Don't tell Chief Maven I was here, eh?"

They were both smiling and shaking their heads when I left. I got in the truck, sat there for a long moment, tried to figure out what the hell to do next. Finally, I crossed the bridge over the canal, went down the business loop to Three Mile Road. The Riverside Motel didn't look any better in the daytime. And it hadn't moved any closer to the river.

I could see that room six was still off limits, the yellow tape still on the door. I didn't imagine it was helping the man's business any. I found him in the office, sitting behind his desk watching TV.

"Good morning," he said. "Checking in?" I remembered seeing him that night, standing there in the cold night in his pajamas and boots.

"No sir," I said. "My name is Alex McKnight. I'm a private investigator. I was . . . I was here on Saturday night. I'm the one who called the police."

"I see," he said. He turned the sound down on his TV.

"I don't mean to disturb you," I said. "I was just wondering if you had noticed anything unusual prior to that night. Did you see any strangers here?"

"Most everyone is a stranger," he said. "This is a motel. The only person I ever saw more than once was Mr. Bing. He lived here for almost a year."

"I understand," I said. "But was there anyone here that day who looked . . . unusual or out of place in some way?"

"He always had men coming over at all hours of the day," he said. "I told the police that. I knew he was a bookmaker, but beyond that it was none of my business. He paid his bill every week."

"This may sound strange," I said, "but have you seen anyone wearing a large blond wig lately? A man, I mean."

"A man in a wig? What are you talking about? Why do I have to answer more questions, anyway? I told everything I know to the police."

"I know, sir. I know how difficult this must have been. I'm just following up on something personal."

"No men in wigs," he said. "No women in wigs, either." He turned the sound back up on his TV. I took the hint, thanked the man, and left.

Before I got back in my truck, I went over to the door to room six. I stood there and tried to imagine how it had happened. The door was unlocked, Edwin said. Bing looked like he had just stepped out of the bathroom. Was the silencer already on the gun, or did he stand right here on this spot and screw it on? Walk right in, shoot the man in the face. Take out the knife, cut his throat from ear to ear. I looked down at the ground. They had cleaned the blood off. I wondered what the room looked like now. Could they have possibly gotten all that blood off the floor? Could you walk into the room and not *know* that somebody had been killed there? I tried the doorknob. It was locked. I thought of going back to the office, asking the man if he could open it for me.

But then I thought, no, I don't want to see that room again. In fact, I don't ever want to see *any* motel room again.

I went back up to the north side of town, stopped at the Mariner's Tavern again. I figured I'd try that bartender again, see if he had remembered anything about the night Edwin met Tony Bing there. That's what I told myself anyway. When I got there, it was open and the bartender was there, but of course he hadn't remembered anything else. I sat by the window again, looking across the locks into Canada. I finally had my morning coffee, with a little something in it just to get me going. It had been another long night. And it didn't look like my nights were going to get any easier any time soon.

LANE UTTLEY WAS on the phone when I got to his office. He hung up as soon as he saw me. "There you are!" he said. "Get in here, for God's sake! Sit down!" He grabbed me by both arms and stuck me in his guest chair. The chair was a lot softer than the one in Maven's office. "Edwin called me and told me what happened. Did Maven really call you from your cabin?"

"Yes, he did."

"Edwin said it had something to do with a knife. That's all he knew about it."

Uttley sat on top of his desk while I went through the whole story. When I got to the part about the letter on my door he blew up. "What the hell was he doing at your cabin, anyway?"

"He said that he called me when they found Dorney behind the restaurant. I wasn't there, so he sent a man out to see if I was all right."

"Yeah, I'm sure he was just looking out for you," he said. "But you're telling me he saw that letter before you did?"

"Yes."

"Did he have a warrant?"

"No," I said. "But the letter wasn't in an envelope. It was stuck to my door in plain view."

"It still stinks," he said. "And then he dragged you down to the station to question you?"

"I went voluntarily," I said. "I wanted to find out about Rose." I told him the rest of the story. The shooting, how we finally caught Rose, up to Maven's phone call.

"Are you telling me," he said, "that Roy Maven *called* the prison this morning to see if Rose was still there?"

"That's what he did," I said.

"And he is there."

"He's there," I said.

"This is incredible."

"That's one word for it."

"Alex, I'm concerned about this whole business with Maven. Do you want me to talk to him?"

"About what?"

"About not harassing you," he said. "I wish you'd at least let me go with you the next time you go talk to him."

"Maven's harmless," I said. "He's just an old blowhard cop. I've seen a million of them."

"It sounds like he's got a major hard-on for you, Alex. I'd watch him very carefully."

"I'm not worried about Maven," I said. "I'm worried about Rose."

"You mean whoever this guy is who's *pretending* to be Rose."

"Yeah, whatever," I said.

"This can't be Rose himself," he said. "You said that yourself. Rose is in prison."

"I know, it's just . . . "

"What, Alex?"

"I don't know," I said. "It's just a funny feeling. Is there anything more we can do? To find out if he's really still in prison?"

"What are you talking about? Maven called them, didn't he?"

"Yes, he did. But I don't know, maybe somebody made a mistake. Maybe the man they *think* is Rose isn't really Rose."

"What, Rose has a stand-in doing his jail time?"

"I know it sounds crazy," I said. "It's just that note. . . . Some of the things he said in that note . . . "

"So what do you want me to do?"

"Can we file a habeas corpus or something?"

"You file a writ of habeas corpus if you think somebody's being illegally detained," he said. "I don't think you could file one just because you want to make sure a man is really who they say he is."

"We can contact him, can't we? Can I talk to him on the phone?"

"Maybe," he said. "He'd probably have to agree to it."

"Can you try?"

"I'll see what I can do," he said. "If you really want me to."

"Yes, I do. Just to make sure."

"I think you should go home," he said. "You look awful."

"I will," I said. "Although I think I should stop in at the Fultons' first. You said you talked to Edwin? How are they doing?"

"They're just worried about you. You ran out of there last night after Maven called."

"I asked them to think about leaving the area for a while. You know, just go back downstate until this thing is over. Do you think it would do any good if they heard it from you, too?"

"I told them the same thing," he said.

"No go?"

"They're staying put, Alex. I think they just don't want to leave you here to face this by yourself."

"That's crazy," I said. "Hey, Mrs. Fulton is probably expecting me to spend the night there again. But I have to be at the cabin. Do you know somebody else who can stay there?"

"Not off the top of my head, no."

"How about your old investigator, Leon Prudell?"

"Oh God," he said. "I'd rather do it myself."

"Do you have a gun?"

"As a matter of fact, I do," he said. "I've got a nice little Beretta."

I was surprised to hear that. I wouldn't have expected Lane Uttley to own a gun. Although if he *did* have one, it figured it would have to be an expensive little Italian import. "Can you shoot?"

"I've been to the range with it a couple times," he said. "I'm not a bad shot."

"Sounds like you're talking yourself into it," I said. "It could be worse. It's a nice house, and Mrs. Fulton will make you dinner. You just sleep on the couch and keep half an ear open."

"What happens if he shows up?" he said. "What if he comes into the house?"

"That's easy," I said. "You kill him."

CHAPTER NINE

IT WAS ANOTHER calm night, the November winds mysteriously absent. I figured that was a good thing. I would be able to hear him outside if he came to my door.

The policeman had stopped by in his unmarked vehicle to set up the watch. I felt bad for the guy, having to sit there all night in his car. I remembered having to do that myself in Detroit.

I plugged in the phone unit Maven had given me. Any incoming calls would automatically trigger a trace record, and the recorder would turn on. All I had to do was pick up the phone and talk. If it was the same guy and he wanted to know what I thought of his latest murder, I would play along, get him to tell me all about it. That was the plan, at least.

The cop gave me a walkie-talkie, too. I called him as soon as he had taken up his position on the logging road, just around the bend. "I hear you loud and clear, Mr. McKnight," he said. "If anyone shows up, I should be able to see him from here. But give me a yell on this thing just in case you hear anything."

"You got it," I said. "I hope they're paying you double overtime for this." I signed off and put the walkie-talkie and my revolver on the table next to my bed. All I could do now was wait.

I lay on the bed, listening to the silence. It felt like a long time. I looked at the clock. It wasn't even eleven yet.

And then the phone rang. I sat up and grabbed the gun. Easy, Alex. For God's sake.

I heard the machine click on automatically. The number would be traced before I even answered it. And the faint whirring sound meant that the tape recording had already started.

I picked up the receiver. "Yes?"

"Alex, it's me, Lane. I'm at the Fultons' house. We had a nice dinner, sorry you couldn't be here. You were right, Mrs. Fulton is a great cook."

"Say hello to her for me," I said.

"I will. Listen, I just wanted to make sure you were all right over there. Is everything set up?"

"Yes, it is."

"Good. Okay, I'll get off the phone then. Hey, by the way, I tried calling the prison today. They were having a lockdown. There was some sort of disturbance on Rose's block. The guy sounded like it happens once a week. Anyway, I couldn't get through to Rose. I'll try again tomorrow."

"Okay, thanks," I said. "I appreciate it."

"No problem, Alex. You call me if anything happens, okay?"

"You got it."

"I mean, call the police first, of course. Ha! Then call me."

"Of course," I said.

"All right, I'm off to guard the palace. I'll talk to you tomorrow."

I lay back down on the bed. The gun was still in my hand. I looked at it closely, checked that it was loaded. It looked exactly like the gun I once carried as a policeman. I suppose that's why Lane bought it. He figured I'd be accustomed to a service revolver. But holding it in my hand only made me think of one thing. Why didn't I go for my gun right away? Could I have gotten it out of the holster in time? Would he have shot me first instead? Maybe I'd be dead now and Franklin would still be alive. Would that be such a bad thing?

The phone rang again. The machine turned on. Another trace, another recording. I answered it.

"Mr. McKnight? This is Theodora Fulton."

"Mrs. Fulton," I said. "Is everything all right over there?"

"For the moment, yes. Although I have to say, I would feel much safer if you were here."

"I'm sure you'll be fine," I said. "Lane is a good man."

"He's Edwin's lawyer, isn't he?"

"Yes, he is, ma'am."

"Do they allow lawyers to carry guns?"

"Uh . . . sure. Of course," I said. "Why not?"

"It doesn't seem right to me. Lawyers are dangerous enough without being armed, wouldn't you say?"

"Ah, you're being funny now, Mrs. Fulton."

"Please forgive me," she said. "I just had to hear your voice and to say good night to you, Alex. . . . You don't think that person will show up here, do you?"

"No," I said. "I really don't think so."

"All right, Alex. Do take care of yourself. Good night."

I walked around the cabin for a while, stood looking out each window into the night. I picked up the walkie-talkie and hit the button. "You okay out there?"

"No problem," he said. "I'm gonna just step out of the car a second to water the bushes, but don't worry, I'll have the radio with me at all times."

I signed off and put the unit back on the table. I checked the gun again. Alex, you are going to drive yourself fucking insane before this night is over.

The phone rang again. It was almost midnight. I picked it up.

"Alex, it's me, Edwin."

"What's wrong?"

"Nothing," he said. "Everything's fine. I just wanted to see how you're doing."

"Edwin, for God's sake. Uttley already called, and so did your mother."

"You're kidding me. I didn't hear them. I was in the jacuzzi."

"I'm fine, Edwin."

"You should try this jacuzzi sometime," he said. "It really helps you to relax."

"I can't imagine what relaxed feels like right now," I said. Truth was, I *had* been in his jacuzzi. It was the one time I had actually spent the night over there with Sylvia, when Edwin had gone down to Detroit to accept some kind of humanitarian award. All the other times were just quick exchanges in the afternoon, or maybe a stolen hour in the night when we were sure he was out at the casinos. Just thinking about it made me feel bad again. It was guilt, yes. But also the horrible realization that I would do it again if I had the chance. And the equally horrible realization that I *wouldn't* get the chance.

This is just what you need to be thinking about, Alex. While you wait for a killer to come pay you a visit. Now the night is complete.

"Are you still there, Alex?"

"Yes, sorry," I said. "I guess I'm a little on edge here."

"I shouldn't wonder. I'll let you go. Just wanted to say we're all thinking about you."

"You sure you guys don't want to go back to Grosse Pointe for a while," I said.

"No dice, Alex. You're stuck with us. Good night."

I put the phone down. Sylvia will be next, right? Just a quick good night and I hate your guts. Then I will have spoken to everyone in the house.

She didn't call. I finally lay back down on the bed with my clothes on. I turned the light off. I knew that having a light on inside might make me feel better, but that it was better to wait in the dark, where I could see him as well as he could see me.

I drifted off, thinking about that day in Detroit again. Whatever I had said into my radio was enough for them to finally find us there. My memories shifted from the ceiling of that apartment to the ceiling in the hospital. A doctor looking down at me, shining a light into my eyes. More darkness. Then another doctor and a nurse.

And then my wife looking down at me, biting her lip. I tried to speak, but I could not. I closed my eyes. The next time I opened them, she was gone.

And then a reporter, I think, trying to ask me questions. And then a nurse shooing him away.

I don't know how many days I spent in that hospital bed. Finally I was able to focus my eyes for more than a fleeting moment. And then soon after that I could lift my head up. I felt a thick wrapping of bandages on my right shoulder. A doctor came in and sat in a chair next to my bed.

"Mr. McKnight," he said. "How do you feel today?"

"How long has it been?" I said. "What happened?"

"It's been six days," he said. "You were shot three times."

"My partner," I said. "Franklin."

"He was gone when they found him."

"Yes," I said. I let my head fall back on the pillow. "I thought so."

"They had the funeral on Sunday," the doctor said.

"What about the man who shot me. Us. Did they catch him?"

"No," he said. "I don't believe so."

I nodded. "Was Mayor Young there? At Franklin's funeral?"

"Yes, he was."

"Good," I said. "Franklin always liked Mayor Young. It was one of the things we argued about."

"Mr. McKnight, I need to tell you what's going on. We were only able to remove two of the bullets."

"Two of them? Where's the third one?"

"It's still inside you," he said. "As a matter of fact, it's right next to your heart. It apparently bounced off your collar bone and stopped just outside the pericardial membrane."

"What does that mean?" I said.

"What that means is that you are a very lucky person. Although I don't suppose you *feel* very lucky right now."

"Not really."

"If the bullet had gone maybe a quarter of an inch more, it would have ruptured the membrane. Your heart would have drowned in its own blood."

"Why can't you take it out?"

"Well, we may be able to. We're going to have to think about this. You had lost a lot of blood when they brought you in. It took a long time just to stabilize you. Later we went in and took the two bullets out. One of them just nicked your lung and stopped at your shoulder blade. The other went into your rotator cuff. I'm afraid you'll never pitch again."

"I'm a catcher," I said.

He looked up from his chart. "Excuse me?"

"Never mind," I said. "Go on."

"I don't like where that third bullet is, Mr. McKnight. It's in what we call a retrocardiac location in the inferior media stinum, which means that it's between the heart and the spinal cord. An operation would be a matter of risk versus benefit at this point. We decided to hold off on it, see how you're doing. If there had been any sign of danger, we would have gone right in, of course."

"So now what?"

"Believe it or not, that bullet doesn't seem to be doing you any harm right now. It certainly wouldn't be the first time we left a bullet in somebody. When it's imbedded deep in a muscle, for instance, we often decide that we'd cause even more damage going in to get it."

"But this is next to my heart," I said.

"Yes," he said. "That's a little unusual. Like I said, you're very fortunate to be alive."

Very fortunate. That's me, all right.

Five months later, my right arm was still in a sling. I had just left the police force. My marriage was all but over. And then they caught Rose one night over at the other hospital across town. My old commanding officer came to my house and picked me up, drove me to the station. They led five men into the lineup room. I had stood on the other side of the glass a few times while a witness looked at all the faces. Now I was the witness.

Rose was the second man from the left. Even without the big blond wig, I would know him anywhere.

At the trial, I sat in the box and I pointed to the man named Maximilian Rose sitting at the defense table, and I said, that's the man right there. He looked at me with those same penetrating eyes.

They found him guilty and they sent him away. I watched the two bailiffs lead him out of the courtroom. He was going to prison for the rest of his—

A sound. The phone.

The phone was ringing.

I woke up. I grabbed the gun off the table, my heart pounding. The clock read 2:57.

The phone rang again. The machine went on. The call was traced. I could see the number right there on the readout.

I picked up the receiver. I didn't hear anything.

"Hello?" I said.

Silence.

"Are you there?"

Silence.

"Say something," I said.

Silence.

"Goddamn it, say something!"

Silence.

"Tell me about what you did," I said. "I want to hear about it. Tell me everything."

Silence.

"You motherfucking piece of shit, *who are you*?"

He hung up.

I was just about to throw the phone, but stopped myself. I picked up the walkie-talkie. "Come in," I said.

"Right here, Mr. McKnight. Is everything all right?"

"He just called." I gave him the number from the machine.

"Hold on," he said. I heard him calling in the number. I knew it would only take a few seconds for them to look it up, then another couple minutes to get to the phone. Something in my gut told me that it would be a pay phone. Two squad cars would come racing into the deserted parking lot of a gas station or a restaurant. The pay phone would stand alone under a street lamp, not a soul in sight.

I thought about what the note had said. I didn't have it with me, of course. I couldn't look at it to convince myself that it was real. I couldn't read it to try to make sense of it. What did it say? What were the exact words?

It can't be Rose. He can't be here. He's in prison. There's no way he could be anywhere else.

The note. What did it say? Something about microwaves, about the chosen one, about me being in disguise.

I never told anyone about that.

I didn't tell my wife. I didn't tell the shrink the department sent me to. I never told anyone.

There were only three people in that room when he said those things. Rose, myself, and Franklin. And Franklin is dead.

CHAPTER TEN

I STOPPED BY to see Maven the next day. He had the phone record on his desk. "It was a pay phone on Ashmun Street," he said. "It's only a block away from the second murder site."

"I don't understand why he didn't say anything," I said.

Maven rubbed his chin. "It's almost like he *knew* he was being recorded."

"How would he know that?"

"You tell me," he said.

I shook my head. "You're something else, Chief."

He picked up the piece of paper and looked at it again. "Funny, you got three other calls last night. They're all from the same number."

"The Fultons'."

"Yes."

"So what?"

"It's just funny," he said.

"Uttley called me, and then Mrs. Fulton, and then Edwin."

"Mr. Uttley is baby-sitting them now?"

"We didn't have much choice, Chief," I said. "I'm stuck in my cabin now, remember? And you didn't seem too willing to post an officer over there."

"Oh, I'm sure they're safe," he said.

"I don't follow you," I said. I felt the acid building in

my stomach again. How long would I have to keep seeing this bastard every morning?

"This is your own personal psycho, McKnight. Why would he bother your friend? He even said in his note that he likes the guy, didn't he?"

I just looked at him. "Am I *ever* going to get a coffee in this place?"

"Maybe some day, McKnight. The next time I'm in a good mood."

That was enough of Maven for one morning, so I got myself out of there. While I was in town, I stopped by to see the pay phone. A detective was still there, finishing his work. He had dusted for fingerprints. I could still see traces of the powder on the phone.

There was a little bookstore nearby, a gift shop next to that. But I didn't imagine there would have been anyone around at three o'clock in the morning. And even if there was, would they have noticed a man making a call at a pay phone?

If the man was wearing a big blond wig, maybe. Ha ha.

Angelo's restaurant was just down the street, so I walked down to see it again. It was still deserted. I walked around to the back alley. The police had cleaned the place up pretty well. I had to get down on my hands and knees to see the faint residue of blood on the bottom of the grease barrel.

What was I doing here? Here I was in a dirty little alley, on all fours like a dog. My pants were probably ruined. What was I looking for? I didn't even know. All I knew was it was driving me crazy, just sitting around wondering who this person was and what he would do next.

On the way back to Paradise I gave the Fultons a call on my cell phone. Everyone was fine, although Uttley had a stiff neck from sleeping on the couch. He told me he'd try the prison again when he went in to the office.

I went home and slept for a couple hours. Later I stopped in at the Glasgow. Jackie was the only person in the place, but that was fine by me.

"Haven't seen ya in a couple days," he said as he cracked a cold Canadian for me. God bless him.

"Things have been a little crazy," I said.

"Have you seen the paper today? They had another murder in town."

I took the newspaper from him. The headline read, "Local Man Slain Behind Restaurant, Second Murder In Three Days." I read the story, but it didn't tell me anything I didn't already know. They tried to get Maven to say something about it, but he gave them the usual line about it being too early in the investigation to comment. Maven's picture was on page two. He didn't photograph well.

"Damnedest thing," Jackie said. "Hey, didn't I read something about Edwin and that first murder? The one in the motel?"

"He just found the body," I said. I was about to tell him all about it. He certainly knew how to listen. But I didn't. I just felt too tired and confused to go through it all again. Maybe next time, I thought. We'll go sit at a table and I'll lay it all out for him. He might be able to help me make some sense of it.

I went back to the cabin and called Uttley. "The lockdown's over," he said. "I was able to get a message through today."

"Great, so what happened?"

"Well, I wasn't quite sure what to say. I just asked them to double-check on Rose, make sure they take a mug shot with him."

"Maybe I should visit him," I said.

"You actually want to go down there and see him?"

"Maybe that's the only way I'll know if it's really him," I said. Although I couldn't imagine actually being in a room with him again. Even with four inches of wire-reinforced glass between us.

"I can give it a try," he said.

"Thanks," I said. "Are you spending the night at the Fultons' again?"

"Mrs. Fulton wants *somebody* there. As long as they refuse to leave, I figure I'll keep staying there with them." ·

"You're doing a good thing," I said.

He laughed. "Just wait until they see my bill."

THE NIGHT CAME again, and with it another small dose of the fear. I found myself thinking about those pills in the back of the medicine cabinet. But I couldn't afford to take them. I had to be ready.

The same cop waited all night in the same place. His name was Dave. He had a wife and two kids at home. I felt for the guy, having to spend all night sitting in his car. I made him some coffee and a couple sandwiches this time. It was the least I could do.

Uttley spent his night on the Fultons' couch. I spent my night lying on my bed, looking over at the phone every five minutes. I got up a few times and looked outside.

He didn't call. Not even just to hear my voice. Not even just to let me hear the silence on the other end. The night passed without a sound. Even the wind stayed quiet.

THE NEXT DAY I had no reason to go see Chief Maven. That gave me two choices. Either pick some daisies and show up at his office anyway, or give myself the day off. It was a tough choice, but I stayed home.

I split some firewood and delivered it to the other cabins. On my first run I stopped at the bend in the road, just to see where Dave was spending his nights. It looked like he had chosen a thick stand of jack pine trees. You could just barely make out my front door.

I came back to the woodpile and finished my last load. It felt good to swing the ax, but it didn't make me forget my troubles. Out of the corner of my eye I caught a flash of something that looked like blond hair. It turned out to be a doe making a break through the brush. I had to stand there leaning with both hands on the chopping block for a full minute before I could move again.

I gave Uttley a call at his office. "You sound pretty beat," he said.

"You sound a little rough around the edges yourself," I said. "I was just wondering if you had heard anything from the prison."

"Just talked to them. The guy's going to go check himself. I haven't heard back yet."

"Did you tell them I want to visit him?"

"Alex," he said. "This man shot you. I gotta tell you, the man at the prison thinks it's a *bad* idea to try to visit him."

"Don't worry," I said. "What's he going to do to me in a prison?"

"Alex, it just seems . . . unhealthy."

"I'll tell you what's unhealthy," I said. "Somebody killing people and writing me love notes about it."

"But Alex, *that can't be Rose.* You know that. A man can't be in two places at one time."

"What if he has a twin brother?"

"What? Are you serious?"

"It's just an idea," I said. "What if his twin brother is in prison and the real Rose is up here?"

"If he had a twin brother, why would he even . . . never mind. I don't even know what to say."

"I'm sorry," I said. "I know this sounds crazy, but I have to start somewhere."

"Look, I'll see if I can locate any records. Birth certificate, school records, whatever. And I'll let you know as soon as I hear back from the prison, okay?"

"All right," I said. "Thanks for humoring me."

"Maybe this will be the night," he said. "Maybe he'll show up at your front door."

"I hope so," I said. "I know it sounds strange, but this is one murderer I really want to meet."

ONE MORE NIGHT. Dave in his car, me in the cabin, just waiting there. How long would we have to keep doing this? If this guy wanted to torture me, he had found the best way. Just make me sit there on my butt all night long.

The wind started to pick up a little bit that night. Then it died down again. In the long hours I tried not to think about the past too much. I didn't want to see Franklin dying again. I didn't want to see that look in Rose's eyes. And yet, who else's eyes would I see at two o'clock in the morning, as I lay on my bed feeling the cold weight of my gun?

And then suddenly, a light. It swept across the wall. Headlights.

I reached for the walkie-talkie, pushed the button, and spoke in a hoarse whisper. "Dave," I said. "It's a car."

Silence.

"Dave. Come in."

Nothing.

"Goddamn it, Dave! Are you there?"

No answer. Outside I heard a car door shut. Then footsteps. I gripped the revolver with both hands. The footsteps stopped.

I took a step toward the door. The floor creaked beneath me. I stopped.

There was no sound except for my breathing and my heartbeat. What was he doing out there?

Bang! The silence was ripped apart. My heart leapt into

my throat. Bang! The pounding on my door sounded like he would smash it into splinters. I put my back against the wall, keeping clear of the door. Surely it would bust open with the next blast. Bang! I could feel the impact shake the entire cabin.

And then a voice, bellowing in the night. "McKnight!" He was right there at my doorstep. I could practically feel the heat of his breath through the door. "Get out here, McKnight!"

I quickly weighed my options. Stay put, see what he does next? Throw the door open and surprise him? What if he's armed? Am I prepared to shoot? Goddamn it all to hell, can I shoot him this time?

I checked the gun. All right, you fucking lunatic. This is it. I'm opening this door right now. And if I see a gun in your hand I'm gonna shoot you right between the eyes. On the count of three. One. Two.

"Freeze!" Another voice. Outside. "Get down now! Put your hands behind your head! On the ground! Now! Move it!"

I threw the door open. There was a man facedown on my doorstep. Dave was standing above him, both hands on his gun. "Mr. McKnight, put the gun down!"

I just stood there.

"Mr. McKnight! Please put your gun down!"

I looked down at my hand. The gun was shaking. I pointed it to the ground.

"Are you all right?"

"What?"

"Are you all right, Mr. McKnight?"

"Yes," I said. I looked at the man on the ground. He was fighting for breath. I couldn't see his face. "Where were you? I tried to call you on the radio."

Dave kept his gun trained on the man. "I didn't hear you," he said.

I didn't take my eyes off the man on the ground.

"Backup is on the way," he said. And then to the man, "You just keep lying right there. Don't move a muscle."

The man groaned.

He looked familiar. That hair. "Wait a minute," I said. I bent down to look at him.

"Mr. McKnight, don't go near him!"

"It's all right, Dave," I said. I grabbed the man's red hair and pulled his face up into the light of the doorway. "I know this man."

"Goddamn you, McKnight," he said. He was drunk.

"Dave," I said. "I'd like you to meet Mr. Leon Prudell."

"You must be pretty goddamned afraid of me, Mc-Knight," he said. A thin line of drool ran from his mouth to the ground. "You went out and got police protection just in case I showed up?"

"Yeah, that's right, Prudell. I was afraid you'd use your chin to bruise my knuckles again."

THEY DRAGGED PRUDELL'S sorry drunken ass down to the station for the night. The next morning, I still hadn't started to feel sorry for him yet. I figured he deserved at least a few more hours with Chief Maven.

I stopped by Uttley's office around ten o'clock. He was just finishing a good phone slam. For the first time in memory, his hair was messy.

"I can't take too much more of this," he told me. "Everything's falling apart here. I'm losing clients. You remember that guy at the trailer park? I missed a couple of calls from him so he went out and got somebody else."

"You don't look so good," I said.

"I hope I don't look as bad as you do," he said.

"You might want to stop in at the station today," I said. "They've got your man Prudell there."

"He is most definitely not my man," Uttley said. "What did he do?"

"He came by my cabin last night. I think he wanted to continue our discussion from last week."

"Oh for God's sake," he said. "Does he actually blame *you* for him losing his job?"

"He's out, I'm in," I said. "That's all he cares about."

"What a jackass," he said. "So I suppose Maven thinks he's our killer now? Because he came to your place last night?"

"He did for about five minutes," I said. "I set him straight."

"So why's he still there?"

"I think he's just drying out," I said.

"Fine, let him stay there," he said. "God, what a jackass."

We both let ourselves laugh a little bit. It was the kind of laugh that comes out when you haven't slept in days and you feel like one big exposed nerve.

"Where are we on Rose today?" I said.

He held up a pad of legal paper, taking a moment to focus his bloodshot eyes. "Maximilian Rose, born in 1959." He looked up at me. "He did *not* have a twin brother. Sentenced in December of 1984. Life plus twelve years, no parole. I told you I talked to a corrections officer down there yesterday. It took a little while to make him understand our situation."

"Did he have a picture? A mug shot or something he could use to positively identify him?"

"Yes, he did. He told me that he went to Rose's cell personally and double-checked on him. As far as he's concerned, that man in the cell is Maximilian Rose."

"How about the request to visit him?"

Uttley looked at me and exhaled. "This guy did pass that request along, yes."

"And?"

"And Rose refused to see anyone."

"What? Are you kidding?"

"That's his right," he said. "He doesn't have to receive any visits if he doesn't want to."

"But can't we *make* him?"

"*We* can't, no. I suppose the police can."

"Great," I said. "I'm sure Maven will love this idea."

"I don't know what else to do."

"Can I talk to this guy? The corrections officer?"

"If you really want to," he said. "He seemed like a good man. But I don't know how much patience he's going to have with this."

"I don't know," I said. "Maybe I should just forget it. I mean, it's crazy, right?"

Uttley sat down behind his desk and looked at the ceiling. "I don't know what's crazy anymore, Alex."

I STOPPED BY Angelo's restaurant again. The owner had opened the place up again. He was sweeping the floor when I went in and ordered a couple slices. He had been there the night of the murder, but he didn't remember anything out of the ordinary. I sat there at a small table, maybe in the same chair as the murderer, the would-be Rose, whatever I wanted to call this guy. Vince Dorney was here, I thought, maybe over there by the bathroom, talking on the phone. He overhears Dorney talking, thinks he hears something about microwaves. Wasn't that what the note said? He decides Dorney is a bad man, a man who needs to be removed. But how does he get him into the back alley? The owner of the restaurant didn't have any ideas about that. He didn't seem too anxious to even think about it anymore.

A couple hours later I was still in town, sitting on the

hood of my truck on Portage Street, looking out at the vast expanse of Lake Superior. I sat there for a long time, thinking about the night before. Dave didn't hear me calling him because the radio wasn't even on. Didn't I even notice that the unit was dead? No static, even?

And then when Prudell was knocking on my door, the way I grabbed that gun. What if I had opened the door before Dave got there? Would I have shot him? Prudell could be dead right now, on top of everything else. What was happening to me?

And why in God's name won't Rose see me? It doesn't make any sense. Unless . . . unless it's not really Rose. The man is afraid I'll know it's not him if I see him.

Listen to yourself, Alex. Listen to what you're saying.

But what else can explain it? Rose is the only person who could have written that note.

Stop it. Just stop it.

I could see the dark clouds building in the western sky. The wind began to pick up. It stung my face and brought tears to my eyes.

I FINALLY MADE it into the Glasgow for dinner, after killing a few more hours driving around, going nowhere. I didn't want to go back to the cabin yet. I dreaded the thought of another long night there.

Jackie was behind the bar when I got there. "What the hell happened to you?" he said. "You look worse than I do, and that's saying something."

"It's a long story, Jackie. I'm not going to tell you until you slide a beer this way."

He cracked a Canadian for me. "Couple men in here asking about you last night."

"One of those men would be Leon Prudell, I take it."

"Yeah, he came in later. Said he had some unfinished

business with you. Drank a good twenty dollars' of whiskey before he finally left. I keep overcharging that guy but he doesn't seem to notice."

"Who else was here?"

"What's his name, the chief of police over in the Soo."

"Roy Maven?"

"Yeah, that's the guy. He was asking all sorts of questions about you. You know, how often you come in, who you hang out with."

I raised my bottle. "Here's to Roy Maven," I said.

"So are you going to tell me what's going on or aren't you?"

"Get your no-good son out here so we can go sit down," I said. "This is going to take a while."

His son poked his head out of the kitchen. There was a phone in his hand. "Hey, is McKnight here?"

"Depends on who's calling," I said.

"Do you know a woman named Theodora Fulton? She sounds like she's ready to kill you."

I jumped off the barstool and grabbed the phone from him. "Mrs. Fulton?"

"Alex! My God, where have you been? I've been calling you for two hours."

"Take it easy, Mrs. Fulton. What's the problem?"

"It's Edwin!"

I felt a needle in my gut, sickly and cold. "What about Edwin? What's the matter?"

"I knew this would happen," she said. "I had such a horrible feeling when I woke up this morning."

"Mrs. Fulton, tell me!"

"He's gone," she said. "He told me he'd be back in a little while. But he didn't come back, Alex. He . . . " Her voice broke for an instant while she struggled with the panic. "He's gone, Alex. Edwin is gone."

CHAPTER ELEVEN

MRS. FULTON WAS already standing in the doorway when I got there. She grabbed the front of my coat and pulled me into the house. "What in God's name took you so long?" she said as she steered me onto the couch. "I called you twenty minutes ago." She didn't sit next to me. She just stood there looking down at me.

"I came as fast as I could, Mrs. Fulton." I wasn't about to tell her that it had only been fifteen minutes. "Please, you have to tell me exactly what happened."

"He's gone," she said. "My son is gone."

"Gone where? When did he leave?"

"It was around noon. He said he needed to go into the office for a little while. He said he'd be back for dinner."

I looked at my watch. It was almost seven o'clock. "He's not that late," I said. "It's just starting to get dark out."

"No, no," she said. "He's never late. Edwin is never late for dinner. He should have been here two hours ago."

"I'm sure he's fine," I said. "Did you call his office?"

"Yes, of course I did." She made a fist with her right hand and rubbed it with her left, like she was getting ready to belt me.

"Then he's probably on his way home right now."

"I called at five-thirty. Don't you understand? He should be home by now!"

I grabbed her hands and pulled her onto the couch. "Please, Mrs. Fulton. I'm sure there's a reasonable explanation."

"He shouldn't have left the house," she said. "He should have stayed here. It's too dangerous."

"No, Mrs. Fulton, no. You can't think that way."

"He had a fight with *her*," she said. Her voice turned cold. "She was yelling at him. I could hear them from down here. That's why he had to leave. He just had to get away from here."

"He had a fight with Sylvia?"

"Yes," she said. "That woman drove him out of the house."

"Well then, that explains why he hasn't come back yet, doesn't it."

"What do you mean?"

"He's probably just sitting in a bar somewhere."

"Do you think so?" Finally, the first hint of hope in her voice.

"Of course," I said. "He's talking to a bartender right now, telling him all about it. You know, trying to figure women out. We've all done that."

From behind me a voice said, "He's at the casino." I turned and saw Sylvia standing there.

"How do you know that?" I said.

"Because he told me that's where he was going," she said. The expression on her face was totally unreadable. I didn't know if she was angry or smug or God knows what. "That's why we were fighting."

Mrs. Fulton just stared at her. For the first time, I sensed some of the history between them.

"Edwin told me that he was through with gambling," Mrs. Fulton said.

"He told that to everyone," Sylvia said. "But it was

only a matter of time. He needed his fix. I couldn't stop him."

"Which casino is he at?" I said.

"He starts at one casino and then moves on when he thinks his luck is turning bad," she said. "You know that. You've gone and found him before."

"Alex," Mrs. Fulton said, "you know how to find him? You've done it before?"

"Yes," I said, looking at Sylvia. I remembered the last time I had gone looking for him. It was a summer night, as warm as it ever gets up here on the lake. Sylvia had wanted me to spend the night, to use this rare chance to wake up in the same bed together. He won't come back, she had told me. You know he'll be gone all night. And even if he does come back, then so what, so he finds out. Maybe that wouldn't be so bad.

I told her it was time for us to put an end to it. And then the warm night got even warmer.

"Please," Mrs. Fulton said, "go find Edwin. Will you do that please?"

"Yes," I said. "I'll go find him."

Uttley came in the house. Why did he always show up five minutes after I could really use him? "What's going on?" he said. "Alex, shouldn't you be at your cabin?"

"Edwin is gone," Mrs. Fulton said. "Alex is going to go find him."

"It's all right," I said. "He's at one of the casinos."

"I thought he said—"

"I know," I said. "So he had a little relapse. It's perfectly normal. I'll go get him and then we can all beat on him until he admits he needs to get some help with his problem."

"Do you want me to come with you?" Uttley said.

"No, you stay here," I said. "See if you can make Mrs.

Fulton some tea or something. I won't be long. There aren't that many places he could be."

"Maven's not going to like this," he said.

"Maven doesn't like *anything* I do. So it doesn't matter."

On my way out, I grabbed Sylvia by the elbow and pushed her into the hallway. "Goddamn it," I said in a whisper. "What's the matter with you?"

"Let go of me," she said. Her green eyes shone with enough venom to kill me seven times over.

"Why did you let him go out gambling?"

"I told you, I tried to stop him. What does it matter, anyway? You don't care what happens to him."

"Why are you still here?" I said. "Why don't you tell him you want to leave, go back home to Grosse Pointe?"

"I don't think you really want me to leave," she said.

"Is that what this is about? Are you making him stay here because you think there's still a chance for us? Because if you are—"

"Oh please," she said. "That is so pathetic. And so transparent. You're the one who's missing it, Alex. It's so obvious."

"Whatever you say, Sylvia. Now if you'll excuse me, I'm gonna go find your husband."

She caught my arm as I turned to go. "Alex," she said, her voice low and even, the anger seemingly turned off in an instant. I could smell her perfume. I knew it would cling to me. Her scent would stay with me all night. "What's going on? Why is she so upset about Edwin being gone?"

"I can't talk about it right now," I said.

"Is he really in danger? Tell me the truth."

"I promised her I'd bring him back," I said. "And I'm going to."

"Your promises don't mean anything." She said it

without malice, like it was nothing more than simple truth.
"I should know."

I HEADED TO the Bay Mills Casino first, Edwin's
favorite place to play blackjack. On the way I gave Maven
a call. He wasn't in, so I left a message that I wouldn't be
at the cabin for a while. If he really wanted to, he could let
an officer sit by my phone. Dave had a key. He could pretend to be me for a night.

It almost made me happy to imagine how upset he
would be when he found out I wasn't at home. I was sure
Edwin was just sitting at a blackjack table, spending
money as fast as he could. He didn't even know how to
play the game. I once saw him draw two sevens against a
dealer showing a six. He didn't split them. He didn't even
stand. He hit the fourteen and busted. Most compulsive
gamblers at least give themselves a fighting chance once
in a while.

I'm sure that's where he was. Or in a bar somewhere.
Just like I told his mother. This prickly little ball of dread
rolling up and down my back, that was just a product of my
overworked imagination. God knows I had every right to it
by now.

The casino is on the Bay Mills reservation, just north of
Brimley. No big sign in front, no lights all over the place.
The outside is all cedar, the inside is all high wooden
beams and ceiling fans. It looks nothing at all like a casino,
not like in Vegas or Atlantic City where they try to dazzle
you into coming inside and staying. Only the noise is the
same, that distinctive casino noise that hits you as soon as
you walk into the place. The slot machines with that hollow electronic music, the coins hitting the metal trays, a
payoff somewhere in the room every few seconds. The
keno wheel spinning and clacking, slower and slower until

it stops. Dealers calling out every exchange of money for chips, the pit bosses answering. A thousand voices at once, begging for the right card or the right turn on the roulette wheel, celebrating, cursing, winning, losing. You just stand in the middle of the room for five minutes, that noise starts to make sense. It starts calling your name. Tonight's your night, it says. As long as you're in this room, nothing can touch you. You're better than everybody else. You're smarter, you're luckier. You deserve to be a winner.

A guy like Edwin doesn't stand a chance here.

They had about twenty blackjack tables going, a Bay Mills tribe member standing at each one, dealing the cards with detached precision. I didn't see Edwin at any of them. I pulled a pit boss over and asked him if Edwin Fulton had been in. I knew he'd know the name.

"Just got here myself," he said. "Let me go ask somebody else."

I watched a few hands of blackjack while he was away. The players were a strange mix of downstaters. One man was wearing the kind of clothes you only see in casinos anymore: the polyester blue sport coat, the pinkie ring, the tie as wide as a lobster bib. The man next to him looked like he walked right out of the woods: the mandatory orange pants and jacket, the hunting license pinned to his back. They were both pushing piles of chips onto the table and staring at the cards as though they were hypnotized. I wondered if they pumped extra oxygen into the air here like they do in Vegas, just to keep the bettors from getting tired.

The pit boss reappeared. "Mr. Fulton was here," he said. "He left about two hours ago. I understand he made quite a little performance on his way out."

"Oh beautiful," I said. "You guys didn't throw him out the window or anything, did you? Not that I'd blame you."

"I wouldn't know. Like I said, I wasn't here."

"Is Vinnie LeBlanc here? Red Sky? I'm sorry, I don't know what he calls himself here. He lives down the road from me."

"Red Sky, huh? He's gonna hear about that one. No, I think he's on his dinner break. He should be back soon."

I thanked the man and left. When I was outside I took a deep breath of the night air. The casino sounds were still buzzing in my head. From the west I caught a blast of cold wind that smelled like rain.

I raced down Six Mile Road toward the city, hoping I was right behind him on his rounds through the casinos. Just before I got there, my cellular phone rang. I had a good idea who it was, but I picked it up anyway.

"McKnight, what the hell is wrong with you?"

"Chief Maven, what a pleasant surprise."

"You're supposed to be in your cabin."

"I'll be there. I just have to find Edwin first."

"Goddamn it, McKnight, are the two of you queer for each other or something?"

"Would that upset you, Chief? That I was already taken?"

"Go fuck yourself, McKnight."

"You have a nice night, too, Chief."

The casino was just up ahead. I hung up before he could say another word.

The Kewadin Casino is right in Sault Ste. Marie, on a little piece of land owned by the Sault tribe. They're Chippewas just like the Bay Mills tribe, but they're less traditional and less restrictive on the bloodlines. And they have a lot less restraint when they build casinos. The Kewadin is huge, with giant triangles on the front that are supposed to remind you of tepees. You can see that damned thing ten miles away. It has a four-star hotel, live entertainment every night, the works.

I looked at my watch. It was almost nine o'clock. Okay,

Edwin, you've got to be here somewhere. They threw your ass out of the other place and this is the only other game in town. I started working my way up the rows of blackjack tables. I knew I had to hit them all, even the five-dollar tables, because that's where he liked to start, see how the cards were falling that night. I remembered telling him once that he should just throw five-dollar bills out his car window on the way there. The effect would be the same.

I didn't see any sign of him. I took a quick look through the roulette tables and the craps tables. Sometimes out of desperation he'd go give them a try when he felt his luck needed a little jolt. I didn't see him anywhere.

I didn't know what to do. I walked back and forth between the two big rooms, looking at all the blackjack tables again. I slowed down near the horse-racing game, watched that for a couple minutes. There were a good twenty people gathered around it, one in every chair, watching the little mechanical horses go around the track. The horses weren't more than two inches tall, probably driven by magnets under the table, and yet these people were screaming at them like it was the Kentucky Derby. On another night I would have found it pretty damned hilarious.

I got in the truck and drove all the way back to the Bay Mills Casino, hoping to catch Vinnie this time. I spotted him at one of the blackjack tables and sat down. The woman next to me had a nice little pile of five-dollar chips going. Her husband stood over her shoulder, obviously ready to offer his expert advice.

"Alex," he said, barely looking up from the cards. "Good to see you. You come to clean us out?"

"I wouldn't want to break this place," I said. "Then you'd be out of a job. Actually, I was just looking for Edwin Fulton. The pit boss told me he was here around dinner time. Did you see him?"

He smiled and rolled his eyes. "Oh, I saw him," he said. He dealt two cards to the woman and then waited for her decision. Her husband leaned in and told her to take a card. She waved him away like a mosquito.

"He left here about when, six o'clock?"

"Sounds about right," he said. "He was not a happy man." The woman said she was good, thank you. The husband threw his hands in the air. Vinnie turned up his cards, drew to his fifteen, and busted. He matched the woman's chips while her husband massaged her shoulders. "Alex, you gonna play a hand here at least while we're talking? You're gonna get me in trouble."

I slid him a ten-dollar bill. "Give me two chips."

"I don't know if we can handle that much, Alex. I'm gonna have to call the man for more chips."

"You're one funny Indian," I said. "Just tell me what happened."

"Same thing as always," he said, dealing the cards. "He lost a ton, he drank a ton, he got ugly, we booted him."

"That much I heard already."

"You know, if it wasn't for that losing a ton part, I don't think they'd even let him in the door anymore."

"Any idea where he went? Did he say he was going home or anything?"

"I don't know. They did offer to call him a cab so he didn't have to drive. He said he had a chauffeur waiting outside."

"He doesn't have a chauffeur," I said.

"I didn't think so. I guess he was just trying to show off."

"All right. Thanks, Vinnie."

"Do the guy a favor, eh? The next time he feels like playing blackjack, lock him in his room. Hey, you want a card here or what?"

I doubled on the seven and four, drew a ten for twenty-one.

"Looks like the cards are going your way," he said as he paid me.

I slid the chips right back at him. I needed to get back out there to look for Edwin, wherever he might be. I wouldn't be able to sleep until I found him, until I knew he was safe at home with his goddamned wife where he belonged. "You got that right," I said to Vinnie as I stood up. "This is my lucky night."

CHAPTER TWELVE

I SAT IN my truck in the Bay Mills Casino parking lot, looking out at the lights on a freighter anchored across the bay. There must be a big storm coming, I thought. They're waiting for it to blow through before they make their last run of the season.

At least they had a reason to be sitting there doing nothing. With some idea of how long they would wait until they began moving again.

I picked up the cell phone. In the darkness it gave off an eery green glow. If I call his house and he's there, I thought, then I can just stop this nonsense and go home. I'll save his ass-kicking until tomorrow. But if I call his house and he's *not* home, then I just end up getting Mrs. Fulton even more frantic.

Please, Uttley, pick up the phone. He didn't.

"Alex, is that you? Did you find him?" It was Mrs. Fulton.

"Not yet, Mrs. Fulton, but he was just here at the casino. I'm sure he's fine."

"Where is he now?"

"He's probably on the way home right now," I said. "I'm going to swing by a couple more places, just to make sure."

"I have a bad feeling, Alex," she said. "I told you that already, didn't I? I'd really like you to find him immediately."

"There's no need to worry, Mrs. Fulton," I said. "Can you please put Mr. Uttley on the phone?"

"Why do you want to talk to him?" she said. "Is there something you aren't telling me?"

"No, Mrs. Fulton."

"Something has happened, hasn't it?" The command in her voice finally giving way.

"No, Mrs. Fulton, I swear, everything is okay. I just want to talk to Lane for a minute."

"Alex, I'm here," Uttley's voice came on. "What is it?"

"Lane," I said, taking a couple beats to calm myself down, "will you please make sure you answer the phone next time?"

"Of course, Alex. I'm sorry, she beat me to it."

"You have my cellular number, right? Give me a call if he comes home. I'm going to go check a few more places."

I didn't feel much like doing that, but I didn't see much choice. I knew he was probably sitting in a bar somewhere, feeling sorry for himself. All that talk about being a new man, it lasted, what? Seven days? I should leave the guy alone, I thought. Let him crawl home in the morning, and then tomorrow just tell him to look in the phone book under Gamblers Anonymous. But I can't do that. I promised Mrs. Fulton I'd find him.

And that feeling. That little tickle up and down my back. I kept wishing that it would go away. It wouldn't.

I stopped in at the two bars in Brimley. Then I headed back east toward the Soo and stopped in at the Mariner's Tavern. I knew that had been his bar back when he was placing bets with Tony Bing. They had a good Saturday night crowd in the place, but no Edwin.

There's got to be something like twenty bars in Sault Ste. Marie. I hit every one of them I knew of, and even found a few new ones. I looked for his silver Mercedes in the parking lots first, then took a quick look inside just in case he had left his car somewhere else. I did that myself a few times back in Detroit, after I left the force and my wife left me. I'd start at one bar and sit there over a drink for a while until it didn't feel like the right place to be anymore. Then I'd go to the next one. By the end of the night I was walking through the darkness, just aiming myself at the next bright light down the street. I'd have to go find my car the next morning.

When I had run out of bars in the Soo, I stopped at the Kewadin Casino again, looked over all the tables. I asked a couple pit bosses if they had seen him there that night. They hadn't.

On a hunch I decided to go down to St. Ignace, check out the casino down there. It was a good hour's drive south, but at least it kept me moving. I took I-75 all the way down, crossed the line into Mackinac County. It was almost midnight by then, not many cars on the road. I saw a car with a deer tied on the back, lifeless eyes staring at me as I passed. The glow of a cigarette in the passenger's side window.

I found the casino in St. Ignace, another one of the Sault tribe's. I walked blinking in the sudden brightness, looked at every table, cursed myself for wasting my time with such a stupid idea, got back in the truck, and headed right back to the Soo. Another hour of driving, the wind picking up, bringing the storm in from the lake.

God, I am so tired. Why am I doing this?

My eyes were burning. I felt like somebody had hit me with a bag of sand. But I had to find him. Not just for Mrs. Fulton, but for myself. I had to know that he was safe.

The phone rang. It was Uttley.

"Alex," he said. "Any sign of him?"

"Not yet," I said. "I'm going to keep looking. How's Mrs. Fulton?"

"I think she might be asleep finally. No, wait, I think I hear her. I better go. Good luck, Alex."

I hit the Kewadin Casino one more time. They were open all night, after all. He could walk right back in any time. I got some funny looks this time. I must have seemed like a stray dog, coming back again and again and just wandering through the tables.

The bars would be closing soon, but I knew there were a few places open in Canada. I crossed the bridge, paid the toll, pulled into the customs lane. The man in the booth asked me all the usual questions. No, there are no drugs or firearms in the vehicle. I shouldn't be in Canada more than an hour or two. Before he let me go he asked me if I had been drinking that night. I said I had not. He looked me in my bloodshot eyes like he wanted to make an issue out of it, but then he finally just let me go through.

I looked in every bar I could find in Soo Canada. They didn't have any casinos in Canada, but they did have a few places with exotic dancing. That's what they called it, anyway. The women didn't look very exotic to me, but then I wasn't exactly in the right mood for it.

It was almost three o'clock when I came back over the bridge. I could see the Algoma Steel foundry below me, the fires burning even at this hour of the night. The wind was getting stronger. A gust hit the truck sideways and for a moment I thought it would blow me right off the bridge.

I stopped at the Kewadin Casino one more time. It was the only place in the Soo still open. The crowds had thinned out but there were still more people gambling at that hour than you would expect. There are no clocks in a casino, of course. No windows. Nothing to tell you that you're spending the entire night throwing your money away.

I headed west. I could barely keep the truck on the road. My eyes were refusing to focus. I made myself stop at the reservation, take one more look in the Bay Mills Casino. Vinnie had finished his shift and gone home.

And then as one last futile gesture, I drove up through the reservation to the Kings Club. It was a tiny little place, nothing more than one room with some slot machines in it. Maybe that's what hitting bottom would look like for him, I thought. Just standing there feeding quarters into a slot machine at four in the morning.

He wasn't there. He wasn't anywhere.

I went home. I just couldn't face seeing Mrs. Fulton yet. Let her sleep a couple more hours, assuming that she got to sleep at all. Maybe Edwin will show up on his own, anyway. By the time the sun comes up, maybe he'll be home on the couch, wrapped up in a blanket and drinking hot chocolate. And I'll actually be glad to see him before I remember what he put me through tonight.

When I was in my cabin, I called Dave on the radio and apologized for missing most of the night there.

"No problem," he said. "It was another quiet one. No sign of anybody. Chief Maven called me, though. He's not real happy with you."

"I'm too tired to name all the places on his body he can blow it out of, Dave. Good night." I lay down on the bed. I was asleep before I could even think of fighting it.

THE PHONE RANG. The sound gave me a heart attack. When this is all over, I thought, I'm going to get rid of my phone forever. If somebody wants to reach me, they'll have to come and find me.

It was light out. I looked at my watch. It was just after seven o'clock. I rubbed my eyes as the phone rang again, got up, and looked at the readout on the trace machine. The call was coming from the Fultons'. I hoped to God it was Edwin calling to apologize.

"Alex? It's Lane." Uttley paused for a long moment. I

could hear a faint noise in the background. It sounded like a glass breaking on the floor. "He didn't come home."

"All right," I said. "I think we should call the police."

"Did you find any other trace of him last night?"

"No, not since I talked to you after I checked at Bay Mills. They said he was there around dinnertime."

"Alex, I'm sure he'll show up today," he said. "I'm sure he just had to sleep it off somewhere."

"I hope so," I said. "Now go tell Mrs. Fulton that."

"I will," he said. "Are you going to call the police? Or do you want me to?"

"Dave might still be here," I said. "He usually calls me on the radio before he leaves. I'll have him call it in. I don't feel like talking to Maven right now."

"Are you going to come over here?"

"Yes," I said. "Let me just clean up a little bit. I'll be over as soon as I can."

"Take your time, Alex. We're not going anywhere." I could hear yelling in the background now as he hung up.

I caught Dave on the radio just as he was getting ready to leave.

"I'll call it in right now," he said. "I don't think the twenty-four-hour rule applies here."

"It's probably nothing," I said. "But under the circumstances . . ." I didn't even know how to finish the sentence.

"Don't worry, Mr. McKnight. We'll find him."

I signed off and just sat there looking out the window for a few minutes. Then I took a hot shower and shaved and put on some clean clothes. I almost felt human again. If something happened to Edwin last night, I said to myself, if *he* got to him, then he would have called me to tell me about it. I had to believe that. I had to hold onto that hope.

On my way to the Fultons' house, I stopped in at the

Glasgow for a cup of coffee. As I went in, I looked up at the clouds building in the western sky. It wouldn't take long for the storm to hit us.

Jackie came out of the kitchen and poured me a cup. "Morning, Alex," he said. "You look pretty used up. Whatever happened last night, anyway? After that phone call, you ran out of here like a crazy man."

"Ah, Edwin's disappeared," I said. "He fell off the wagon, went and blew his wad at the casinos again. He's probably just too embarrassed to show his face."

Jackie shook his head. "That bastard. If he wasn't so goddamned rich, I might feel sorry for him."

"He's not so bad, Jackie."

"Whatever you say, Alex." He put the pot of coffee back on the burner. "Hey, by the way, somebody left a letter here for you."

My heart stopped. "A letter?"

"It was taped to the door this morning when I got in."

"How do you know it's for me?"

"It's got your name on the envelope, genius. Most people know you spend a lot of time here. I didn't think anything of it."

"Jackie," I said, trying to maintain my composure, "where is it?"

"Let's see," he said. He looked around behind the bar. "I put it here somewhere."

"Jackie, this could be important . . . "

"Relax, Alex, I know it's here." He looked through a pile of papers next to the cash register. "Now where the hell did I put it?"

"Jackie, please think." I tried to swallow.

"Oh for God's sake," he said. He fished through the front pockets of his white apron. "It's right here." He pulled out an envelope and set it down in front of me.

There were four capital letters typed on the front. ALEX.

"Jackie," I said. My face felt hot. I could barely breathe. "Do you have a pair of rubber gloves?"

"Probably," he said. "In the kitchen."

"Go get them please."

He went back and rummaged through the kitchen, leaving me there to stare at the envelope. He finally came back out with a pair of yellow rubber gloves. "What do you want these for?"

"Just give them to me." I took the gloves from him and put them on. "I'll need a plastic bag, too." My voice sounded like it was coming from somewhere else.

"What's the matter, Alex?"

I didn't say anything. I just opened the envelope slowly and unfolded the single piece of paper that was inside.

ALEX

It hurts me so much to see you building a wall around yourself with a policeman hiding in the bushes like a cat waiting for a mouse. I had to ask myself why is this happening? You know I am only here to serve you. How many other mouse-traps do you have that I have not even seen yet? I was sad for two days until it came to me that you have been poisoned against me. I should have seen from the beginning that he is no good for you. He is like Judas waiting to betray you with the kiss of death before you are handed over to the enemy. I made up my mind that I had to be a brave mouse one more time and remove the betrayer. It was not so easy because he knew who I am and he tried to summon all the forces of darkness to his aid but I was stronger and he did not have a chance in the end. You are free of him now and I have found a new way to remove them and not leave so much blood behind. The blood is what sends the signals. It is not the microwaves. That is my discovery. Now there is so much cold water on top of him. He will never be seen again. All that cold water Alex. Just think of all that cold water. I hope this pleases you. I think that you owe me a blessing now. Don't you think so? I think it is finally time for us to be together.

Yours forever

ROSE

I made myself put the letter in the plastic bag. I made myself go behind the bar and pick up the phone. When Maven answered I said two things: "I have another note from him. Get out to the Glasgow Inn right now." I couldn't say anything else. I couldn't say anything about Edwin. I couldn't even say his name.

I went outside. To get away from the note, to breathe some fresh air, I don't even know. The first angry raindrops hit me in the face. In the distance I could hear the approaching storm whipping the waves into whitecaps.

I couldn't see the lake through the trees. But I knew it was there.

All that cold water.

CHAPTER THIRTEEN

I WAS STILL standing in the parking lot when Maven got there. The rain had stopped and then started again, driven by the northwest wind. I just stood out there and let it hit me like buckshot.

"Where is it?" Maven said as he slammed his car door.

"Inside."

"Did you open it?"

"Yes," I said. My voice sounded like it belonged to someone else.

"You know it's evidence, McKnight. Why in the hell did you open it?"

I just looked at him. "It was addressed to me," I said. "I wanted to read it."

"Well, goddamn it, what are we standing out here in the rain for?"

He started for the door.

"Are you coming in or not?" he said.

"You don't need me," I said.

He shook his head and then went inside. I stood out there alone in the parking lot, looking at nothing. I felt cold all the way through my body. The bullet inside me seemed to vibrate in time with my heartbeat.

Finally, Maven came back out. He had the plastic bag in his hand, the letter inside. He looked at me, then down at the letter, and then back at me again. "McKnight," he said, "you get more fucking stupid every day, did you know that?"

I didn't say anything.

"Why the fuck didn't you tell me?"

I just looked at him. I couldn't comprehend what he was saying.

"We could have had the whole force out looking for him thirty minutes ago," he said.

I heard the front door to the Glasgow open and close behind us. Maven kept standing there, staring me in the eyes. As he spoke I could see a small bead of spit forming on his bottom lip.

"You're standing out here in the fucking rain while your friend is on the fucking bottom of the lake, McKnight."

I just stood there.

"What the fuck is wrong with you?" he said. "Don't you care that your best friend is feeding the fucking fish right now?" The spit hit me in the face as he gave me a good shove in the shoulder.

And then it all came apart. I grabbed him by the neck with both hands. I squeezed with all my strength, with everything I had left inside me. If I could have, I would have torn his head right off his body.

His knee came up and caught me in the groin, and then his hand was on the back of my arm, driving me down onto the ground. I twisted free and started swinging. That's when Jackie tackled me.

"Alex, for God's sake!" he yelled as he sat on top of me. He still had his white apron on.

"Get off me," I said.

"You need to go look for Fulton," he said. "You don't need to get arrested right now."

"Too late," Maven said, rubbing his neck. "You should have told him that before he assaulted me."

Jackie got off me and pulled me to my feet. "Maven, I'm a witness to what happened here. You struck him first and then he retaliated. I would have done the same thing myself. Now, will the two of you just cut this shit out and go find the guy? Maybe he's still alive. Has that occurred to you?"

Maven went back to his car and pulled out the radio. I went to my truck. "McKnight," I heard him say, "where do you think you're going?"

"I'm going to go find Edwin," I said.

"The fuck you are. Get back here."

I didn't even look back at him as I got in the truck and sent the gravel flying. In my rearview mirror I could see him with his hands in the air.

I sped down the main road toward the highway. I knew I needed to get back to the reservation, start at the Bay Mills Casino. That was the last place Edwin was seen. I picked up the cellular phone and called the Fulton house. Please answer it, Uttley. Don't let Edwin's mother get it.

Uttley answered. "Alex," he said. "I just called your cabin."

"Lane, listen very carefully," I said. "I received another note from . . . him. Rose. Whoever he is."

"Oh God."

"He got Edwin, Lane. At least that's what the note said."

"I can't believe this."

"Lane, you've got to put up a good front for Mrs. Fulton. Until we find out for sure."

"Where are you?"

"I'm on my way to the casino," I said.

"You called the police?"

I checked my rearview mirror, half-expecting to see Maven's car speeding to catch up with me. "Yes, they know about it," I said.

"I'm coming out there, Alex."

"Lane, no. I think you better stay with Mrs. Fulton and Sylvia."

"I can't do that, Alex. I have to help you. Besides, if I stay here, Mrs. Fulton will know that something is wrong. It's like she can read my mind."

"All right, all right," I said. "I'll meet you at the casino. Hurry."

I hung up and kept driving. I thought about what Maven had said. Why didn't I tell him about Edwin when I called? He was right, they could have started searching right away. Why did I just go stand out there like that, listening to the wind and the waves?

Just like in that apartment. When Rose drew that gun. I froze. I am so fucking pathetic.

I tightened my grip on the steering wheel until my knuckles turned white. For some reason, Sylvia came into my mind. The way her skin felt the last time we were together. The look in her eyes as she watched me watching her robe slip to the floor.

God help me. Why am I thinking about this? I am losing my mind.

When I got to the casino, I saw Soo Police cars. Maven must have called them from his car. The tribal police were there, as well, probably wondering what the Soo Police were doing on the reservation. I had just been there a matter of hours ago, but that was when I expected to find Edwin throwing his money away at the blackjack tables. Now the morning light, muted by the rain, made the casino look sinister and out of place, like a madhouse.

I pulled up next to the front entrance and went inside. The place was maybe half-full even on a miserable morning like this one. As soon as I got inside the door, a Soo officer stopped me. "Mr. McKnight," he said, "you're not supposed to be here."

I recognized the officer. It was the same man I saw at

the motel and then again behind the restaurant. "I'm just trying to help," I said. "We have to find him."

"The chief said if I see you I'm supposed to arrest you."

I grabbed him by the shoulders. "Then you didn't see me, okay? Please."

"I think you should go home," he said. "We've got every officer out looking for him."

"You know he drove a silver Mercedes, right?"

"Yes," he said. "And we have the plate number."

"Good," I said. "Have you found out anything here? I know he was here last night around six o'clock. Do you have anything else?"

"Mr. McKnight . . ."

"Tell me, damn it," I said. "Have you found out anything else?"

"No," he said. "Everybody who was here last night has gone home. They're calling some of those people right now."

"All right," I said. "Keep at it. I'm going to go start working some of the roads."

"You were a police officer once, weren't you?"

"Yes."

"Go," he said. "I didn't see you."

"Thank you," I said.

Outside, I searched the main parking lot. There was no sign of his car. I walked around the building, looking through all of the cars in the employee lot in back.

When I got back to my truck, Uttley had just pulled up in his red BMW. When he got out of the car he was out of breath like he had just run the whole way. "Alex, my God," he said. "Tell me this is just a bad dream."

"I'm going to go start looking for his car," I said. "Why don't you do the same. We'll split up."

"No, let me come with you," he said. "I have a good map. We can be more thorough that way."

"Fine, get in," I said.

He grabbed his map and jumped in my truck. As I left the parking lot I looked over at him. He closed his eyes and shook his head.

"Is Mrs. Fulton okay?" I asked.

"Not really," he said. "I think she knows something is wrong."

"How about Sylvia?"

"I don't know," he said. "I didn't see her before I left. I think she was in her room."

I tried to breathe. Think, Alex. Think of what to do. "The water," I said. "Let's start working the shore roads, look for his car."

"Go up through the rez," he said, unfolding his map. "We've got to start with Lakeshore Drive."

When we hit the shoreline we started to see Soo Police cars, as well as a few state cars and even some county cars. Maven had apparently called everyone.

The sky was growing darker. The rain came down even harder.

We worked up Lakeshore Drive all the way to Iriquois Point. We stopped there at a little parking lot overlooking the lighthouse. I tried to picture Edwin sitting there in his car, looking out at the water. I tried to *make* it happen in my mind. But his car wasn't there.

"I think we need to go out more," I said.

"What, away from town?"

"It's just a feeling," I said. "There's too many people around here. Even late at night. I would think he'd want something more isolated."

"Makes sense," he said, shifting the map. "So just keep going. We'll work our way all the way around the bay."

We headed west. There were a lot of cottages and vacation homes overlooking the water. Another state car passed us.

"At least we've got everybody out here looking," he said.

We looked down long driveways and through the pine trees for some sign of his car. There was no sound apart from our breathing, the rain, and the rhythmic stroking of the windshield wipers.

"This is my fault," I finally said.

"What are you talking about?"

"All of it. It's my fault."

"You can't think that way."

"I brought it here."

"No," he said. And then we were silent again.

We kept driving, kept looking. The trees grew thicker here as we made our way into the heart of the forest. "His car has to be here somewhere," Uttley said.

"There's not much out here until we hit the road to Paradise," I said. "Maybe we should just go right there and start—"

"Wait, I think I saw something," he said. "Go back to that driveway." I pulled the truck over and put it into reverse. We both looked down at a small cottage. There was a silver car parked next to it, but it wasn't a Mercedes.

"Sorry, false alarm," he said.

"This is hopeless," I said. "We're never going to find his car. Even if we do . . ." I couldn't finish the sentence.

"Just keep going," he said. He looked me in the eyes. "Go."

We kept working our way down the road. There weren't many driveways this far out in the woods. We slowed down by each one and then sped up to the next.

I don't know how many driveways we checked. I lost all track of time. The rain came on harder.

Finally, Uttley said, "Alex, look." There was a cottage that looked closed up for the winter. Parked next to it was a state trooper's car.

And next to that was a silver Mercedes.

"Oh God, Alex."

I took the truck down the driveway and pulled in behind the trooper's car. We got out to look at the Mercedes.

"This is Edwin's car," Uttley said. We looked through the windows. Nothing seemed out of the ordinary.

"It's unlocked," I said.

"We shouldn't touch it, though, right?"

I nodded. My whole body was numb.

"Where are the troopers?" he said. The place was deserted.

"Let's go see," I said.

We made our way down a dirt path to the beach. As soon as we got near the water we could see the troopers. They were standing over a rowboat. One was bent over it like he was looking at something. The other was looking up at the rain, sheltering his face with one hand and holding a radio with the other. We could hear the faint crackling and then a metallic voice breaking in.

I ran down the beach, working hard to make my way over the stones. Uttley was right behind me. As we approached the boat, the troopers looked up at us. "Who are you?" one of them said.

"What did you find?" I said.

"I need to know your name, sir," he said.

"I'm Alex McKnight," I said. "I'm . . ." What do I say? "I'm a friend of Edwin Fulton. What did you find?" I looked into the rowboat.

"Please, sir," the trooper said, "you can't touch anything."

"I know that," I said. "I just want to—"

I saw blood. On the side of the boat. It was mixing with the rain and washing down into a pool of faint pink.

And floating in that pool, driven by the wind into a slow spiral, was a single red rose.

The second trooper, the one who was bent over the boat, looked up at the first. "Call them again," he said. "This rain is messing everything up."

"They said they're on their way."

"Damn it all."

I went closer to the boat. I stood right over it and looked down at the blood. Uttley stood behind me, his arms wrapped around his body to keep his coat from whipping in the wind.

"Sir," the trooper said, "you really need to step away from that."

I ignored him, looking down at the oarlock. I got down on my knees and looked at it closely. I tried to find my voice, but I could not speak.

The troopers needed to do something about this. They needed to collect this evidence before the wind blew it away.

Wrapped around the oarlock were several strands of long blond hair.

The hair was thick and coarse. Like the hair that would come off a long blond wig.

CHAPTER FOURTEEN

THERE WERE TWO policemen at the Fultons' house when Uttley and I got there. They were Soo officers I had never seen before, and the way they were standing around in the kitchen made it obvious that they wished they were somewhere else. When Uttley and I came in, one of them looked us up and down and said, "Which one of you is McKnight?"

"That's me," I said.

"Chief Maven wants you to stick around until he gets here."

"Fuck him," I said. I was tired, my face burned from the cold wind. But I didn't care how I felt, or what Maven would do to me when he found me. I was beyond caring about anything.

"Where is everybody?" Uttley said. Aside from the cop, the place was empty. There was a broom leaning against the kitchen counter, next to a pile of broken glass.

"Mrs. Fulton is in her bedroom," the cop said. "The older one, I mean. The younger Mrs. Fulton is outside."

"Outside?" Uttley said. "What are you talking about?"

"Um . . ." The cop looked at his partner. "I'm afraid the two Mrs. Fultons had a bit of a fight when they . . . you know, when they found out about Mr. Fulton."

"Where did she go?" Uttley said. "You just let her go out there?" He looked out the big picture window overlooking the lake. The rain was beating against the window like it meant to harm us.

"She was in no mood to listen to us," the cop said. "There was nothing we could do. And your name would be?" He slipped into his cop voice while he hitched up his belt. That was the last thing we needed right now.

"This is Lane Uttley," I said. "He's the family lawyer. He's the guy who's going to have your badges if you don't get out there and find Mrs. Fulton."

"I don't like that tone of voice, Mr. McKnight."

"You're not going to like my boot up your ass, either," I said. "The woman just found out that her husband is dead and you let her go running out into the freezing rain. Did she have a coat on even?"

The cop just looked at me.

"If you don't get out there and find her right now," I said, "I swear to God, I'll beat you so bad you won't even recognize yourself."

"Alex, come on." Uttley moved in between us.

"The chief is on his way over here," the cop said. "You can deal with him."

"Let's go find Edwin's mother," Uttley said. He led me out of the kitchen. The door closed behind us as the cops went outside.

We went through the house to the guest wing, and stood outside her room. We could hear the faint noise of her sobbing. Uttley tapped on the door. "Mrs. Fulton? It's Lane and Alex."

There was a long silence. Then the door opened. Mrs. Fulton looked ten years older. "What do you want?" she said. Her voice was raw.

"Mrs. Fulton," Uttley said. "I don't know what to say. I'm so sorry."

She looked at me. "What about you? Are you going to say you're so sorry, too?"

"Mrs. Fulton . . ." I said.

Her open hand hit me across the face. I didn't even try to stop her. "You were supposed to protect him," she said. "That was your responsibility."

I didn't say anything.

"I hate you," she said, her voice breaking. "I hate this place. I always hated this place. It's cold and dark and full of backwoods trash and Indians and . . . oh God, Edwin. Please. This can't be happening."

Uttley put his arms around her. I left the two of them there in the hallway.

At the window I could see that the rain had let up into a steady drizzle. But the wind was still howling and it kept whipping up the surface of the lake. I could see the waves crashing on the rocky shoreline below the house. It wasn't even a lake anymore, not on a day like this. It was a sea, the kind of sea that wrecks ships and pulls men to their deaths. And now Edwin was out there, somewhere at the bottom of all that cold water. The state would drag the lake near where the boat was found, I knew, but it would be hopeless. These waves would pull his body down to the deepest, coldest heart of Lake Superior, down where the crew of the *Edmund Fitzgerald* lay. All twenty-nine men would welcome him into their midst.

Rose did this. Rose killed Edwin and then he dumped his body in the lake. The water was calm enough last night, before the storm hit. He could have taken him out a good mile or more if he knew how to row. He heaved Edwin's body over the side of the boat and watched him sink. And then he rowed back to shore. It must have been dark. Maybe the rain was beginning to fall already. Maybe the water was already turning ugly. Maybe it was hard rowing all the way back to shore.

But he did make it back. I know that because I read his

note. I saw the boat and the blood and the long blond hairs. It was Rose. Somehow it was Rose.

And he's still out there.

I rubbed my face where Mrs. Fulton had hit me and watched the two police officers outside. They had come around the house and now they were working their way down the path to the beach. When they got to the shore, they split up, one going in each direction.

A minute later I saw Sylvia come around the opposite side of the house. She started down the path where the officers had gone. And then she stopped. She turned around and looked right at me, as if it suddenly came into her mind that I must be standing there at the window watching her. She didn't have a coat on, just a sweater. It was wet and it clung to her body. Her hair was tangled by the wind. She was shivering.

I was just about to go out to her, to offer her my coat and to try to convince her to come inside. But something stopped me. Why in God's name I didn't go out to her, I don't know. I just kept standing there looking at her until she finally turned away and went down the path toward the lake.

God help me, I still wanted her. After all that had happened I still wanted her.

"McKnight," a voice said from behind me. It was the last voice in the world I wanted to hear. And along with that voice came a hand on my shoulder.

I turned around and faced Maven. His hair was wet, his face bright red from the wind. I could see a couple welts on his neck from where my hands had been. There was another man standing next to him, a man who looked like he was ordered from the same catalog. He was a little younger than Maven, he had a little more hair, a better mustache. But that same hard-ass cop look in his eyes, that same little power-trip gum-chewing swagger. And he was just as wet and windblown as Maven. I was expecting to get a double-barrel shot from both of them at once, but instead Maven said, "Alex, how are you doing?"

I looked from one face to the other. I didn't know what to say.

"Listen, Alex," Maven said. "I know this is difficult for everybody. I just wanted to apologize, first of all, for our . . . disagreement earlier. And I want you to know that I am truly sorry about the loss of your friend. This is Detective Allen from the Michigan State Police."

"Mr. McKnight," he said, reaching for my hand. "I'm sorry we have to meet under these circumstances."

I shook his hand. I still didn't know what to say. I couldn't figure out why he was talking to me like an actual human being. He must be putting on a little show for this state guy, I thought. Although I couldn't imagine Maven sucking up to anyone.

"Detective Allen has been trying to get a couple boats out to drag the lake in the vicinity of the crime scene, but I'm afraid the weather is not being very cooperative."

"Even if this lets up," the detective said, "you realize that it's a long shot, of course. It's a big lake out there."

I nodded.

"In any event," the detective said, "we just wanted to let you know that both agencies are on this case now."

"You have the hair?" I said. "From the boat?"

"From the oarlock, yes," he said. "We have some blood samples, as well. Although there's probably not much doubt about whose blood it is."

"Did Maven tell you about Rose?"

"Yes, I've been apprised of that situation."

"We need to talk to him," I said. "I mean, whoever it is that's in that jail cell. You can make that happen, can't you?"

I saw him give Maven a quick look.

"What is it?" I said. "You guys aren't telling me something."

"Mr. McKnight . . ."

"You know something about Rose, don't you."

"Alex," Maven said, "we'd like you to come down to the station with us. I think we all need to work together to get to the bottom of this."

"Just tell me what's going on," I said.

"Not here," Maven said. "Please, Alex." He looked around. "We don't want to disturb anyone else. Where's Mrs. Fulton, anyway?"

"She's lying down," Uttley said as he came into the room. "What's going on?"

"This is Lane Uttley," Maven said to the detective. "He's the Fultons' lawyer."

"I'm Detective Allen from the State Police," he said as he shook Uttley's hand. "We were just going over some matters with Mr. McKnight."

Uttley looked back and forth between them and then at me. "Going over *what* matters?"

"They may have some information about Rose," I said. "They want me to go back to the station to talk about it."

"I'm coming with you," he said.

"No," I said. "You've got to stay here, Lane. Mrs. Fulton needs you here. And Sylvia—" I turned around and looked out the window. "Sylvia is out there."

Lane came to the window and looked out. "Where is she?"

"On the beach," I said. "She doesn't have a coat on."

While we stood there, the two Soo officers came back into view. They walked up the path toward the house, and when they saw all four of us standing at the window watching them, they stopped. I felt a lump in my stomach, and I pictured Sylvia wading out into the cold water, shivering and blue. But then finally I saw her walking down the shoreline. She walked right behind the officers, but they were oblivious to her. They just stood there looking at us looking at them.

"For God's sake, Lane," I said. "Will you go out and get her?"

"Why don't we both go get her?" he said.

"Just go," I said. "I need to go to the station."

He looked at both Maven and Allen. They had already started toward the door. "Alex, something's not right here."

"We're just going to talk about Rose," I said. "Don't worry about me."

He shook his head. "Call me when you're done, Alex."

I went outside with the two men. "I'll follow you in my truck," I said.

They looked at each other. That look, it should have tipped me off. "Why don't you ride with us?" Allen said.

"Then I'll be there and my truck will be here," I said. "Go on, I'll be right behind you."

"Mr. Uttley can take care of that, can't he?" Maven said. "His car is back at the casino, anyway, isn't it? He can bring your truck into town and then you can go get his car."

I didn't feel like arguing about it, so I just threw my keys on the front seat of my truck and got in the back of Maven's car.

It had been a long time since I had seen the back of a police car. When we were on our way I sat up and laced my fingers through the wire cage and looked at them. "All right, so what's going on with Rose?" I said.

Maven just sniffed and kept driving.

"Come on, tell me what's going on," I said.

"We'll talk at the station," he said. It finally sank into my thick head. They were taking me in.

"Maven, what the fuck do you think you're doing?" I said.

"Please, Mr. McKnight," Allen said, turning his head. "Just relax. We'll all be more comfortable at the police station."

I sat back in the seat. After all that had happened in the last twenty-four hours, I couldn't make any sense of it. Surely they don't think I had anything to do with what happened to Edwin, I thought. They didn't arrest me. They didn't read me my rights.

I looked out the window at the pine trees. Edwin is dead. I poked my finger through a hole in the seat. Somebody was smoking back here and they burned a hole.

When we got to the station I tried to open the back door. It didn't open, of course. I had forgotten, the back doors don't open from the inside on a police car. I waited for Maven to open it for me. "Come on in, Alex," he said. "Right this way."

"I know the way," I said. But instead of taking me to his office, he led me into an interview room. There was a table in the middle of the room, with four chairs. Another table stood against the wall with a coffee pot and a small refrigerator. A map on the wall showed the different types of fish in the inland lakes.

"We'll have more room in here," he said. "Have a seat."

"Is somebody going to tell me what's going on here?"

"Of course, Alex," Allen said. "Please sit down." He pulled a chair out for me.

"Now how did you say you like your coffee?" Maven said. "One sugar, no cream?"

I sat down. "Yes," I said. "That's right." The man is finally going to make me some coffee. This is getting worse by the minute.

He poured the coffee in a mug and put it down in front of me. Then he sat down across from me, next to Allen. I looked from one face to the other while a curl of steam rose from the coffee.

"Mr. McKnight," Detective Allen said, "tell me about this man Rose."

"I thought you said Maven told you all about him," I said.

"I want you to tell me," he said. "Chief Maven might have left something out."

I went over the whole story, starting at the hospital in Detroit, Rose's apartment, the gun, the shooting. I told him how Rose went away for life, how I never figured on hearing from him again, until the phone calls and the notes started coming.

"These notes," Allen said. "They all seem to have been typed on the same typewriter."

"Makes sense," I said.

"Why do you say that?"

"Because the same man wrote them."

"Yes," he said. "Of course."

"What are you getting at?"

"Just thinking out loud," Allen said. "Let's talk about the dead men. The first two, I mean." Maven just sat there, watching me.

"I didn't know them."

"Tony Bing, a local bookmaker," Allen said. "Your friend Edwin found him in his motel room."

"Yes," I said.

"I understand he called you before he called the police."

"Yes."

"You were on the scene, in fact, before the police even got there."

"Yes."

"That strikes me as rather odd," he said.

"It *was* odd," I said. "Edwin did an odd thing."

"A very odd thing," he said. "Wouldn't you call that odd, Chief Maven?"

"It was odd at the time," Maven said. "And it's still odd now."

"The next man was, what was his name?"

They both looked at me.

"Dorney," I said. "Vince Dorney. At least that's what the chief told me."

"Yes, that's right. Vince Dorney. Another local character, from what I'm told. In fact, I believe Mr. Dorney was known to engage in a little bookmaking himself, wasn't he?"

They both looked at me again.

"I don't know anything about the man," I said.

"It's just another odd thing," Allen said. "Here's another bookmaker who ends up dead."

"Another odd thing," Maven said.

"Your Mr. Rose seems to have a specific dislike for bookmakers, Mr. McKnight. Funny, I didn't see any mention of that in his notes."

I could feel a line of sweat starting down my back. Both of the men had their forearms on the table. As they shifted their weight it made the coffee splash out of the cup.

"I don't like where you're taking this," I said. "A homicidal maniac has been terrorizing me for the last week. Three men are dead, including the most harmless man I've ever known. But instead of trying to find this guy, all you're doing is sitting here grilling me like I'm your lead suspect."

"We're just having a conversation here," Maven said. "Although we can give your man Uttley a call if you really want us to. If you think you need a lawyer, I mean."

"I don't need a lawyer, Maven. What I need is for you to start doing your fucking job."

"Now, Mr. McKnight," Allen said. "Is that kind of language necessary?"

"You guys aren't even doing it right," I said. "It's supposed to be good cop, bad cop, not asshole cop, dickhead cop."

"Keep going, McKnight," Maven said. "Just keep digging that hole."

"If you don't get out there and start looking for this guy, I swear to God, Maven—"

"You swear what, McKnight? You swear you'll try to choke me to death again?"

I grabbed the cup and threw it. It hit the fishing map and exploded, leaving a great brown streak right across the whole county. Maven and Allen just watched me, not even blinking.

"My, my," Allen finally said. "Your man has a temper."

"He was a baseball player once," Maven said. "Did I tell you that?"

"No, you didn't."

"I assume he had a better arm then."

"I would hope so. That was a weak throw."

"Never made the big leagues," Maven said.

"That's a shame," Allen said.

"So he became a cop instead."

"So I gathered."

"He never made detective," Maven said. "In fact, he had to leave the force after the Rose incident."

"Another failure to deal with," Allen said. "It's painful to think about."

"So here's what I think happened, Detective Allen, if you'd care to hear it."

"By all means, Chief Maven. Please proceed."

"It's no secret that Edwin Fulton had a gambling problem. More than once, in fact, he had to be escorted off the reservation. I'm thinking maybe he got into a little trouble with these bookmakers."

"But I thought Fulton was a wealthy man," Allen said.

"Very much so," Maven said. "But you know how bad they can get once they get their hooks into you. Maybe they saw him as an easy mark."

"Good point."

"So Mr. Fulton asks his friend Mr. McKnight if perhaps he can help him with this problem. Perhaps Mr. McKnight even owed these men some money himself."

"Could be, could be."

"Mr. McKnight decides that there's only one way to eliminate the problem, and that's to eliminate the two bookmakers themselves."

"Seems pretty drastic to me," Allen said.

"Drastic, yes," Maven said. "But we've both seen men killed over much smaller matters. And in this case, Mr. McKnight had the perfect plan. He would write these notes to himself to make it look like this man Rose had come back to haunt him."

"Very original. But all this just to knock off a couple bookies?"

"There could be more to it," Maven said. "Maybe this Rose thing helped to satisfy some sort of craving. Some sort of sickness. It must be hard to live with yourself all these years. Knowing that you froze when it really counted and your partner ended up getting killed."

"It must be a living hell," Allen said.

"It's just a theory, of course. But it would certainly explain a lot. Like why the phone calls he claimed he was receiving suddenly stopped when we started tapping his phone."

"So what about Mr. Fulton, then? What happened to him?"

"Ah, that's the interesting part," Maven said. "After Mr. McKnight has killed the two bookmakers, he has this idea. Maybe it just occurs to him then, or maybe he had been planning it all along."

"Are you suggesting that Mr. McKnight killed Mr. Fulton?"

"He wasn't in his cabin that night. He was out looking for him, remember. Or so he said. All those other nights, when we had an officer over there, nothing ever happened. The one night he goes out, Fulton is killed. And this time, he dumps the body in the lake. I'm guessing that they had already disposed of the gun. So he didn't want the body to be found. That way, it wouldn't seem out of place that he was killed by something else."

"The rose in the boat was a nice touch. And the blond hairs."

"Give him points for that one, yes."

"But why would he kill his own best friend?"

"Ah, Detective Allen. I'm surprised you even have to ask that question. Why does *anyone* kill his best friend?"

"Of course," Allen said. "You kill your best friend so you can have your best friend's wife."

I had heard enough. "If you guys are about done," I said. "I think I'll be leaving now. I mean, unless you have a good reason to keep me here."

"We can't keep you here," Maven said. "We can't charge you yet."

"Then why are you telling me all this?" I said.

"All those years on the force," Maven said, "and you never saw a suspect get worked over?"

"He never made detective," Allen said. "He never learned this stuff."

"Good point," Maven said. "He never got past parking tickets."

"Tell him how it works, Chief."

"Sometimes when you know a suspect is guilty," Maven said, "but you don't have enough evidence, you just bring the guy in and you lay it all out for him."

"You tell him that you know he did it," Allen said, "and you know that's he going to give himself away."

"You tell him that you're going to be watching him."

"You tell him that it's only a matter of time."

"But you only lean on him if you *know* he's going to fold," Maven said.

"Otherwise," Allen said, "you're just wasting your time."

"I don't think we're wasting our time here, McKnight."

"I can see the fear in his eyes," Allen said. They both leaned over to look at me. They were close enough for me to catch the scent of cigars and aftershave. "Can you see it, Chief Maven? Can you see the fear?"

"I certainly can, Detective Allen. I can see it all over him."

"You know how an owl does his hunting, Mr. McKnight?" Allen said.

They both sat there for a long moment. I didn't say anything.

"He listens. He waits."

"As long as you don't move," Maven said, "you're safe."

"But as soon as you move," Allen said, "he hears you."

"You want to stay still, McKnight. But you can't."

"You know the owl is there, waiting."

"You have to run, McKnight. You can't help it."

"You're too scared not to run."

"Then he *swoops* right down on you." Maven shot his hand out and picked up an imaginary animal. "And he eats you."

"Eats you for dinner."

"Makes me hungry just thinking about it," Maven said.

I stood up.

"Pleasure to meet you, Mr. McKnight," the detective said. "We'll be seeing you soon."

"*Very* soon," Maven said. "I'll bring the ketchup."

CHAPTER FIFTEEN

WHEN MAVEN AND Allen had finished with me, I called Uttley. I didn't answer any of his questions. I just told him to come and get me. I stood outside the station house waiting for him, looking out past the courthouse at the locks and beyond them the bridge to Canada. The storm had passed, but the remaining clouds filtered what sunlight there was into an otherwordly glow. Everything looked wrong and I felt sick to my stomach.

That bridge marks the northern end of one of the longest highways in America, Interstate 75. You can take it dead south more than a thousand miles, right out of Michigan, through Ohio, Kentucky, Tennessee, Georgia, all the way to Florida. Forget what Maven had said about not leaving. I could just get on that road and go. Never come back.

Would Rose follow me? How long would it take for him to find me again?

Uttley finally showed up in my truck. "God, Alex," he said when I opened the driver's side door. "What happened to you?"

"Just move over," I said.

I pulled out of the parking lot and headed across town. Uttley watched me for a while and then finally said, "Where are we going?"

"To your office."

"I told Mrs. Fulton we'd come back," he said. "And my car. It's still at the casino."

"We'll get it later," I said.

We came to a red light and sat there for a full minute. I closed my eyes and took a long breath. "How are they doing?" I said.

"Mrs. Fulton is a mess," he said. "I guess that's understandable. Sylvia finally came inside, but she refused to change out of her wet clothes. When I left, she was just standing at the window, looking out at the lake."

I didn't say anything.

"Are you going to tell me what happened at the station?" he said.

"They think I killed Edwin. And everybody else."

"What? Are you kidding me?"

"I'm not kidding you." I told him everything that had happened.

He listened to the whole story, shaking his head. "So they didn't charge you?" he said.

"No. But they told me to stay in town."

"Goddamn it, I *knew* I should have gone with you."

"What good would that have done?"

"You need a lawyer, Alex," he said. "This is insane."

"Well, you're right, I do need you to help me," I said. "But I'm not going to worry about those two clowns right now." I stopped the truck in front of his office.

"What are we doing, Alex? Why are we here?"

"We need to call the prison again," I said. I got out and waited for him. He sat there rubbing his forehead for a long moment and then he finally got out of the truck.

When we got into his office, he sat down behind his desk and looked at his watch. It wasn't even noon yet. I winced as I sat down in the guest chair. Everything hurt. I felt a hundred years old.

"Where was that guy's number?" he said. He went through a pile of papers on his desk and finally found it. After he had dialed, he turned on the speaker phone and put the receiver down.

A voice answered, "Corrections, Browning speaking."

"Mr. Browning," Uttley said. "This is Lane Uttley in Sault Ste. Marie. We spoke a couple days ago."

"Yes, you were asking about an inmate."

"Maximilian Rose," he said, looking up at me. "I have Mr. McKnight with me here in the office. We're sorry to bother you again, but I'm afraid our situation has gotten much worse. I mean, we've had another, um—"

I picked up the receiver. "This is McKnight," I said. "I want you to listen to me very carefully. I have good reason to believe that Maximilian Rose is here in the area, and that he's responsible for three murders."

"That's impossible," Browning said. "That man is here in prison. We've gone through this already."

"I don't care what you've gone through," I said. "You have to believe me. *Something* is not right down there. I don't know how it happened, but I don't think that man you have is Rose."

"Mr. McKnight, I told this to Mr. Uttley and now I'm going to tell it to you. I personally took the man's mug shot and went and stood in front of the man's cell. He has grown a pretty big beard since then, but—"

"What? A beard? Nobody told me about a beard before." I looked at Uttley. He just shrugged his shoulders.

"Yes, the man has a beard now. But it's the same man."

"How can you know for sure?" I said. "He must look totally different now. I mean, whoever that is. He must not look like the picture."

"Mr. McKnight." I could tell he was fighting down his anger. He spoke as slowly to me as he would to a child. "If I stopped shaving, a month later, I would have a beard.

A year later, I'd have a *big* beard. But I'd still be the same man."

"Why won't he see me? Explain that to me."

"I don't know why he won't see you. It doesn't matter why. We can't force him."

"I want you to fax me his mug shot," I said. "And then I want you to go take a Polaroid of the man in the cell and fax me that, too. I'll give you Uttley's fax number."

"If a law enforcement officer makes that request, then I'll do it, sir."

"I don't think that's going to happen," I said. "Why can't you just do it for us?"

"If there's a murder investigation going on up there and you think somehow Rose is involved, why aren't the police talking to me?" he said. "You have to admit, this looks mighty strange."

I didn't know what to say. They aren't calling you because they think I did it? How far would that answer get me?

"I don't have time to explain it," I said. "Please, you have to believe me. Three people are dead."

"Have the police call me."

"I'm begging you," I said.

"I'm sorry."

"Then go to hell." I slammed the phone down.

I just sat there looking at the floor. Uttley didn't say anything for a while. And then finally, "So now what?"

"We take you back to your car," I said. "So you can go back to the Fultons' house."

"You're not coming with me?"

"No. I don't think I should be there right now."

"So what are you going to do?"

"I'm going to go try to find him."

"Where?" he said.

"I don't know. Everywhere."

"The police should be doing that."

"They aren't."

"Are they going to keep the man outside your cabin, at least?"

"No," I said. "Why should they?"

"Goddamn it," he said. He picked up the phone. "I'm going to call that bastard right now."

"Don't call him."

"What?"

"I don't want a man there anymore."

"Why not?"

"In his note, Rose said that he knew the man was there. I don't know how, but he knew."

"I don't get it," he said.

"Don't you see? It's not safe for an officer to be there in his car if Rose *knows* he's there."

"But what happens if he shows up now?"

"Then I'll be waiting for him," I said.

"Alex, you can't do this. Not this way. Let me be there, at least."

"No," I said. "This is between me and him."

"Look at you," he said. "Why don't you let me stay with you one night at least, so you can get some sleep?"

"I don't need sleep," I said. "I'll sleep when this is over with."

He argued some more, but he knew he wouldn't win. Finally, I took him back to the casino to pick up his car. He wanted to come help me look for Rose, but I convinced him that Mrs. Fulton and Sylvia needed him more than I did that day. I don't know if he believed that, but he left me there and went back to their house.

I looked around the Bay Mills Casino for Vinnie. I figured he'd be the right man to start with. He had seen Edwin the night before. Maybe he had seen someone else there with him. Or at least he could point me to the men who actually threw Edwin out of the place. Maybe *they* had seen someone.

Someone.

How did he find me? How long had he been here? Has he been watching me? If it had ever occurred to me to check my rearview mirror before the last few days, would I have seen him in the car behind me? That little restaurant by Uttley's office, the place I often had breakfast after stopping in to see him, was he ever there in a booth across the room, watching me eat? If I had put down the paper and looked up at him, would I have even recognized him?

I couldn't find Vinnie at any of the blackjack tables, so I just stood there for a few minutes watching the action. I told myself I was waiting for Vinnie to show up for work. But that was a lie. The only reason I kept standing there was because I had no idea what to do next.

When I finally left the casino, I got in my truck and drove west along the shoreline to where the boat had been found. It was good a place as any. Start at the end and move backward. As I drove, I tried to imagine how it happened. His car was found at the cottage, so Edwin must have come down this very road. Was he alone then? I couldn't imagine why he would come this way. Was Rose in the car with him? Edwin driving, Rose sitting next to him with a gun in his ribs? Or maybe Rose was driving. Maybe Edwin was lying in the backseat, already dead. Although I didn't remember seeing any blood when Uttley and I looked into the car.

The trunk. He was in the trunk. Right now they've got his Mercedes down at the police station and they're opening up the trunk. How much of Edwin's blood will they find there?

I tried to drive the thought out of my mind, but I didn't have much luck. I kept thinking about Edwin's blood.

When I got to the place where we found the boat, I drove down the long driveway and stopped next to the cottage. It was still deserted. Nobody would be here until the next summer. There was a weather vane on the top. I hadn't noticed that before. It was spinning madly in the wind.

I got out of the truck and walked slowly down the beach. The boat was gone. They had taken it, along with the car. There was no trace left, nothing to tell you what had happened here.

I looked out at the water. The rain had stopped. There were high clouds moving fast across the sky. The wind stung my face. It felt like all the heat had gone out of the world. It felt like I would never be warm again.

I hoped he didn't suffer. I hoped by the time he got here, he was already gone. Just a body to be dumped into the water. I hoped he didn't lie bleeding in the boat, watching Rose working at the oars. I hoped he didn't know that his life was almost over, that he would soon feel the icy shock of the water, that he would struggle with whatever strength he had left but that it wouldn't be enough.

Why did he have to pick Edwin of all people? All the money in the world and yet he was the most helpless man I had ever known. I wanted to hate him for being married to Sylvia, but I couldn't. I thought about that night in the bar when he told me I was the only real friend he ever had. Everyone else just wanted his money, he said.

The only real friend he ever had. I fucked his wife and then a madman out of my past came all the way up here and killed him.

Find Rose. That's the only thing left to do. That's the only thing you *can* do now. Find Rose.

He has to be staying somewhere. Judging from the phone calls and the notes, he probably doesn't come out much during the day. But he has to eat. I looked up and down the beach. I couldn't see any other cottages from where I was standing, but I knew they were scattered through the trees. He could have broken into one of them. There might be food there. And nobody would find him at this time of year. But there were hundreds of cottages on the shore. It would take weeks to look at all of them.

But no, he wouldn't break into a cottage. Somehow, I just knew that. I was trying to think like him, see the world through his eyes. All around you, evil aliens. You can't trust anyone. You hide during the day. Where do you hide? Someplace safe. Behind a solid door with a good lock. I remembered how we had to wait outside his apartment door while he undid all the locks. If you break into a place, then you've broken that door, or that window. You won't be able to close it behind you and lock it.

I went back to the truck. He's in a motel. The lock on the door isn't enough, because the man at the desk has a key and the maid has a key. But there's a dead bolt on the door. Something that you can only unlock from the inside.

I backed out of the driveway, drove back into the Soo. He killed Bing there, after he saw him at that bar. And the restaurant where he killed Dorney, that was just a few blocks away. Maybe he was staying on that side of town, over by the bridge. It made sense. Or as much sense as it was going to make.

I drove into town, trying to think of all the motels. The summer crowd was long gone. It had to be mostly hunters now. Would Rose stand out from that crowd? Would a desk clerk remember him? The first killing was, what, only seven days ago? How long was he here before that? How long has he been watching me?

I worked my way through town, stopping at every motel I could find. I didn't have much to work with. No badge. No picture to show them even. Just a vague description. A strange man, eyes you wouldn't soon forget. May or may not be wearing a big blond wig. Obviously, yes, if he had the wig you'd remember him. Been in town at least a week, probably more. I must have looked pretty strange myself. I hadn't slept, I hadn't shaved. I still had the same clothes on from the day before, my shirt rained on and then dried into a map of wrinkles.

Most of the desk clerks were kinder than I had a right to expect, and they seemed to believe that I was a private investigator. Even without a card. But nobody had seen anyone with a blond wig or with eyes you wouldn't soon forget.

I kept at it all day, working my way to the western side of the city and then right out to the highway. I lost count of how many motels I visited. It would have been discouraging if I had stopped to think about it. But it was something to do, at least. Something else besides just waiting. I drove by the Riverside Motel, where it all started. I didn't think Rose would be staying there. He saw Bing in that bar and then probably followed him back to his motel room. It would have been too much of a coincidence if Rose was staying there, too. But I drove by, anyway. I just had to see it again. The place was closed down, a big "For Sale" sign taped to the office window.

I pulled into the empty parking lot and sat there for a while. I had spent most of the day looking for him, but now I was running out of ideas.

Wait a minute, I thought. I started in the Soo, because that's where the murders happened, and then I worked my way west. Maybe that's backward. Rose found me somehow, and he knows that I live in Paradise. So maybe he's staying in Paradise. It was worth a shot.

I drove around the bay and up to Paradise. On the way, I stopped in at the casino again. Vinnie was there, but he wasn't able to tell me anything useful. He hadn't seen anyone suspicious. He found the security men who had escorted Edwin to the front door, but they were no help, either.

Paradise is a small town, but there's enough tourist trade to support a dozen motels. They were all little family-run places, eight or ten rooms, nice views of the water. Brochures in the lobby for the Shipwreck Museum and the Tanquamenon Falls State Park, hiking in the summer, hunting in the fall, snowmobiling in the winter. I knew most of the owners, at least well enough to nod to them if I saw them at the post office. But none of them could help me. If Rose was in Paradise, he was doing a damned good job of hiding.

The sun was just starting to go down. I stopped in at the Glasgow, figured I'd grab some dinner, collect my thoughts, prepare myself for another long night of waiting. Some of the regular crowd was there, but nobody even spoke to me. They all must have heard about the note that was left there, about me and Maven going at it in the parking lot. About Edwin. Jackie put a plate down in front of me, gave my shoulder a quick squeeze, and then left me alone.

It was dark by the time I got home. I walked around the cabin before I went in. I wasn't sure what I might find. It just seemed like the right thing to do. Inside, I looked at the machine still hooked up to the phone. I picked up the walkie-talkie, turned it on and listened to the static, turned if off. These things weren't going to do me any good now. I was surprised that Maven hadn't asked me to return them. He must have forgotten. He's probably at home right now, I thought, sitting in front of the TV, slapping himself in the head. Damn it all, he's saying to his wife, I forgot to make McKnight give back the phone machine and the radio. That stuff is police property.

The gun was still on the table next to the bed. I picked

it up and held it. There was nothing more I could do, except sit here in this cabin and wait. It was all up to Rose now.

I sat on the bed for a while, but then I realized that was a mistake. Too easy to fall asleep. I got up and sat in one of the hard wooden chairs at the kitchen table. The time passed slowly. I looked at my watch. It wasn't even eleven o'clock yet. I got up and looked out the window, saw nothing but my own reflection. I turned off all the inside lights and tried again. The one light I had outside above the front door didn't do much good. I could only see the edge of the road, my truck, the woodpile, the first few pine trees. Beyond that, the forest stretched in all directions. The moon was just a rumor behind the clouds.

It was quiet. The crickets were long gone, the tree frogs asleep for the winter. No wind. The trees were still.

I sat back down in the chair. Before long, my head started to feel heavy. Uttley was right. I needed to sleep. I should have let him come over for one night.

Maybe I can still call him. Maybe I can call Uttley. The phone. Get the phone. Pick up the phone and call him. I'll pick up the phone now.

I saw myself picking up the phone. There was blood on it. I looked at the blood on my hands. There was a pool of it on the floor. Blood everywhere.

This is a dream. I must wake up. I cannot sleep now. I cannot sleep.

I raise my head from the table. I am not in my cabin. There is a window in front of me. I rise and go to it. There is a great courtyard. Four great walls around it, a thousand windows. In the center of the courtyard there is a man. I can barely see him, the courtyard is so big. His back is to me. He is hunched over something.

He turns and looks at me. Out of a thousand windows, he knows that I am right here. He is looking right at me. I see that he has been sharpening a knife on an old-fashioned turning stone. He caresses the knife while he looks at me.

I run. I am in a hallway. It is the hallway in the apartment building in Detroit. I run past a hundred doors and then I open one. Franklin is lying on the ground. He is covered in blood but he is looking up at me. Don't leave me here, he says. The walls are covered with aluminum foil.

I close the door. I hear Franklin calling to me even as I keep running. My legs will not work. I cannot run fast enough. The hallway will not end.

Finally I open another door. Edwin is there, lying on a white table. He is wet and covered with seaweed. I look down at him and say that I am sorry. He tries to open his eyes. But he has no eyes. The fish have eaten them.

There is a pounding on the door. Edwin grabs at me. He cannot see but his hands find my arm. He is pulling at me while I try to back away from the door.

More pounding. Hard enough to break it down. He will be here soon. I cannot hide from him any longer.

I woke up.

I was sitting at my kitchen table. There was no sound except for my breathing and the faint ticking of a clock.

And then the pounding on the door.

I jumped out of the chair. My gun. Where is my gun?

More pounding.

Goddamn it, my gun. I don't know where it is. Not on the table, not on the bedstand. *Where the fuck is my gun?*

Pounding, pounding.

There, under the kitchen table. It was in my hand when I fell asleep. Down on my hands and knees, get the gun. Check it. Ready to go. Get back up. Go to the door.

The pounding stopped.

I stood there by the door, listening.

Silence.

I waited. Nothing.

I raised the gun and unlocked the door. Opened it a sliver and looked out into the night.

Sylvia looked up at me. "Alex."

She had the same clothes on, the sweater I saw her wearing as I watched her from the window that day. It was dry now, but she still wasn't wearing a coat. I could feel her shivering as I grabbed her by the shoulders and pulled her inside. "What are you doing here?"

She didn't say anything. She just stood there and looked around my cabin. All the time we had spent together, she had never been here.

I grabbed a blanket and wrapped her up. "Sit down," I said. "I'll make you some tea or something."

She sat down at the table, in the chair where I had just been sleeping.

"You shouldn't be here," I said as I put some water on the stove. "You should be home with Edwin's mother."

"She's gone," Sylvia said, looking down at nothing.

"What?"

"She went back down to Grosse Pointe. She said she couldn't stay here another minute."

"But what about . . . I mean, what if they find him?"

"Then they'll send him down there," she said. "That's where the service is going to be."

I didn't know what to say. I just stood there watching the water. The cabin was silent until the water finally started to boil.

"Where's Uttley?" I said.

"I sent him home," she said. "I don't like him. How can you work for him, anyway? He reminds me of a used car salesman."

"Sylvia, goddamn it all."

"What, Alex?" She finally looked up at me. "What?"

"I don't know," I said. "I'm sorry."

"What are you sorry about?"

"Everything," I said. "About everything."

She started to say something but just shook her head and looked down again. I made her tea and put the cup on the table in front of her.

"He's gone," she said. "He's really gone."

"Yes."

"It's just what I wanted to happen," she said. "I wished for it every night."

"Sylvia, don't talk that way."

"It's true, Alex. I wanted him to disappear forever. And now he has."

"You didn't make it happen," I said.

"I think I did, Alex. I think I wished for it so hard, it finally happened. And you know what the funny thing is? I don't feel a thing. If I was a bad person, I'd be happy. If I was a good person, I'd feel guilty. But I don't feel anything either way. I'm just . . . I don't even know what. I just feel nothing."

"You're still in shock," I said. "You're going to need some time."

"And you'll be here to help me through it, right? Is that what you're getting at? Now that he's gone? Now that I'm not your friend's wife anymore?"

"I didn't mean that."

"The hell you didn't," she said. She threw the blanket off her shoulders and stood up. "Why did I come here, anyway? What the hell am I doing here?" She looked around her. "This is a pretty tiny fucking cabin, you know that, Alex? I think my bathroom is bigger than this cabin."

"Sylvia, stop it."

"I should have known it would be this small. You built this yourself, didn't you? I'm surprised it's still standing."

"I said stop it." I went to her and grabbed her by the shoulders again. This time I squeezed a little harder.

"Let go of me," she said.

I just looked at her.

"Let go of me," she said again. But she didn't struggle. She didn't try to get away.

I kept looking at her eyes, her hair, her mouth. I could feel the warmth of her body. Goddamn it all, I wanted her more than ever.

She just stood there. I couldn't imagine what she was thinking. Her eyes gave nothing away.

"You shouldn't be here," I finally said. "It's not safe."

"What do you mean, it's not safe? You've got a policeman outside keeping watch."

"No," I said.

"Yes, you do," she said. "In the unmarked car, hiding in the woods."

"No, Sylvia. He's not there anymore."

"Yes, he is," she said. "I saw him."

"What are you talking about? When did you see him?"

"Tonight," she said. "Just now, I mean. When I pulled in. He's out there right now."

CHAPTER SIXTEEN

THE FEAR CAME to me. There was no way to stop it. I could feel it unfolding in my stomach, cold and alive. "Sylvia, please," I said. "Tell me exactly what you saw. Did you see anyone inside the car?"

"No," she said. "I just saw the car. I don't know what kind. Just a plain car. He's not doing a very good job of hiding, either. I could see half his car sticking out of the trees."

"Where? Exactly where is the car?"

"It's right out there," she said. She started toward the window.

"No!" I grabbed her. "Stay away from the window."

"What's the matter with you?"

"That's not a cop, Sylvia." I held her in front of me and looked her in the eyes. "That's not a cop out there."

Something changed inside her. I could feel the anger leaving her body. "Who is it?" she asked.

"It might be Rose," I said.

"He's the man who shot you?"

"Yes."

"He's the man who . . ." She didn't finish it.

"I think so," I said.

"Why is he here?"

"I don't know."

She looked toward the window. "What are you going to do?"

"I'll call the police," I said. "Here, get down on the floor."

"Why do I have to get down?" she said. The fear was starting to overtake her. I could hear it in her voice.

I pulled her down behind the couch. "Just sit right here."

"Alex, this is getting a little scary."

"I'm calling the police right now," I said. I picked up the phone.

Nothing. It was dead. I just stood there looking at it. "I can't believe this."

"What's wrong?"

"He cut the phone line. He actually cut the fucking phone line."

"Alex, this is getting a *lot* scary now."

I didn't say anything.

"Alex . . ."

I picked the gun up from the table and turned off the light in the kitchen. There was a flashlight hanging on the wall. I took that and then I turned off the lamp by the bed. The cabin was dark except for the dim glow coming through the front window from the outside light above the door.

"Alex, what are we going to do?"

I got down on my knees. "We're going to wait a few minutes, let our eyes get adjusted to the dark."

She folded her arms around her knees.

"All right," I said. "I'll be right back."

"Where are you going?" She grabbed my arm.

"I'm just going to look out the window."

I crawled over to the front window and peered over the sill. The outdoor light lit up the clearing in front of the cabin, and the first row of pine trees. On the right side of the clearing, just off the road, I could see the front of his car. Sylvia was right. It wasn't even hidden at all. Anyone could see it. Although I couldn't tell if anyone was in the car. On the left side of the clearing I saw the woodpile, my truck, and Sylvia's black Jaguar.

Both hoods were up.

I crawled back to Sylvia. "When you drove in, was the hood up on my truck?"

"I don't remember," she said. "I don't think so."

"You didn't lock your car, did you?"

"No, I didn't. Alex, what are you talking about?"

"He's got both hoods up," I said. "He must have taken out the distributor caps or something. He obviously doesn't want us to go anywhere."

"So now what?"

I thought about it. He was out there somewhere. He knew that Sylvia was here in the cabin with me. No phone. No vehicles. My other cabins were a quarter mile up the logging road. But there were no phones in those, anyway. Nearest phone was in Vinnie's cabin. That was a good·half mile away in the other direction, down by the main road. If I snuck out the back I might be able to make my way down there, but I didn't want to leave Sylvia alone. And I didn't want to take her out there, either. "I think we should just sit tight for a while," I said. "See what he does."

"What if he tries to come in?"

"Then I'll shoot him," I said.

"I don't like this," she said.

"I'm not too crazy about it, either."

She leaned her head back against the rough wall. A long minute passed, and then another, and then I lost track of the time altogether. It was just the two of us sitting on the floor behind my couch, listening to the silence.

Finally, a sound. A car starting, a roar and a rattle. The car needed a new muffler. And then the sound of the car on the logging road. The noise grew smaller and smaller until it disappeared.

"I think he's gone," I said. "He just drove away."

"Why would he do that?"

"Who knows? The guy is nuts."

"But why would he just leave?"

"Sylvia, he's absolutely fucking crazy. There's no reason for anything he does."

"Are you sure it was him?"

"Had to be," I said. "Who else would it be?"

"So what do we do now?"

"Stay here," I said. I went to the window again and looked outside. Nothing. His car was gone. I turned off the outside light. We were in total darkness now.

"Alex, why did you do that?"

"I want to go see what he did to our cars. But I don't want that light on. I'll use the flashlight."

"Don't go out there!"

"Sylvia, if I can get one of the cars started, I'll pull up next to the door. As soon as I'm close, come out and get in. We'll get out of here."

I opened the door a crack and looked outside. The cold air rushed into the cabin. I stepped outside and then made my way to the vehicles, the gun in one hand and the flashlight in the other. I didn't want to turn the flashlight on unless I had to. There was just enough moonlight to see where I was going.

When I got to the truck, I took a quick look inside the cab. The cellular phone was gone. I looked under the hood, snapping the flashlight on just long enough to see the engine. He hadn't taken out the distributor cap after all, but all the spark plug wires were loose. I put the gun and the flashlight down and tried to reconnect them in the dark. Just relax, I told myself. Relax and think. How do these things go on? One through four on this side. One here, two, three, wait a minute. Is that right? Goddamn it. If I could just see what I was doing. . . . I turned the flashlight on for a second, looked it over, turned it off, and tried to keep the image burned in my mind. The fourth one was right here. I could feel a thin line of sweat running down the side of my face. Where's that fucking wire? All right, five is where? Where the *fuck* is five? I turned the light back on for a second.

A sound! I threw myself to the ground, fumbling with the flashlight. When I finally got it turned off, I just lay there on the ground, listening. My heart was pounding in my ears.

It was just a bat, whistling by in the air above me. A motherfucking bat.

I got up and tried to find my place among the spark plug wires. My hands were shaking.

All right, five goes here. Six, seven. Is this right? Am I doing this right, goddamn it all to hell? Is this fucking truck going to start now? Eight is next. One more wire. Where is it? Where is eight? Where the fuck is eight? I turned the light back on for a moment. There it is. Connect it here. I'm all done. I hope.

I eased the hood down, didn't even bother to close it all the way. Just get it out of the way so you can drive. We'll get out of here, go down to the main road, maybe go to the Glasgow if it's still open, call the police. Have a drink or two or five. Let's go let's go let's go.

I opened the door, slid into the seat. The key! Where the fuck is the key? I put the flashlight and the gun down on the seat next to me, fished around in my pockets. Motherfucking keys! Here they are. I pulled them out, felt through all the keys on my ring for the car key. Why the fuck do I have so many fucking keys on here? The car key, the key to the cabin, that's all I need. What are all these other fucking keys for?

That's when the window exploded. The sudden blast of the gunshot, the spray of glass, the scream that came out of my lungs all on its own, they all seemed to happen in the same instant. I threw the door open and dropped to the ground. Was I hit? Was I bleeding? I didn't even know.

No, you're not hit, Alex. You're still alive. For the moment. Get a grip on yourself. Try to breathe. I can't breathe. Breathe, damn it! The gun. Where's the gun? I picked my head up. There, on the car seat, covered with a million small shards of glass. The gun and the flashlight. I grabbed them. I could feel the glass cutting into my hands. All right, you have a gun. You have a flashlight. Now just breathe. Make yourself breathe.

Where is he? He shot out the passenger's side window, so he must be on the other side of the car. Is he over in the woods? What is that, twenty yards, maybe thirty? By the woodpile? Or is he standing right there next to the car, waiting for me to show myself?

What do I do? Do I wait? Do I make a run for it?

Speak. Say something to him. Make yourself talk.

"Rose!" I yelled. "Rose, are you there?"

There was no response.

"Rose, is that you?"

Nothing. I shook my head. The gunshot was still ringing in my ears.

"Rose, goddamn it, say something!"

I heard laughter. How far away? I think from the woods. I moved down toward the back of the truck and peeked over the edge. Too dark. I ducked back behind the truck, turned the flashlight on. I raised my hand, waiting for the next bullet.

Silence.

I peeked over the edge, keeping the flashlight as far away from my head as I could. If he's going to shoot, let him shoot at the light. I couldn't see him anywhere. I trained the light on the pine trees. No sign of him.

"Rose, where are you?" He had to be there somewhere. In the trees. "Show yourself!"

More laughter. Yes, from the trees. He was there.

"Rose, I've called the police! They'll be here any second! Come out and throw your gun down now!"

"Nice try, Alex!" That voice. Is it him? It was so long ago. What did his voice sound like? On the phone, he spoke in a whisper. It was so hard to tell.

"I know you cut the phone line, Rose! But I have a radio!" It was a bluff, but I figured it was worth a shot. "The police are on their way!"

There was a long silence. "I don't think so, Alex," he finally said. "Just give it up."

"What do you want from me?" I said. How can I reason with him? What do you say to a madman? "What do you want me to do, Rose?"

"I want you to be scared, Alex. That's all I want. Are you scared?"

"Yes," I said. I kept moving the flashlight across the tree line. Where was his voice coming from? Which tree is he hiding behind? "Yes, I'm scared."

"That's good, Alex."

"So now you can leave, right?"

He laughed. "I'm not even here now, Alex. I can't be. I'm in prison, remember?"

"All right, Rose," I said. "I've had enough." Anger. I need to feel anger. I need to stand up and do something for once in my fucking life. I'm not going to just sit here and wait for him to shoot me again. "I want you to put your gun down, Rose. Put the gun down and get your ass out here."

"What are you going to do, Alex?"

"I'm going to come get you, Rose. I swear to God, I'm going to come in there and find you."

"You don't have a gun, Alex."

Wait a minute. He doesn't think I have a gun? What's *that* all about? Do I go along with it? Try to surprise him? No, fuck it. "I have a gun, Rose. Now get out here."

"That's not a real gun, Alex." He laughed. "I know that's not a real gun. *Now* what are you going to do?"

God, now what? This doesn't make any sense? Why he would think—

Forget it. He's crazy. Don't try to get in his mind. Just move.

I stood up. The flashlight in my left hand, the gun in my right. I put them together into a double-handed grip, just like they taught me at the academy a million years ago. The beam of light and the sight of the gun were one now. Anything I could see I could shoot. "I'm coming in there, Rose. Put the gun down."

More laughter. Which tree is it?

"Put the gun down." I moved closer to the tree line. I wanted him to laugh again. I was getting close enough.

I heard something. A footfall. Leaves. A small branch snapping.

"Put it down, Rose!"

There. From behind that tree. There he is.

"PUT THE GUN DOWN!"

I saw the blond wig. I saw the gun in his hand. He raised it. I fired. Four times, chest chest head chest.

I stood there for a long time. The noise from my gun dissolved into the night. But it kept reverberating in my head. My hands tingled from the shock of it. I could smell the burnt powder. I didn't move.

Finally, a car. I didn't look up. The car pulled into the clearing, the tires scraping the grass. A door opened and closed. Footsteps.

"Alex, what happened?"

I looked up. It was Uttley.

"I thought I heard shots," he said. "I was on my way

down from the Fulton house. I tried calling you, but I couldn't get through. So I thought I should—" And then he saw the legs on the ground. The rest of the body was knocked back behind the tree.

More footsteps. It was Sylvia. She came out of the cabin and stood next to me. She looked down.

"Is it him?" Uttley asked. He didn't even seem to notice that Sylvia was there. "Is it Rose?"

I stepped forward and shone my flashlight on his face. The headshot had blown the wig away and taken out a small piece of his scalp.

"No," I said.

"What?"

"I don't know who this is," I said. "I've never seen him before."

Chapter Seventeen

I WAS SITTING in the same interview room. The fishing map was still on the wall. Someone had made a half-hearted attempt to clean off the coffee, but there was still a pale brown streak from Lake Nicolet all the way down to Potagannissing Bay.

Uttley had called the police on his cellular. Maven showed up not long after the first officers. He brought me down here himself, made me go over it a couple times. When Detective Allen got there, they made me go over it a couple more times. And then they made me go over it eight or nine times more, just for good measure. I imagined Uttley had been put in another room to give his statement, Sylvia in yet another room to give hers. I hoped they were both long gone by then, home in their beds. Or eating breakfast. I couldn't guess how long I had been there. I didn't even know if it was night or day. There was no clock in the room. I didn't know where my watch had gone. I couldn't even remember if I was wearing it the night before. I suppose I could have gotten up and opened the blinds, but I just sat there in the chair, my arms on the table, staring at the map.

The last time through my story, a uniformed officer stuck his nose in the room, told Maven and Allen he had something important for them. As I watched them get up and leave the room, I noticed that they both had that stiff, middle-aged cop way of moving around. Put a couple of hats on them and they'd be Joe Friday and Bill Gannon. That's the kind of thing you think about when you're as tired and shell-shocked as I was.

I didn't think about what had happened. I didn't think about what it meant, that I had killed the man, whoever he was. That I would have to deal with later, when I had the strength to face it.

Finally, the door opened again. Maven and Allen walked in and sat down across from me. Allen took a long breath and looked me in the eyes. Maven just stared right past me at the wall. He had a look on his face like he was trying to pass a kidney stone.

"Mr. McKnight," Allen said, "does the name Raymond Julius mean anything to you?"

"No," I said.

"That's the man's name."

"The man I shot?"

"Yes. You've never met him before?"

"No."

"You don't know anything about him?"

"No."

"Well," Allen said, "apparently Raymond Julius knew a lot about *you*." Maven kept staring at the wall. He wouldn't look at me.

"I don't get it," I said.

"Apparently, Mr. Julius spent a great deal of time thinking about you. Following you, watching you. Writing about you."

"How do you know this?"

"There were certain items found in his residence."

"I still don't understand," I said. "Did he write the notes? Did he kill Bing and Dorney? And Edwin?"

"That seems fairly obvious," Allen said. "From the physical evidence, I mean." He snuck a sideways glance at Maven, who still hadn't said a word. I was finally be-

ginning to see what was going on here. Maven had convinced Allen that I was their man. Allen agreed to help
double-team me. Now that he knew the real story, Allen
was embarrassed. And not too happy about helping Maven
in the first place.

"What kind of physical evidence are we talking
about?"

Allen took out a pocket notebook and paged through it.
"Traces of blood. We'll run those, see who they match. A
silencer for a nine-millimeter pistol, consistent with the
weapon found on Mr. Julius. We'll do ballistics on both,
of course. See if they match the bullets removed from
Bing and Dorney."

"He didn't use the silencer last night," I said.

"No," Allen said. "He left it in his gun case."

"Doesn't make sense."

"Who knows. You live in the middle of the woods. He
didn't figure he'd need it."

I just shook my head.

"There was a typewriter on the desk," Allen went on.
"We found several pages of text, describing his move-
ments over the last few months. You know, like a jour-
nal. A diary. At first glance, the actual type on those
pages seems to match the type on the notes."

"You were there? You saw all this?"

"Yes," Allen said. "That's where we were while you
were detained here for the last couple hours." He snuck
another look at Maven. Maven didn't say anything.

"What did the diary say?"

"I can't go into too much detail at this point. But I can
tell you that Mr. Julius was a very disturbed individual.
There were several news clippings on his desk, as well.
Copies of stories that appeared in the *Detroit News* and the
Detroit Free Press, summer of 1984."

"Summer of 1984?" I said. "Were they about . . ."

"About Rose, yes. About the shooting. There was one column, in particular. About your recovery."

"I think I remember," I said. "The guy from the *News* got into the hospital."

"That one was pinned on his wall. Right next to his bed."

"Wait a minute," I said. "This is just too weird."

"Like I said, Mr. McKnight, this was a very disturbed individual. He apparently thought you have some sort of special . . . power or something. He thought you were some sort of messiah."

"The chosen one," I said. "He said that in the notes."

"Yes, exactly."

"But what about the other stuff in the notes?" I said. "How did he know about what Rose said to me? There's no way he could have known that, unless . . ."

"There appears to have been a connection," Allen said. "In the diary, he referred to some sort of communication he might have had with Mr. Rose."

"While Rose was in prison? What kind of communication? Letters? Phone calls?"

"That's not clear at this point," Allen said. "He wasn't specific. He did write something about *becoming* Rose, about taking over his identity in some way."

"I have to see this stuff," I said. "Do you have it here at the station?"

"No, Mr. McKnight," he said. "You know how this works. Right now, it's all still at the residence. We need to go through it all very carefully."

"I thought you said it was obvious."

"It is," he said. "But we have to follow our procedures."

"Can I go to his house?"

"No, Mr. McKnight. Please, just let us work on this. I promise you we'll let you see it when it's all over."

"I still don't get it," I said. "I don't even know this guy. How did he even know about Rose?"

"He just picked you," Allen said. "Who knows why? He just did. I've seen a couple cases like this before. There was one I remember very well. A man was out driving, and he cut somebody off at an intersection. Turns out the guy he cut off, he followed him to his house, found out who he was, started calling him, sending him notes. It escalated to the point where the man had to move out of the house. Even then, the guy found him again, finally tried to kill him. Fortunately, we caught him in time. I think that's the type of individual we're talking about here. It's usually just a little thing that triggers it. He sees you. Something clicks in his head. Suddenly, he has to know everything about you. In your case, he finds out that you had been shot, he goes back and finds the old news clippings. He just makes up this whole little universe with you at the center of it."

"How long has this been going on?" I asked. "When did it all start?"

"Judging from his diary, it looks like five or six months ago."

I shook my head. "Why me?"

Maven cleared his throat. "Just because," he said. Finally, he had opened his mouth. "Maybe it was your dynamic personality. Maybe your incredible personal charm. Maybe it's the way the whole room lights up when you walk in."

Allen gave him a long icy look and then turned back to me. "Mr. McKnight," he said. "Alex. Although you were never formally charged in this matter, I just want to say on a purely personal level that as painful as this ordeal must have been for you, the treatment you received in this office obviously made it even worse. For whatever part I played in that, I just want to apologize to you."

"Fair enough," I said. I looked at Maven. "Is there anything you'd like to add to that, Chief?"

He just sat there chewing on the inside of his mouth for moment. "Just one thing," he finally said.

"I'm all ears."

"This didn't have to happen."

"You got that right," I said.

"No, I mean what happened to Mr. Fulton. He didn't have to die. If you had just cooperated for one minute on this case, we might have had this Julius guy's ass behind bars before that ever happened. Of course, then you couldn't have had your little cowboy shoot-out last night. Mrs. Fulton wouldn't have been there, scared out of her mind because her husband's killer is at the front door. Although what she was doing at your cabin while they're still out dragging the lake for his body is another story."

"Chief Maven," Allen said, "is this really necessary?"

"No, it's not necessary," Maven said. "If ex-policemen who get their partners killed don't decide to retire here and make my life miserable, then *none* of this is necessary."

"You're way out of line, Chief."

"Just get out of here," Maven said. "Go back to your little state office. You've been a big help."

Allen stood up and shook my hand. "Alex, please let me know if I can be of any assistance in the future." He looked down at Maven. "You'll be hearing from me, Chief."

"I can't wait," Maven said.

When Allen had left, we both just sat there at the table, looking at each other.

"I assume I'm free to go?" I finally said.

"You're free to kiss my wrinkled white ass," he said.

I stood up. "I'm going to miss these little chats," I said. "Maybe we can go fishing some time."

I WALKED OUT of the station into daylight. It was late morning already. The sun was actually trying to shine a little bit, but it wasn't doing anything to warm things up.

I stumbled around in the parking lot for a minute until I realized that my truck was still parked next to my cabin, minus one passenger-side window. If I had had the strength to laugh, I would have. I certainly didn't feel like going back into the station and asking for a ride. So I just started walking. I wasn't sure where I was going, but it felt good to be moving.

I walked around the courthouse toward the river, then followed the sidewalk that ran along the water as far as I could go. When I got to the edge of the park, I turned around and came back to the locks. There was a large freighter going through. My ears were starting to hurt from the cold so I climbed the steps to the observation deck. It was empty.

The ship was about seven hundred feet long. It was entering the southern-most lock, so close to the deck that it was like looking across the street at a slowly moving building. The flag was three horizontal stripes, red, white, and black, with some kind of golden bird in the middle. I guessed Egypt. There were a dozen dark-skinned men standing on the ship, wrapped up tight in their coats, looking back at me as they passed. They were so far from home. This must have seemed like a new and strange world to them. And now with a full load of iron ore, they were on their way back out to sea, down through the Great Lakes to the St. Lawrence Seaway and out to the Atlantic Ocean.

I could jump on that ship, I thought. It's close enough. They could take me back to Egypt with them.

"Alex, I've been looking all over for you." Uttley appeared next to me. "The officer at the station said you just walked off."

"Just watching the ship go through," I said.

He looked out at it. "Where's it from? Whose flag is that?"

"Egypt, I think."

He nodded. "Detective Allen called me. He told me everything."

I didn't say anything.

"You really don't know who this Raymond Julius guy was?"

"No," I said.

He let out a long slow breath. "That ship's got a long way to go," he said. "How many days you figure it takes to go to Egypt from here?"

"Couldn't say."

"You know they built the first lock here in 1797? It was destroyed in the War of 1812. They had to rebuild it."

I kept looking out at the ship. They had closed the lock and started to lower the water level. When the boat had come down twenty-one feet, they would open the other end and let the boat go on its way to Lake Huron.

"In World War Two, this was the most heavily defended part of the country. If somebody was going to drop bombs on us, the government figured they'd start here. You know, mess up the iron supply, stop us from making tanks. That's why they built two Air Force bases way up here in the middle of nowhere."

"Why are you telling me this?" I said.

"Because I don't know what else to say."

Neither of us spoke for a while. We watched the boat sink as the water left the lock.

"It's got to be a little easier to deal with now, isn't it?" he said.

"How do you mean?"

"You thought it was Rose before. Even though everybody else was telling you he was still in prison. It must have been driving you crazy."

"So instead it's just some guy off the street," I said. "And for some reason he decides to spend his whole life just following me around, watching me, finding out about my past. Trying to *become* my past, for God's sake. It doesn't make any sense."

"Of course it doesn't make any sense."

"They say he was in contact with Rose somehow. I guess that would mean mail, right? You can't just call a guy in prison."

He thought about it. "Or he could have visited him."

"Right. But either way, they'd have a record of it, wouldn't they? Don't they screen your mail in prison?"

"I'm sure they do," he said. "I'm sure Detective Allen will look into that. Or Maven, if he ever gets his head out of his ass. Allen didn't go into details, but it sounds like you and Maven haven't kissed and made up yet."

"What would happen if I called that Browning guy again?"

"The corrections officer? He'd stonewall you again and you'd get mad again. Why would you even want to call him? What are you going to find out? Alex, it's over. The guy is dead."

"It doesn't feel over."

"You've got to give yourself some time," he said. "Take a vacation. Go someplace warm for a few days."

The freighter had moved through the other end of the lock. We could see the back of it now. There was some Arabic writing and next to that it read "Cairo."

"You were right," he said. "That *was* the Egyptian flag. Come on, let's get out of here."

He took me home in his BMW. I stared out the window at the pine trees. Pine trees and more pine trees. I was starting to get sick of pine trees. We rode in silence the whole way, and then we were at my cabin. It felt strange to be looking at it again after what had happened. It was the same place. A small cabin made in the woods. And yet everything was different now.

"You want me to stick around for a while?" he said. "Help you clean up?"

"No, thanks," I said. "I need to be here by myself for a while."

"I understand," he said. "Give me a call if you need me."

"Okay." I got out of the car.

"Hey Alex?"

I looked back in.

"It's over," he said. "It's really over."

"I know," I said.

I watched him leave and then I turned around to face it. My truck was sitting there, the hood still ajar, the seat still covered with glass. Where Sylvia's car had been, there was just an impression in the grass.

And where the body was. Over in the woods, past the woodpile. They had taken him away, of course, but I wasn't ready to go look at where I had killed him.

I went into the cabin, wondering if I'd ever feel at home there again. I remembered back when I was a police officer in Detroit. They told us if we ever had to kill somebody, no matter how justified it might be, there would eventually be a price to pay. At some point, an hour later, a day, a week, it would suddenly hit you, the fact that you killed another human being. I kept waiting for it to hit me. But I felt nothing.

I picked up the phone. It was dead. I had forgotten, he had cut the line. I'd have to go down to the Glasgow to use the phone. But first I'd have to go out and clean all the glass out of the truck. Or else I'd have to walk all the way down there. I couldn't imagine doing either. I needed to sleep. Let me just get a little sleep first. If I can. If it's possible to sleep, ever again.

I needed those pills. Just one more time. After all that had happened, who could blame me for needing them?

Hell, maybe I can sleep without them. I'll give it a try.

I lay down on my bed. I put my head back on the pillow and looked up at the rough wooden ceiling. And then I was out.

I WOKE UP a few hours later from a dreamless sleep. It felt like something *beyond* sleep, like a temporary total shutdown. It was late afternoon. I had never felt so hungry in my life.

I went outside with the broom and tried to sweep most of the glass out of my truck, knocked out the few fragments of glass that were still stuck in the window frame. I tried starting it. Nothing.

I threw the hood up and looked at the wiring. Just standing there, it all came back to me, the way I felt when I had tried to put the wires back, wondering how long I had to live. In my rush, I had gotten two of the wires crossed. I switched them and tried again. The truck started.

I left the truck running while I took a quick look around the place for my cellular phone, hoping he had just thrown it into the woods. When I came to the spot where I shot him, I stopped and looked down at the ground where he had fallen. There were pine needles on the ground, a few pine cones. I could have gotten down on my knees and looked for blood, but I didn't. I just stood there and re-played it in my mind. He didn't think my gun was real. Did that give me an unfair advantage? Should I have fired a warning shot into the trees? But then what would have happened? Would he have thrown his own gun down? Am I going to have to wonder about that now for the rest of my life?

There will be no trial, no chance to sit in a courtroom and hear an explanation for it all. I'll never find out why he picked me.

Five or six months ago, they said. That's when this all

started. What did I do to him? Why was he so obsessed with me?

As I got back into the truck I felt a sharp sliver of glass slice through my finger. I pulled it out and looked at the thin line of blood. There is nothing so red as blood, nothing so simple. And I had seen quite enough of it for one lifetime.

I ordered a steak at the Glasgow, the biggest damned steak Jackie could find, medium rare, with grilled onions and mushrooms and four ice-cold Canadian beers. Jackie slipped me a quick smile. I think he knew I was on my way back. If I wasn't quite myself yet, he knew it would only be a matter of time. I borrowed his phone, started to dial the phone company, then I realized it was probably too late in the day. I'd call them tomorrow to have my phone line restored. And an auto glass place to have my window replaced.

I sat there tapping my beer bottle for a few minutes and then I picked up the phone again. She answered on the third ring.

"Sylvia," I said, "I'm just calling to make sure you're okay."

"Why wouldn't I be okay?" she said. "I'm so okay I'm way past perfect."

Her voice wasn't right. "Are you drunk?"

"I'm way past drunk," she said. "I'm just sitting here in this big old house on the edge of the world all by myself getting way past drunk."

"Do you want me to come out there?"

"Why would I want you to come out here?"

"Because you shouldn't be alone."

"Why shouldn't I be alone?"

"Because you shouldn't. Damn it, Sylvia, you came all the way out to my cabin last night. Why did you do that?"

"You know, that's a good question. I'm not sure why I came out there. But obviously it was such a wonderful thing to do. Another brilliant turning point in my life. I got to meet the man who killed my husband, after all. Well no, I didn't get to meet him really. I did get to see him on the ground with half his head blown off."

"You didn't want to be alone," I said. "That's why you came to my cabin, all right? It's okay. After everything that's happened, there's nothing wrong with that."

"Yes there is, Alex. There's something very wrong with that. I'm not sure what, but I'm sure if I think about it—Christ, where did that bottle go?"

"I'm coming out there."

"So help me God," she said. Suddenly, she sounded sober. "If you come here I will kill you. I will kill you or I will kill myself. Or I will kill both of us. And believe me, I can do that now. I've been watching the experts."

"All right, Sylvia," I said. "All right. Take it easy."

"Don't tell me to take it easy. Just leave me alone. You got that? Leave me the fuck alone."

I didn't know what else to say. I closed my eyes and listened to the faint sound of her breathing.

"What have we done, Alex?" she finally said, her voice drained of all emotion. "What have we done?"

She hung up before I could answer. I just sat there with the phone in my hand. And then I had Jackie bring me another beer.

A couple hours later, I was back at my cabin. It was dark. I walked around the outside of the cabin a couple times. I couldn't bring myself to believe that nobody was watching me anymore, that nobody was waiting to kill me.

My gun. I didn't have my gun anymore. It was still at the police station. But that was okay. I didn't need it anymore, right?

I went inside and found the phone book. I tried to look up Raymond Julius. He had no listing.

Five or six months ago. What happened five or six months ago?

You're not going to figure this out tonight, Alex. Just go to bed. You need to cut some wood tomorrow, clean up the place. Get some food in the house, for God's sake. Become a human being again.

I slept. Two hours, maybe three. And then I sat up in my bed and turned on the light. It was just past midnight.

Five or six months ago.

The phone book was still on the kitchen table. I paged through it until I found Leon Prudell. The address was in Kinross, a little town south of the Soo, down by the airport. I threw some clothes on and got in the truck. With the cold air whipping through the open window I raced toward Kinross. It was late, but Leon and I had something to talk about.

It didn't take long to find his house. Kinross is almost as small as Paradise, one main road and a few side streets. It was a little clapboard house, not much bigger than my cabin. There was a faint smell of dead fish in the air. A tire swing hung from a tree in the front yard.

I knocked on the door, waited, knocked again. Finally the porch light came on and a woman looked around the door at me. "Who is it?" she said.

"I need to speak to your husband," I said.

"He's not here. Who are you?"

I thought for a second. "I want to hire him," I said. "I understand he's a private investigator."

"He *was* doing investigations," she said, "but he don't do that no more."

"I hear he's good," I said. "Are you sure he won't take a case? I'll pay five hundred dollars a day."

That got her to open the door all the way. I saw a lot of

woman and a lot of red bathrobe. The way she was built, I was glad that Leon had come after me in the bar that night and not her. "He's working up at the truck stop on I-75 tonight," she said. "In the restaurant."

"The one by the Route 28 exit?"

"Yeah, that's the one."

"I appreciate it, ma'am."

"He works nights," she said. "Ever since he lost the investigating job."

"I see."

"Do you know a guy named Alex McKnight?"

"Can't say that I do," I said.

"That's the man who got him fired. You see him, you tell him he's an asshole, okay?"

"I'll do that, ma'am. I'm sorry I had to disturb you at this hour."

"For five hundred dollars a day, you can disturb me anytime you want."

"Thank you, ma'am. Good night."

I got out of there and made my way back to the highway. The truck stop was a few miles north on I-75, one of those places you see from the road, lit up all night long, a hundred trucks gassing up or just sitting there while the drivers have their apple pie and coffee.

I found Prudell clearing off a table, a big white apron hanging over his gut. As soon as he saw me, he set his pile of plates down with a clatter.

"Well, look who it is," he said. "Don't tell me, you came to take this job away from me too, right?"

"Sit down, Prudell."

"Here, let me take my apron off for you. You'll be needing this." There were a couple truckers at the counter, a waitress serving them, another one just sitting in a booth. They all looked over at us.

"Just sit down," I said.

"All you got to do is keep these tables clear," he said. "And once an hour you gotta go clean up the bathrooms. I'm sure you'll be able to handle it."

"Prudell," I said. I was trying to control myself. I was really trying. "If you don't shut up and sit down, I'm going to hurt you. Do you understand me? I'm going to beat the hell out of you right here in the restaurant."

"McKnight, if you don't get out of here right now—"

I grabbed his left hand and bent it back against his wrist. It had always been a great way to convince someone to get into the back of a squad car. Not as dramatic as an arm behind the back, but just as effective. Prudell gave out a little yelp and then he sat down in the booth. The whole place was watching us now, but I didn't care.

"What the fuck is wrong with you?" he said. "You trying to break my wrist?"

I sat down next to him. It was a tight fit. "Listen to me very carefully," I said. "Do you remember that night in the bar, the first night you came after me? I know you were drunk, but try to remember what you said to me."

"What are you talking about?"

"You said I took your job and now you were going to go broke and you had a family to take care of, remember? You gave me the whole sob story about your kids not going to Disney World and your wife not getting a new car and all that shit. And then you said something else, something about a man who was helping you out. You said he was down on his luck and the only thing keeping him together was running errands for you and feeling like he was doing something important. Do you remember that?"

"I remember," he said. "It was all true. You really fucked over a lot of people. Not just me."

It had been five months and change since I took Prudell's job. He had nursed his grudge for a few months until he had finally worked up the nerve to face me.

"Okay, fine," I said. "Whatever you say. I ruined all your lives. Now just tell me his name."

"The guy who was working for me?"

"Yes," I said. "Tell me his name."

"His name is Julius," he said. "Raymond Julius."

CHAPTER EIGHTEEN

A LONG SILENCE passed while it sank in. Prudell slipped me a quick elbow in the ribs, but it didn't get him out of the booth. It just made me even madder. "Do that again and I'll take your head off," I said.

"You've got a lot of nerve, McKnight. Just let me out of here."

"Where does he live?" I said.

"I don't know," he said.

"The hell you don't. The guy worked for you."

"I only saw his house once," he said. "That was a long time ago, before you—"

"Yeah yeah, before I fucked you both over. We've been through that already. You were at his house, but you don't know where it is? What, were you blindfolded?"

"It's in the Soo," he said. "On the west side of town somewhere. I don't remember exactly where, all right?"

"Have you talked to him since then?"

"No, I haven't."

I sat there and thought about it. Finally, I got up out of the booth and said, "Let's go."

"What are you talking about? I'm not going anywhere."

"Yes you are. We're going to go find his house."

"Like hell I am. I'm in the middle of working here."

"Go tell your boss you need to take a little break. Call it a family emergency."

He worked his way out of the booth, adjusted his white apron, and picked up a plate. "You can go fuck yourself," he said.

I counted to ten in my head while he cleared the table. "Prudell," I said. "You got two choices. Number one is I bounce you off every wall in this place and then throw you through a window. I'm sure I'll get arrested. I don't care anymore. Number two is you help me find Julius's house, and I pay you five hundred dollars for your time."

He looked up at me. "You expect me to believe that? You're going to pay me?"

"You're a private investigator, aren't you? Consider it a case."

"I *was* a private investigator," he said. "Now I'm a busboy."

"What's your choice, Prudell?"

"You're something else, you know that? You're a real piece of work."

"Choose, Prudell."

He dropped the plates on the table and went back through a couple of swinging doors to the kitchen. I didn't know if he was calling the police, or getting a big knife, or sneaking out the back door. Finally, he burst back out through the doors, untying his apron. A frowning little man who had to be his boss came out behind him.

We walked out to the parking lot without saying a word. He wasn't happy about the missing window in my truck, especially when he sat down on some of the glass I hadn't quite cleaned up.

I started the truck and pulled out of the parking lot. "Start talking," I said. "Tell me about Raymond Julius."

"God, it's freezing in here," he said. It was about thirty degrees outside. I'm not sure what the windchill would be if you were riding around at sixty miles an hour in a truck with no passenger side window. The man didn't even have a coat on.

"Raymond," I said again, nice and slow. "Julius."

"What can I tell you? He was kind of weird. He was way into all that militia stuff. Hated the government."

"So he belonged to a militia?"

"No. He tried, I think. It didn't work out. He was more into being a detective than being a soldier. Or a patriot or whatever the hell they call themselves."

"He had guns?"

"Yes," Prudell said. "The man had guns. He didn't have permits for them, but he had guns."

"Did he have a nine-millimeter pistol?"

"Don't know for sure," he said. "I wouldn't be surprised."

"Would he know how to get his hands on a silencer?"

"I'm sure he would," he said. "Why are you asking me all this?"

"Which way are we going?" I said. "Three Mile Road? You said the west side of town. Be more specific."

"Hell, I don't know," he said. "I remember getting off there, I think. I had to pick him up one day when his car broke down."

"Old junker? No muffler?"

"Yeah, I think so."

I took the exit and headed west. "Now where?"

"I told you, I don't remember." He peered out at the road, running his fingers through his hair. "I think it was up by the industrial park."

"How did he start working for you?"

"I had a listing in the Yellow Pages. He called me up, wanted to know if he could work for me. I told him no, he kept calling me up again and again. Every day. Said he'd do anything, run errands, take phone calls. Said he wanted to be a private detective so bad, he'd start out working for free."

"What, he expected to work his way up to investigator?"

"That's how he saw it. I explained to him how it worked. You gotta be certified by the state, you gotta get a gun permit. That really set him off. Like I said, that man hated the government so much. Far as he was concerned, the state of Michigan was the only thing preventing him from being an investigator."

"And you let this guy work for you?"

"The man was begging me. Said it was a matter of life or death to him. So I figured, hell, I'll take him with me one day, just make him get me lunch, cover me while I went to the bathroom. I was just watching lifeguards, writing down their routine. I figured he would see how boring it was and forget all about it."

"That was the place out on Drummond Island."

"Yeah," he said. "I watched those lifeguards for three days straight, wrote out a detailed report. I tried to do a good job for Uttley. I guess it wasn't good enough, huh?"

I looked over at him. He was looking out the window into the cold night. The wind was whipping his crazy red hair in every direction.

"Julius is dead," I said.

He didn't say anything. He just kept looking out the window.

"Did you hear me? He's dead."

"I thought so," he said. He looked at me for a second, and then looked at the dashboard. "The way you were talking about him."

"He was stalking me for months," I said. "He killed three men, including Edwin Fulton. He tried to kill me, too."

Prudell just nodded.

"Doesn't surprise you?"

He shrugged his shoulders. "I wouldn't have expected something like that from him, but . . . hell, who knows anymore. I remember, he'd get this look in his eyes sometimes. Made me wonder why I ever let him hang around me."

"I killed him," I said.

He turned and looked at me. He didn't say anything.

"I had no choice," I said.

He just nodded his head.

I came to Fourteenth Street. "Do I turn here?"

"I think so," he said. "I think I came this way. I remember having to look around for his street."

We came to a stop sign. I could keep going north on Fourteenth Street or turn east on Eighth Avenue. "Which way?"

"I'm thinking," he said. We just sat there in the truck. One single street lamp burned above us. It sounded eerily quiet without the rush of wind through the open window. "Go straight," he finally said. "I think it's up this way."

We passed small brick houses built close together, most of them at least fifty years old. This was one of the original neighborhoods in the Soo, back when there was an Air Force base just across the highway, long before the casinos and the tourists. We went up Fourteenth Street, past Seventh and Sixth, and then we ran into a dead end. "I remember now," he said. "I came to this dead end and had to turn around. Go back down to Sixth Street."

I did as he said. I was getting disoriented in this maze of numbered streets. It wasn't like in New York City, where all the numbers make some kind of sense, and where the streets run one way and the avenues run another way. "All right, now go to Thirteenth Street and take that all the way up until it ends." We passed Fifth Street and then the road ended at Fourth. "Let's try a left," he said.

"It feels like we're going in circles," I said.

"Feel free to take over the navigation," he said.

As we worked our way west on Fourth Street, the houses got smaller and smaller. Most of them had every window and door covered with plastic. With the bay and all its violent weather less than a mile away, I couldn't see how some of these places were still standing.

"This is starting to look familiar," he said. As we rounded a bend, a sign told us that were now on Oak Street. "Yes, that's right," he said. "I remember the tree names. There'll be some more tree streets around here. I'm pretty sure his house is on one of them."

We worked our way through Ash Street, and then onto Walnut and then Chestnut. Prudell kept staring out of the open window and then looking back across at my side of the street. "I know we're close," he said. "I know it's in this neighborhood."

"We've been down every street," I said. The man was being more cooperative than I could have hoped, but even so my patience was starting to fray around the edges.

"No, we haven't," he said. "As soon as we see his house, I know I'll recognize it. It had this awful siding on it. I can picture it in my mind. It looked like a mangy dog, that siding. All this hairy stuff on it like it was shedding. That house was such a dump. He was renting it. I remember him complaining about the landlord, all the stuff that was broken. The pipes used to freeze every night in the winter, he said. The way he talked about that landlord, I swear. All the things he said he would do to him if he ever got the chance."

"He never tried anything?"

"I don't think so. I think he was afraid to even talk to him."

I thought about that while he looked down the street. It was a dark corner in an unknown neighborhood. The Soo is a friendly place in general, but you never knew who's going to take exception to a strange truck cruising back and forth in front of the house. I was sure there were a lot of guns around here, high-powered deer rifles with scopes, shotguns.

"How about we keep moving?" I said.

"Wait a minute, now that I think of it, there was a street that I missed the first time through here. I didn't even see it until I doubled back. I think it was another tree name."

I turned the truck around and headed back up Chestnut. We took the right onto Ash, and went all the way down the street to Walnut. "This time, keep going straight," he said.

"It's just a dead end down here," I said.

"No, there's another street down here, see?"

He was right. You didn't see it until you came to the very end, a side street named Hickory.

I took the left and saw the police car immediately. I held onto the wheel and swung the truck all the way through, like I was just turning around. "Where are you going?" he said. "His house is down that street."

"There's a police car in front of the house," I said. "I don't want them to see me."

"Just cruise by like you're looking for something else."

"No, they might be watching for my truck," I said. "I wouldn't put it past Maven." I went back up Walnut Street a few houses and pulled over.

"So what are you going to do?" he asked.

It was a good question. In the back of my mind I knew that there was only one thing I *could* do if I wanted to answer all the questions. There was no way that Maven would ever let me see those papers. The news clippings, the diary. I couldn't think of a way to force him to show them to me. Technically, they were all pieces of evidence that would be used to close the file on three murders.

"I have to go inside his house," I said.

"Are you totally insane?"

"I have to," I said. "If I don't, this is going to haunt me for the rest of my life."

"You're going to break into a sealed house," he said. "You're going to corrupt evidence. That's a felony."

"I don't care."

"There's a policeman right outside the front door."

"I know," I said. It might be Dave, I thought, the same man who was keeping watch at my house. They could be sticking him with more offshift duty. But how would I know for sure unless I went up and knocked on his window? Excuse me, is that Dave in there? Any chance of letting me inside the house for a minute?

"So how are you going to get in the house?" he said.

"When you were here before, did you go inside?"

"Yes, for a second."

"Was there a backdoor?"

He just looked at me for a long moment. "I think so, yes."

"Good."

"You really need to do this, don't you."

"Yes."

"Then I'm coming with you," he said.

"The hell you are."

"I'm not gonna just sit here in this truck while you go breaking into that house. I'm an accessory already. I might as well go with you."

"Why would you want to help me?" I said. "I thought you hated me."

"Who says I'm going to help you? I just want to see how you do it. I want to see how good you are."

"I think you should just stay here," I said.

"Back at the restaurant, you gave me two choices, remember? Now I'm giving *you* two choices. Either we go together or I go wake up that cop."

We went together. Leaving the truck where it was, we made our way through the woods to the back of the house. I brought a pair of work gloves from the truck, a flashlight that I would only turn on if we absolutely needed it, and a set of lock picks. I had ordered them the same week I had gotten my license, but I'd never thought I'd get to use them. If I had, I would have practiced.

The back door was maybe thirty feet from the woods. The night was dark enough, nobody was going to see us. The houses on either side looked deserted. We crept up to the back door and knelt down on the ground. I snapped on the flashlight for a second and took a quick look. There were a couple garbage cans, an old lawn-mower. The siding on the house was just like Prudell described it, rough and shaggy like a shedding dog. There was police tape across the door.

"You don't want to break this tape," Prudell whispered to me.

"I will if I have to," I said.

"Wait, turn the light back on for a second." When I did, he stood up and traced the line of tape to its end. When he pulled on it, it came right off. "Very sloppy work," he said. "It comes right off this siding. They should have run it all the way around the house."

"I'll be sure to give Maven that tip," I said. I took my gloves off, took the set of picks out of my pocket, and began working on the door. With the tension bar set, I tried a couple rakes to see if I could get lucky. The lock didn't give. I settled down to working the tumblers one by one. Prudell stood by, making sounds of impatience. A cold wind kicked up, the kind of wind that starts somewhere near the North Pole, picks up a load of moisture off the lake, and then hits you across the face like a frozen porcupine. I lost the tension on the bar and had to start all over. One tumbler. Two tumblers. Three. And then I lost the tension again. The top half of the door was all window, so I just slipped my right hand back into the glove and took dead aim.

Prudell stopped my hand. "What's the matter with you?" he hissed. "Give me those." He took the picks from me, set the tension bar, and then gave the tumblers three quick rakes. "How'd you ever become a private eye, anyway?" he said as he opened the door for me.

I stepped into the house first. Prudell came in behind me and gently bumped the door closed with his hip. He doesn't want to leave fingerprints, I thought. Not a bad idea. I put my work gloves back on.

"Don't you have a pair of surgical gloves?" he asked.

"I left them with my stethoscope," I said.

"Those work gloves are too bulky to pick anything up."

"They're not too bulky to punch you in the mouth if you don't shut up."

I went to the front window and peeked through the blinds. The police car was still sitting at the curb. Its interior was dark. I pulled the flashlight out of my coat and turned it on, shielding most of the ray with my hand.

"Don't you have a red filter?" he asked.

"Prudell, I swear to God, if you don't shut up . . ."

"Not another word," he said. "Go ahead and do what you got to do. You're obviously the trained professional here."

I fantasized for a moment about hitting him in the head with the flashlight. Relax, Alex. The man is right. Do what you got to do and then get out of here.

It was a small house. It could barely be *called* a house. There was one main room that served as kitchen, dining room, and living room. The bed was separated from the rest of the house by a cheap partition that didn't even go all the way up to the ceiling. The bathroom was too small for more than one person to stand in. The whole place had the distinctive smell of loneliness. Unwashed bed sheets, overcooked food, cigarette smoke.

There was a stack of magazines on the kitchen counter, one of those detective rags on top. "He Mutilated the Cheerleaders and Then Buried Them In His Basement." There were some gun magazines, as well, and a few cheap propaganda pamphlets. "Feds to Bring In Chinese Troops to Take Our Guns Away." The usual antigovernment nutcase garbage.

I circled through the room and came to the gun cabinet. If nothing else, this man knew how to take care of his guns. There were five or six rifles stacked side by side behind the glass. I could smell the gun oil. In a glass case next to the cabinet there were three handguns. A classic service revolver like my own, a .357 magnum, and another gun that I didn't even recognize. There was an empty space where a fourth gun might have rested, and next to that there was a silencer. I was about to open the case, but then I stopped myself. There was no need. I already knew what gun that silencer was designed for.

The police hadn't touched anything yet. I knew the drill. They would bring a team in tomorrow, probably. Take lots of pictures, then remove everything piece by piece. Dust for prints. There wouldn't be any rush. The suspect was dead, after all. All they would be doing was closing the files on the three murders. They might even bring in some young officers, let them look around the place as part of their training.

I had an uneasy feeling, like Raymond Julius would open the bathroom door and walk into the room. Prudell stood by the back door. He hadn't moved. He kept his hands in his pockets. "Do you know what you're looking for?" he said.

"Yes," I said. There it was, on a small desk in the opposite corner of the room. The typewriter.

I went and stood over it. It was exactly as Allen had described, an old beat-up Underwood. Next to the typewriter there were two manila folders. I took a deep breath and picked up the first. It was hard to handle with the work gloves, so I put it all back down on the desk and went through the pages one by one. They were copies of old news clippings, all from the *Detroit News* and *Detroit Free Press,* July 1984. I recognized all the headlines. "Madman Kills Policeman, Second Officer Clings to Life." "Mayor Young Eulogizes Officer, Orders Probe of Mental Health Services." "Madman Cop Killer Guilty On All Counts."

I closed the folder and opened the second. I recognized the typeface immediately. It was his diary, one separate page for each entry. I aimed a small ray of light on the pages and read the dead man's secrets.

CHAPTER NINETEEN

JUNE 11

Alex McKnight. I want those to be the first two words
that I write. As I write them I feel the anger running
through me like a million volts of current. I have not
seen him in person and yet I can see his face when I
close my eyes at night. I am sure it is him. I hate his
face and I hate his name and I hate everything about
him. Now that he has done this to me there is nothing else to do but think about him all day long and
plan the things I will do to him if I ever get my
chance. At least I have something to do now. From
now on my purpose in life is to find out everything I
can about Alex McKnight and then use my knowledge to destroy him. I will say hello my name is Raymond Julius. You do not know me but you caused me
a lot of pain and now I am here to return the favor.
Imagine the look on his face when I say that.

JULY 2

I know more about Alex McKnight now. It feels
good to have this power over him. I feel like he is
right there in the palm of my hand. All I have to do
is close my hand and crush him. He was born in
1950 in Detroit. He was a baseball player at one

time and then a Detroit policeman. He was shot by a man named Maximilian Rose. His partner was killed. Alex McKnight still has one bullet inside him. At least he did when the reporters wrote about him in all the newspaper clippings I have collected. There is a picture of him lying in a hospital bed. There is a picture of Maximilian Rose being led into a courthouse. A strange thing has been happening to me. At night when I close my eyes I do not see Alex McKnight anymore. Now I see Maximilian Rose. I do not know why because it is Alex McKnight that I have been thinking about all the time. I have even been watching him at his cabin and at the bar he goes to almost every night. I only have this one picture of Maximilian Rose and it is not even a good picture of him because it is a copy out of a newspaper. So why do I see his face every night? Maybe because he tried to kill Alex McKnight. Maybe he is like my patron saint now. Maybe he will speak to me and tell me why he is here.

AUGUST 22

I have been bad about writing. So many things have happened. I have been in communication with Maximilian Rose although I just call him Rose now. It sounds so perfect. Everything makes sense now for the first time in my life. The hate in my heart has been turned upside down by what Rose has shown me. I have so much power now because I am plugged into something bigger than myself. Rose has made me see all of this. He told me a secret about Alex. There is something very special and important about him. I do not even know what that means yet but Rose promised he would tell me more. I cannot wait until the next time I communicate with him. Rose is a rose is a rose is a rose.

```
                    R
        R     OSE   RO
      OSE   ROSE   SE
    ROSE   ROSE   ROSE
      ROSEROSEROSE
        ROSE   ROSE
          ROSEROSE
          ROSEROSE
              ROSE
              RO
              SE   E
              ROS
              RO
      R     SE
        OSE
              RO
              SE
              RO
              SE
```

SEPTEMBER 13

I am learning more every day. I am shedding my old self like a snake sheds his skin. I see the reason for all of this and how I fit into the overall design. When I go out now I see people and I can see if they are good or bad people just by looking at their faces and listening to the way they talk. There are so many bad people everywhere I go. Rose says this is to be expected because Alex is here now. I think something big is about to happen. I can feel it. I think Rose is going to give me something very big very soon.

OCTOBER 9

I am Rose. I will say it again and again. I am Rose.
This was the gift that Rose gave me. His spirit flew
to me and came down on my shoulders like a bird
from the heavens. Now I am Rose and Rose is me.
I can see everything now. Alex is the chosen one. I
dare to say it out loud. He is the chosen one because
he was shot three times. This means that the holy
trinity has moved through him. The third bullet is
still inside him. It is a spirit inside him that hums to
the same frequency as the spirit inside me. I have
work to do now. It is important work that I must
finish before the last words are written for all time.

A sickness spread through my stomach as I read. Then a
sudden noise tore me from it. There was someone at the
back door. Prudell looked at me with wide eyes and then
he dove on the floor. I stood there frozen, waiting for the
door to open, for the policeman to come in and to shine his
flashlight in my face. But the door never opened.

I crept to the back door and looked out the window. A
great raccoon had turned over the trashcan. "Get out of
here!" I hissed. "Go!"

The raccoon just looked at me.

"Move it, you big fat-assed bastard," I said as I cracked
the door open.

The raccoon finally pulled himself away from the
garbage and lumbered into the woods. I stood there by the
door for a minute, trying to will my heart rate back into
double digits.

"Do you think the cop heard that noise?" Prudell said.
He was still sitting on the floor.

"I don't know," I said. I went back to the front window

and peeked through the blinds. The police car was still dark. "God, I hope he's asleep or at least hard of hearing."

When I was sure he wasn't on his way up to the house, I finished reading the pages.

NOVEMBER 1

Everything is in motion now. It is all happening so fast. I have removed a bad man. He was speaking evil things to a man named Edwin who is close to Alex. It is no accident that there is so much evil around here with all of the casinos and the men who gamble their souls away. It felt good to remove the man. Finally I can do something real. I called Alex on the phone because it turns out he actually got to see what I had done for him. He saw it with his own eyes. I am filled with happiness because this must be a good sign that he would see it. I wonder when I should tell him who I am now.

NOVEMBER 3

Everything is in a mad rush now but I feel total peace inside myself. I removed another bad man who was speaking the same evil as the first man. I can tell that they are gathering from all corners of the world but I am not worried. I know what must be done and I know that I can do it. I gave a note to Alex right on his door for him to see. I told him I am Rose and I am here for him now. Everything that has been promised will come to pass. I never knew that blood was so red. It is more red than a kiss and even more powerful.

NOVEMBER 6

I barely have time to write. Everything is coming together now just as it should. Even though Alex has so many walls around him I know it is all part of the plan. I know that the man named Edwin who was close to him was like Judas himself. He needed to be removed. I was even more careful with the blood this time. I gave another note to Alex and I even told him my new theory about the blood being more powerful than the microwaves and how Edwin is at the bottom of the lake where he will never stand in the way again. I think it is almost time to go to Alex. I must sleep now so that I will have strength and courage for the final task.

NOVEMBER 7

It is time. I can barely type I am so excited. It is time to go to Alex and to take him through the door. I know he must feel fear and even a little pain but I also know that in the end it will all be worth it. I know I can make it all happen the way it must happen. I know the gun he has is not a real gun at all. It is only an illusion meant to fool bad men and it can never hurt me. It is all part of the plan just like a dance with two parts. Now I will do my part and he will do his. And when it is over we will be together forever.

I read his last words and then I closed the folder. I wanted to see something else that would help me make sense of it. Drugs, a needle, a syringe. Some chemical excuse for this utter madness. There was nothing.

"Let's get the hell out of here," I said.

"Make sure you put it all back the way you found it," Prudell said.

"It is."

"No, I mean exactly. The folders were right on top of each other before."

"It doesn't matter," I said.

"You know they took pictures," he said. "They'll notice if that top folder has been moved a few inches."

"Just get out," I said. "Go." I didn't care if anyone knew I had been here. They could have busted the door down right then, put me in handcuffs. As long as they got me the hell out of that place.

I hustled him out the back door. I stood there breathing in the cold night air as he carefully reapplied the police tape. "Come on," I said. "I told you it doesn't matter."

"Don't be a fool, McKnight." He worked on it until it was perfect, and then we finally made our way back through the woods to my truck.

We got in. I started the engine and pulled away, retracing our way through all the tree-named streets and then the number streets, back to the highway. Neither of us said anything for a long time. There was only the sound of the wind rushing through the open window. It was cold enough to hurt, but I *wanted* it to hurt. I wanted to feel something real, something I could understand.

"What did it say?" Prudell finally asked.

I thought about it for a minute. I didn't know what to say, so I just shook my head. He didn't press it.

When we got back to his restaurant, he got out of the truck and went right to his car.

"Hey," I said. "Aren't you going back to work?"

"I think tonight was probably my third strike here," he said.

"So you're saying I got you fired from another job?"

"This one I don't mind so much," he said.

"Let me pay you your five hundred dollars, at least."

"Forget it," he said. "I don't want your money."

"For what it's worth," I said, "I appreciate your help."

He came back to the window. "For what it's worth," he said, "I'm sorry I roughed you up the other night."

"You mean at the bar? The night you swung at me twenty times and missed and then I put you down with one punch? That night?"

"One punch, my ass," he said. "I slipped on the gravel. I'm talking about when I hit you in the face with my keys. That must have hurt for days."

I laughed. I was surprised I *could* laugh. "You're right, Prudell. You really got me."

"You had it coming," he said. "Just stay out of my way from now on." As he turned to go I thought I saw the beginning of a smile.

I LEFT HIM there in the parking lot, drove away into the night, back down I-75 toward home. Route 28 to 123 to Paradise. I had worn a rut in these roads the past few days, driving into the Soo and back every day. Now it's over, right? Now you go back to your normal life? Demented loser stalks you, contacts the madman who shot you fourteen years ago, thinks he *becomes* the madman for God's sake, kills three people including Edwin, tries to kill you, you end up killing him. Now you're supposed to forget about it and go back to splitting wood and cleaning out the cabins?

I drove. Darkness. The smell of pine trees coming through the window. A car coming toward me. Bright lights blinding me. It passed.

How did he contact Rose? He didn't say *how* he did that.

A sign for the casino. The last place Edwin was seen alive. I could go there now. Play some blackjack. Have a drink. I don't want to go back to that empty cabin. Lie there staring at the ceiling.

The fear should be gone now. Rose is in prison forever. And this other man, this man who made me doubt my sanity, he's dead now. I shot him four times, chest chest head chest. The fear should be gone forever.

I saw the lights on at the Glasgow, thought about stopping in, but kept going. I slowed down at the logging road to my cabin, thought about going home, about trying to get some sleep.

I kept going.

She shouldn't be alone. She sounded so distraught on the phone. Everything that's happened, she shouldn't be alone in that house.

At least, that's what I told myself.

I drove up to the Point, turned west on their service road. I thought about Mrs. Fulton's dream. The car with the lights off, gliding through these trees. The driver watching the house at night. She saw that in her dream. And the blood, as well. It didn't even seem so fantastic anymore. After all that had happened, I could believe anything.

I saw the glow before I made the last turn into their driveway. Every light was on in the house. The yard was bright enough to play baseball on. As I parked the truck I could see all the way down to the beach and into the water. There was probably a seaman on a freighter a mile offshore, looking at the house in his binoculars and wondering where this new lighthouse had come from.

I heard the music as soon as I turned the truck off. When I opened the door it assaulted my ears. It was some kind of opera piece, a soprano climbing the scales in Italian.

I didn't see Sylvia anywhere.

I found the stereo in the study. The speakers were as big as refrigerators. It hurt to go near them but I wanted to turn the music off. It was one of those ten-thousand-dollar stereos with more buttons than a jet airplane, but I finally found the power button and shut the whole thing down. I shook my head in the sudden silence and wondered where Sylvia might be. It didn't take long for me to imagine the worse. Hanging from the curtain rod in the bathroom, or lying on the bed with a bottle of pills clutched in her hand. But then I finally heard her coming down the stairs. "Who turned the fucking music off?"

"I didn't know you liked opera," I said.

She appeared in the doorway, a bottle in her hand. Her hair was a tangled mess, her eyes red and swollen from crying or drinking or God knows what. She looked fantastic. "What are you doing here?" she said.

"I was worried about you."

"I told you to stay away."

"I came anyway."

"You shouldn't have."

"How much have you had to drink?"

"That's none of your business."

I went to her. I took the bottle out of her hand. It was champagne. "Are you celebrating something?" I said.

"I will be as soon as you leave."

"Why did you come to my cabin?"

She didn't say anything.

"Were you scared? Lonely? What was it?"

She looked in my eyes. "Do you have any idea how much I hate you?"

"No, I don't," I said. "Show me."

She slapped my face. Just like Mrs. Fulton had done, only harder. I caught her arm on the next swing.

"Let go of me," she said.

I looked down at her. She was close enough for me to smell her perfume, to feel the heat of her body.

"I said let go of me," she said.

I didn't let go.

CHAPTER TWENTY

I OPENED MY eyes. Through the skylight I could see heavy clouds, a single snowflake, then another. To my left, Sylvia's head on the pillow, turned away from me. I did not know if she was awake.

I got out of bed. I stood there and looked at her. She did not move. When I started to put my pants on, she said, "You're leaving." Not as a question.

"I'll be back," I said.

She turned to look at me. She kept the covers tight around her neck.

"I'm serious," I said. "I'll be back."

She didn't say anything.

"I think it's snowing outside," I said.

She looked up at the skylight.

"Are you going to be all right?" I said. It was a weak offering, but I didn't know what else to say.

"No," she said.

"You drank a lot of champagne," I said, putting my shirt on. I looked around the room for my shoes and socks.

She sat up in the bed, keeping the blanket wrapped around her body. "Are you going to say anything else? Or are you just going to run away again?"

I sat down on the bed. "What do you mean, again? When did I ever run away before?"

"You always did," she said. "Every time."

"That's because Edwin was usually on his way home, remember?"

"He's not coming home this time," she said. In an instant, she had that look in her eyes again. That sudden flame.

"I have to go now," I said.

"Do you expect me to beg you to stay?"

"No," I said. "I don't expect anything."

I was ready for something painful. A cold silence, more venom, violence. Instead, she just looked down at her hands. "Do you think I married Edwin for his money?"

I didn't know what to say.

"I suppose you must think that. Did I ever tell you how I met him?"

"No."

"I had a flower shop in Southfield. I opened the store myself. I guess I wanted to show everybody that I could do it. You know, my family and everybody. I didn't realize what a tough business it was, but I was getting by. I was doing all right. One day, Edwin Fulton walks in the store. He's got this suit on that must have cost five thousand dollars. These incredible leather shoes. The works. So right away, I'm thinking, okay, this guy is gonna come on smooth, try to impress me with how much money he has. He comes up to the counter and he asks me what kind of flower would look good in his boutonniere. Says he's terrible with colors, he's got no idea what would look good with his tie. I had these roses from Central America. Real nice, real expensive. I said, here, you probably want one of these. You know what he said?"

"What did he say?"

"He said no, it looks too expensive. It'll look like I'm showing off. So he buys a big red carnation instead. Seventy-five cents."

I smiled.

"The next day, he comes back, buys another carnation. And then the next day and the next day. He always seemed like he wanted to talk to me, but I don't know, he was just shy. Which was weird, because you don't expect rich people to be shy. Anyway, a few days later, he finally comes in and orders this *huge* bouquet. Every rose I had in the store. Three hundred dollars' worth. It took me forever to put it together. When I was finally done with it, he asked me to fill in the card for him. He said, please make this card out to the most wonderful woman who ever walked the earth. Those were his exact words. And of course, I'm thinking, oh God, how original is this? He's going to make me fill in this card and then he's going to tell me the flowers are for me. So I'm pissed off, because now he's just throwing his money away trying to impress me, and I'm going to say thanks but no thanks and end up putting all the flowers back. But that's not what he did."

"No?"

"No. They were for his mother. It was her birthday. He could see I was surprised, so he asked me if I thought he was going to give them to me. I said yes, to be honest, that's what I was thinking. You know what he said? He said when he finally worked up the nerve to ask me out, he'd buy the flowers at another store. That way he could take them back and demand a refund if I didn't fall in love with him."

"That's great."

She looked up at the skylight. "Do you think he can see us now?"

"God, I don't know."

"You should have heard him talk about you," she said. "He told me you were the best friend he ever had. Did he ever tell you that?"

"Yes, he did."

"I hope he can," she said. "I hope he can see us."

"Why?"

"All that time, he never knew about us," she said. "I should have told him. Not because I wanted to hurt him. Just because he had the right to know."

"Maybe some things you don't *want* to know."

"I don't believe in that," she said. "I don't like things to happen to me without knowing why."

"I suppose I feel the same way," I said. "That's why I need to leave now. I've got one more thing I need to know."

She watched me put my coat on.

"Tell me the truth," I said. "Do you want me to come back or not?"

"No," she said. "Not yet anyway."

"Fair enough."

"I don't think we can just start over," she said. "We can't pretend none of this happened."

"No," I said.

She looked up at the skylight again. The snow was beginning to collect in the corners. I sat there watching her.

"Thank you for being Edwin's friend," she said.

"I don't think I did a very good job of that."

She smiled. It wasn't much of a smile, but it was the first one I had seen from her in months. "He would have forgiven you anything. Even this."

I left. I didn't kiss her. I didn't touch her. As I drove away, I wondered if I would ever touch her again.

I swung by my cabin, took a shower, changed my clothes, had some coffee. And then I got right back into the truck and gunned it into the Soo. The snow was building into a flurry, but none of it was sticking to the ground yet. Some flakes blew into the truck through the open window.

When I got to Uttley's office, I found him packing up a large cardboard box. He looked like his old self again, clean-shaven, his hair slicked back. A nice shirt and tie.

"Alex, there you are," he said. "I was looking for you last night. I figured your phone was still out, so I stopped by your cabin."

"What time was that?"

"Had to be about midnight. I couldn't sleep, so I figured I'd come out and see you."

"You must have just missed me," I said. "I couldn't sleep, either. So I went out looking for Raymond Julius's house."

"Raymond Julius? The man you . . ." He stopped.

"The man I killed, yes. Turns out he did some work for Leon Prudell."

He stopped his packing. "He worked for Prudell? Are you serious?"

"He ran errands for him," I said. "Did you ever meet him?"

"No, I didn't," he said. "I don't remember even hearing his name."

"Prudell says he helped him out on that job he did over at the resort, watching the lifeguards."

"Oh, wait a minute," he said. "I remember that. He said he had a guy helping him, covering for him when he went to the bathroom, stuff like that. I don't think he told me his name. I probably wasn't listening too well. That was toward the end, after I had already decided to fire him. But how does this guy figure into your thing with Rose?"

"He was upset that he lost his job. He blamed me. Started stalking me, looking into my past. He found the newspaper clippings. The rest is kind of crazy."

"My God," he said. "This all happened because I fired Prudell?"

"No," I said. "This all happened because the guy was insane. You didn't do anything wrong."

"I can't believe any of this," he said. "This just keeps getting worse."

"There's one thing that's still bothering me," I said. "This business of how he contacted Rose."

"You mean about whether he visited him or wrote to him?"

"Yes," I said. "In his diary he just said that he 'communicated' with Rose. But he didn't say how."

"How did you see his diary?"

"You don't want to know that," I said.

He raised his hands. "Say no more."

"I'm just wondering how it happened. How did he get through to Rose? How did he find out all the things he wrote about in his notes?"

He shrugged. "Who knows, Alex? Why does it even matter?"

"It just bothers me," I said. "Maybe I should call that Browning guy down at the prison again."

"You won't get anywhere," he said. "You know that."

"Let me just have his number," I said. "I might try him."

Uttley gave out a long tired sigh and went through some papers. He wrote the number down on a card and gave it to me. "You're wasting your time," he said.

"You're probably right," I said. "What's with the box? Are you going somewhere?"

"I need a vacation. I think you need one, too."

"Where are you going?"

"I don't even know yet," he said. "Someplace very far away. Someplace warm. An island somewhere."

"Sounds like a good idea."

"You know, all those nights I spent on the Fultons' couch, I started to think about things. I'm not sure I want to be a lawyer anymore. Not this kind of lawyer, not up here, anyway. I think I might try something nice and quiet for a while, you know, like real estate. Just sit on my butt at a closing and collect my big check."

"You're not coming back, are you."

"I don't think so, Alex. Too much has happened here. I'm surprised you're not thinking the same way."

"Maybe I am."

"So anyway, I guess I probably won't be needing you as a private investigator anymore."

"That's all right," I said. "I'm not sure I ever really wanted to be one."

He nodded and swallowed hard.

"Need help carrying anything out?" I said.

"No, this is all I need," he said. He slapped the box. "Alex, I'm not sure what else to say. You've had to go through so much the last couple weeks. I just hope I was able to help you through it in some small way."

"Of course you did."

He came around from behind his desk and shook my hand. And then he hugged me. He wrapped both of his arms around me and gave me a good squeeze. "Take care of yourself, Alex."

"Good-bye, Lane."

As I closed the door, I looked back at him. He gave me one last thumbs-up and then I was gone.

I went into town and tried to find an auto glass place. The first one didn't have my window in stock. Neither did the second or third. The last man said I could either go over the bridge and try the Canadian side, or he could put it on order and tape up the truck with clear plastic to hold me over. I went with the tape job.

At a pay phone, I called the phone company to see about fixing my cut line. The lady told me they'd try to get out there some time that day, but she couldn't say when. I told her I wasn't going to hold my breath. After I hung up I took out the card with Browning's number on it. I looked at it for a long time and then I put it back in my pocket without dialing.

By the time I headed back to Paradise, the snow had stopped. But it was still a cold, raw day. The sky was as gray as gunmetal. I probably wouldn't see the sun for five months. Maybe Uttley is right, I thought. Maybe I just should go away somewhere, never come back. Maybe even take Sylvia, if I could convince her.

God, listen to yourself, Alex. Just listen to yourself.

I stopped in at the Glasgow for a late breakfast. Jackie made me one of his omelets, with onions, peppers, cheese, the works. It was too early for a beer, but not too early for one of his famous Bloody Marys. Or two or three of them.

I took the card out of my pocket and looked at it again. If I call him, I thought, he's going to hang up on me. I put the card back in my pocket.

When I got back to the cabin, the man from the phone company was up on his ladder. I owed the phone company an apology for doubting them. "What the hell happened to your phone line?" he said. "It looks like somebody cut right through it with a knife."

"Long story," I said. I went into the cabin before he could ask me to tell it.

When he was done, he gave a quick knock on my door. "She's all done," he said. "It'll be on your next bill."

I thanked the man, and then I picked up the phone to make sure I had a dial tone. Without even thinking about it, I dialed Browning's number. I didn't even have to look at the card. I had the number memorized from all the time I'd spent looking at it.

The phone rang. What the hell, I thought. If nothing else, I can at least apologize to the man for yelling at him.

"Corrections, Browning speaking."

"Mr. Browning," I said. "This is Alex McKnight."

"Ah yes, Mr. McKnight."

"Listen, before anything else, I just want to say I'm sorry about the last time we talked on the phone. I was under a lot of stress, and I shouldn't have taken it out on you. I know you were just following the rules."

"That's quite all right."

"Everything's pretty much over up here," I said. "It wasn't Rose, of course."

"Of course," he said. "He's been right here the whole time."

"Of course," I said. "Although it turns out that there was a man up here who had been in contact with Rose. So I was just curious about how that might have happened. I'm sure you keep records on visits and letters. You probably even have to *read* the mail, right?"

"We do."

"Listen, Mr. Browning, I know I don't have any official reason to ask you this. But just for my own sanity, please, is there any way you can tell me if Rose has been contacted by a man named Raymond Julius?"

"Why don't you ask him that yourself?" he said.

"Excuse me?"

"I called your Mr. Uttley this morning," he said. "He wasn't in his office, so I left a message."

"He's gone," I said. "He left for vacation. Why did you call him?"

"I called him to tell him that Maximilian Rose has agreed to see you."

I stood there with the phone in my hand.

"Mr. McKnight? Are you there?"

"Yes," I said. "When can I see him?"

"At your convenience. Believe me, he's not going anywhere."

"I'll come today," I said.

"I thought you were in the Upper Peninsula," he said. "That's got to be, what, six or seven hours away?"

"I'll leave right now," I said.

"Our visitation stops at three o'clock," he said. "You'll never make it."

"Mr. Browning, please," I said. I couldn't bear the thought of waiting. I had had enough sleepless nights for one lifetime. "There's gotta be a way you can let me see him today. I can't tell you how important this is."

I heard him grumbling on the phone. "Mr. McKnight, you are one genuine pain in the ass, you know that?"

"Does that mean you'll let me see him today?"

"Don't kill yourself getting down here, you hear me? The speed limit is fifty-five miles an hour."

"I'm on my way," I said.

"Ask for me at the gate," he said. "Otherwise, they'll never let you in."

I hung up and ran to the truck. I made it to the Lower Peninsula in less than an hour, with about 250 miles to go. I had the speedometer up in the eighties most of the way. If my truck didn't go into a death rattle at ninety, I would have gone even faster.

I didn't want to waste another minute. The answers, the resolution, my own sanity. It was all there waiting for me.

CHAPTER TWENTY-ONE

THE STATE PRISON of Southern Michigan, otherwise known as Jackson State, is sixty miles west of Detroit, past Ann Arbor, out in the middle of the state where the cows and the cornfields are. The prison itself is a city unto itself, a sprawling gray complex of cement and razor wire. I knew there were several wings there, with different security classifications. I was headed for maximum security.

I had driven straight through in just over five-and-a-half hours, stopping only once to fill up the truck and to use the bathroom. I splashed some cold water on my face, got back in the truck, and kept driving. The plastic on my window kept most of the cold air out, but it was still noisy. My ears were still humming when I finally turned off the highway at Jackson.

I gave the man at the gate Browning's name. He looked at his clipboard, asked to see my driver's license, and then let me through. I parked in the visitor's lot and went into the waiting room. There were a hundred plastic chairs lined up in rows. A tile floor, a row of lockers on one wall, a glass trophy case on the other. I had the place to myself because the regular visiting hours were over. I gave my name to the guard sitting behind the bulletproof window. He took down one of the clipboards off the wall. There must have been twenty of them. Somewhere in the city of Jackson there was probably a man who made a nice living supplying clipboards to the prison. The guard looked at his clipboard and told me to have a seat.

I went over to the trophy case and looked inside. It was all marksmanship trophies, given out to the guards with the best scores. There was a trophy for each year, going back a good thirty years. It was interesting psychology, displaying these trophies to the people who were here to visit the inmates.

After a few minutes I heard a door buzz behind me. A man came into the waiting room. He was a large man with a crew cut. He looked like a drill sergeant. "Mr. Mc-Knight," he said. "I'm Browning."

I shook his hand.

"Right this way," he said. He led me back through the same door. We came to another window, with another guard behind it with more clipboards on the wall. "Just step through here," he said as he walked through a metal detector.

"I'm going to set this thing off," I said. I stepped through and heard the beeping.

The guard opened his door and handed me a little plastic tray, just like at an airport. "Put it all in here, sir. Watch, keys."

"It's a bullet," I said. "It's in here." I pointed to my heart.

Browning and the guard looked at each other for a second, and then the guard pulled out his hand unit and waved it over me. It gave out a long wail when he passed it in front of my chest.

Browning stood there in front of me, rubbing his chin. "Rose did that?"

"Yes," I said.

"Are you sure you want to see him?"

"I have to," I said.

"Right this way." He turned and led me down the hallway. I knew there were two types of visitation areas. One for family, with couches and chairs so you could sit with an inmate, even have physical contact if you only went so far. Take away the guards and it would almost look like a living room. But it was empty now as we walked past it. He took me to the other visitation area, the one you picture in your mind because you've seen it in the movies. A thick wall of glass, a pair of telephones. He led me to one of the booths, sat me down, and then left me there. The chair on the other side was empty.

I waited there for a few minutes, thinking about what was going to happen. All the time I was driving down here, I was thinking about what to ask him, about what questions I needed answered. I wasn't really thinking about that day in Detroit when he shot me. But when that metal detector went off, it all came back to me. I'm going to see the man who shot me three times and killed my partner. Fourteen years later, I'm going to see his face again.

I heard a heavy door close. I saw a guard pass by on the other side. Behind him, moving slowly, a man in a prison uniform. He sat down in the chair without looking at me. He had long hair and a long beard. It was all streaked with gray. He was thin. His wrists looked so frail you could snap them like pencils. He finally looked at me.

It was him.

I knew those eyes. Everything else about him had changed, but those eyes were the same. I would have known them anywhere. Even out of context. Forget the jail, forget that I was expecting to see him. Dress him up as a delivery-man, send him to my front door. As soon as I saw those eyes, I would know it was him.

He sat there looking at me, the same way he did before he shot me. The fear came back to me. I knew in my mind that I was safe, but still I couldn't stop the physical reaction to seeing him.

I fought it down, trying to focus on why I had come here. I picked up the phone and waited for him to do the same. When he did, I cleared my throat and spoke to him.

"Do you remember me?" I said.

He just looked at me through the glass.

"I was a police officer in Detroit," I said. "You shot me."

"Yes?" he said. His voice was flat. It barely sounded human. It could have come from a machine.

"You killed my partner," I said.

"Go on."

"That was a long time ago," I said. "That's not really why I'm here."

"I know why you're here," he said.

"You do?"

"Yes," he said. "You want information."

"How do you know this?"

"I have been here a long time. I have become a wise man in many ways."

It was hard to look at him. His face was drawn and haggard. His hair went in every direction, like Medusa's snakes. It made his eyes all the more terrible. "Do you know a man named Raymond Julius?" I asked.

He looked at me like he hadn't even heard me.

"Wisdom is a precious metal," he said. "Information is the ore from which wisdom is, what's the word, smelted?"

"Do you know the man?" I said.

"Is that the right word? Smelted?"

"Raymond Julius. Do you know him?"

"You all want information, don't you," he said.

"Who? Who's all of us?"

"All of you," he said. "Lawyers, psychologists, scientists. You want the information so you may become wise. You all think you can trick it out of me."

I took a deep breath. "I'm not a lawyer or a psychologist or a scientist. And I didn't come all the way down here to *smelt* any wisdom, all right? Can you talk to me like a human being for one minute?"

"When I was first discovered, I said some things. There were two policemen. I remember them. They came to my apartment."

"Oh, for the love of God," I said. "I told you, *I* was one of those policemen."

"Then they captured me and tried to make me talk. A man was supposed to represent me at the trial. He tried to make me say that I was crazy."

"Rose, did you hear me? I said I was one of those policeman."

He shook his finger at me and gave out a little laugh. It sounded like a chain rattling. "Very clever," he said. "I can see why they sent you. You even look like him. An excellent ploy. I must commend you."

"Rose, I was there. You shot me, remember? You shot *both* of us."

"Yes, I shot both of you. Both of *them,* I mean. See, you *are* trying to trick me."

I squeezed the phone. This was hopeless. "Okay, you win," I said. "You're too smart for me. You've obviously been doing a lot of smelting in here."

"You'll never make me tell you," he said. "I'll never reveal my plan."

"Of course not," I said. "Perish the thought."

"I am strong," he said. "Every passing hour, I grow stronger."

"I can see that," I said. "You look great. You've been working out?"

"You mock me."

"You've lost some weight, too. What are you down to, about ninety pounds?"

"You dare to mock me."

"Yeah, Rose, I dare to mock you. You wanna know why? Because you're a crazy motherfucking piece of shit, that's why. You want me to tell you about the man you killed? You want me to tell you about his wife and his two kids?"

"They sent you here, didn't they."

"He had two daughters, Rose. Two little girls."

"I know they sent you here."

"They had to go to their daddy's funeral, Rose. Two little girls standing next to a hole in the ground because you killed their daddy."

"Tell them I can't be bought," he said. "Tell them my information is not for sale."

"What's it like being in prison, anyway?" I said. "Looks like you're in the main population here, aren't you. I bet you've made a lot of new friends."

"I can leave anytime I want."

"So why don't you? Why don't you leave right now? We'll go have a beer."

"I choose to stay for the time being."

"Sure you do. You must like it here. They must treat you real nice here. How many times have you been raped since you've been here?"

For the first time since he sat down, he looked away.

"How many times?" I said. "Give me a ballpark figure. A hundred times? Two hundred?"

He looked back at me, scratching his beard.

"Where does it happen, Rose? In the showers? How many times have you been raped in the showers?"

"You're a fool." His voice had a sudden edge to it.

"They've got an expression for that, don't they? Being afraid of the alligators? That's when you're afraid to take a shower because you know you're gonna get raped again, right?"

"You're *all* fools."

"Tell me about Raymond Julius," I said.

"I don't know this name."

"Yes, you do. You've been talking to him. Or writing letters to him."

"It's an interesting name. I like it."

"Which was it? Did you talk to him or write letters?"

"The name has a good sound to it."

"Did he visit you?"

"Many people visit me."

"Yeah, I bet they line up at the gates every morning."

"I have many friends. They come to see me and ask my advice."

"Advice on what? How to be a crazy fucking headcase?"

"They come from all over the world."

"Two daughters, Rose. Two little girls. You killed their father."

"I killed both of them," he said.

"Both of whom?"

"I shot both of them," he said. "And they both died."

"Who died?"

"The policemen. They both died. I removed them."

"Hey guess what, Rose." I leaned in closer to the glass. "Look at me. I didn't die."

"I removed both of them."

"I didn't die, Rose. You didn't remove me."

"They died. I removed them."

"I was at the trial, remember? I helped put you away."

"I'm enjoying this," he said. "I really am. You should come back more often."

"Look, I don't care if you think you—" I stopped. Wait a minute, I thought. Something is not right here. The man is saying he killed me. He thinks I'm dead. There's no way he would have told Julius all this shit about me being the chosen one if he didn't even think I was alive.

Unless he was just trying to fool me now. Unless he was playing a game with me.

"I'm going to ask you this one more time," I said. "Has a man named Raymond Julius been in contact with you or not?"

"Why do you need to know this?"

"Never mind why," I said. "Just tell me."

"You really do look like that policeman," he said. "The resemblance is remarkable."

I lunged at the glass. "JUST TELL ME, GODDAMN IT!"

Rose went backward in his chair, tipping it over. The phone jumped out of his hand. The sound he made was an inhuman shriek, the look on his face was sudden, complete terror. The guard on the other side had to put him in an armlock and usher him away. I could hear him screaming as he was dragged out of the cell. The door closed with a metallic thud and then there was silence.

I sat there for a long time. I had never seen such fear in a man. For a tenth of a second, I almost felt sorry for him. Then I thought about Franklin and his family and got over it.

Browning was waiting for me when I left the room. "You certainly pushed his hot button," he said. "They're going to have to sedate him."

"I'm sorry," I said.

"Don't worry about it."

"So I'm going to ask you a question now."

"No harm asking."

"Has Rose had any contact with a man named Raymond Julius in the last six months? Letters or visits?"

He exhaled heavily and looked up the hallway. "Walk this way," he said.

"Where are we going?"

"To the exit."

"Fine," I said. "I give up."

He walked me back through the waiting room and out the door. I was expecting a handshake and a good-bye, but he gave me a little bit more. "You didn't hear this from me," he said. "Rose has had no outside contact for the past five years."

"None at all? Are you sure?"

"None. No letters. No lawyer calls. No visits since a mental health follow-up five years ago. Even then, the file says he just sat there, wouldn't say a word. So that's it. I hope that tells you what you need to know. Have a safe trip back." He shook my hand and then he was gone.

I got in the truck, drove through the gate, watched the prison recede in my rearview mirror. When I made the highway I turned the radio on for a minute and then turned it back off. I wasn't ready for noise yet. I needed to think.

Okay, so Julius never really talked to Rose. So what? Maybe it was all in his head. He read the clippings and then he imagined that Rose was talking to him in the shower or in his sleep or wherever the hell else.

So how did he know about the microwaves and the chosen one and all that? Because he was nuts. Because Rose is nuts and Julius is nuts and that's how they think. Paranoia, fear of technology, delusions about a messiah, it all comes with the territory, right? They were both tuned to the same station.

And the rest of it you're just imagining, Alex. If you keep it up, you're going to end up just as crazy as they are. So just find a way to put it behind you. Rose is in prison forever, Julius is in the ground. It's over. O-V-E-R.

I turned the radio back on and settled in for a long drive back. I was in no rush this time. I figured I'd just keep driving until I got hungry or tired. Pull over, have some dinner, maybe get a room for a night. Probably do me some good, a night away from everything.

By the time I reached Lansing, the sun was beginning to go down. I started to relax a little bit. Just a little.

By the time I reached Alma, I started to see a few flakes in the air again. Winter would come quickly, as it always did. Soon the cabins would be buried in two feet of snow. There wasn't much hunting in the winter, just some rabbit and coyote. There'd be mostly snowmobilers renting the cabins, maybe some ice fisherman. The locks would close, the bay and the river would freeze over, so hard you'd be able to walk across it, all the way to Canada if you wanted to.

I stopped for dinner in Houghton Lake, found a little place that served fresh walleye. I thought about Sylvia, what might happen to the two of us. She said she didn't know if we could start over. I wondered if we really could, or if the guilt and the pain would come back to ruin everything. But then as I went back to the truck and breathed the cold night air, I got a little boost from somewhere. A second wind, whatever you want to call it. Back when I was playing ball we'd have a lot of doubleheaders late in the summer. You usually try to split your catchers, but there were a couple times when I had to work both games. A whole day behind the plate, setting up for the pitch, standing up to throw the ball back, setting up again, a good three hundred times. Trying to keep the pitcher's head together, holding runners on base, taking foul balls off the mask. By the middle of the second game, I'd be so drained they'd have to help me off the bench so I could strap the shinpads back on.

But on a good day, I'd find something extra in the last couple innings, some reserve of strength that I didn't know about. That one day in Columbus, my best day as a ballplayer, I drove in the go-ahead run in the eighth inning, and then in the ninth I had to block the plate on their big first baseman. He was coming down that line like a house on wheels. I caught the ball just before he hit me. When I came to, I checked to see if I still had the ball and then I checked to see if my head was still attached. The umpire called him out and we won the game.

It felt good to think about those days again, to think about *anything* else for a change.

And then around Gaylord, it started to come to me. I thought about Julius again. And about everything that had happened. Everything I had seen, everything that had been said. I couldn't keep it out of my mind any longer. For the first time, I had stopped thinking about it, and now that I looked at it again, I was starting to see some things I had missed.

By the time I got to Mackinac, I had it all worked out. I could see how it all fit together, from beginning to end. And what I saw made me mad.

You're a fool, Alex. You're a goddamned fool. How did it take you so long to figure this out?

I crossed the bridge into the Upper Peninsula doing seventy. Suddenly I had somewhere to go.

Chapter Twenty-two

IT WASN'T HARD to find his house. Not like when I dragged Prudell all over town for Julius's house. This house was in the book.

It was a nice neighborhood, up on the hill by the college. Maybe not as nice as I thought it would be. The house was actually quite modest, a little two-story mock Tudor with a small yard. His car was parked in the driveway.

It was just after eleven o'clock at night. But I could see that his lights were on. I felt good about that. I wouldn't have to wake him up. That would have been very rude.

I parked the truck on the street, careful not to block his car in the driveway. That would have been very rude, as well.

I walked up to the front door. I was about to ring the doorbell, but instead I tried turning the knob. It was unlocked. How nice. I walked right in.

There was a little entryway with a stone floor. A living room. There was a fire going in the fireplace. I walked through the room. In the back of the house there was a study. Lots of books on the walls. He was sitting there behind the desk, looking through a pile of travel brochures.

"Alex!" he said when he saw me. "My God, you scared me!"

"Good evening, Lane," I said. "I hope I'm not disturbing you."

Uttley gathered up some of his brochures. "I was just trying to decide where to go on vacation," he said. "I'm leaving tomorrow morning." If he was surprised to see me here, he was doing a good job of hiding it.

"That's nice," I said.

"Alex, are you all right? What's going on?"

"Don't get up," I said. "I'm just going to sit right here and ask you a couple questions." I pulled up a chair and sat down in front of his desk.

"I don't understand," he said. "What questions?"

"I'm not even sure where to begin," I said. "I don't know which question I want answered first."

"What's going on, Alex? What are you doing here?"

"Okay, here's a good one to start with," I said. "A little ice breaker, if you will. Where's Edwin?"

"Edwin is at the bottom of Lake Superior. You know that."

"I'm *supposed* to know that, yes. Just like the police are supposed to know that. And Sylvia. And everybody else in the world."

"I don't get it," he said. "What are you talking about?"

"That night at his house. After dinner, he kept talking about how good it felt to be starting over. I guess he really meant that, huh?"

"Alex, *what are you talking about*?"

"Next question," I said. "How did you get Raymond Julius to kill those two bookmakers? I mean, I knew you were very persuasive . . ."

"What in God's name is wrong with you?"

"And how did you get him to believe that my gun wasn't real, of all things?"

Uttley just sat there looking at me, shaking his head like I was a lunatic.

"And when did this whole thing start, anyway?" I said. "Does this go all the way back to when you asked me to be your private investigator? Was that all a setup from the very beginning?"

"I think you need to see somebody," he said. "I know you've been through a lot. It's obviously gotten to you."

"Here's another question," I said. "This one I really need you to answer. Would you have killed me if you had to?"

He stopped shaking his head. He just sat there. He looked at me without blinking.

"The night you sent Julius over," I said, "he was just supposed to scare me, right? Is that what you told him? Leave the silencer at home, make a lot of noise? Don't worry, his gun isn't even real? You were right there behind him, weren't you. You weren't at the Fultons' house. You didn't call me. You were right behind him and you came along just as soon as you thought it was all over. And fortunately, I guess, everything worked out the way it was supposed to. But what if it hadn't? What if I had just wounded him? What if I had disarmed him? If he had accidentally killed me, that one's easy. You just shoot him. Tell the police you were trying to save me. But what if we had *both* been alive when you got there? Would you have killed both of us? I'm sure you had your Beretta with you."

He opened a drawer in his desk and pulled out the very same gun. "You mean this one?"

"That's the one," I said.

"Please put your gun on the table," he said.

"I don't have it, remember? The police have it."

"I'm not stupid, Alex. You must have another gun."

"No," I said. "Why would I need one? You're no threat to me. And I'm no threat to you."

"What do you mean?"

"You can't kill me now," I said. "That would ruin everything. You'd have to dispose of my body, or try to make up some wild story about me threatening you or something. It would all fall apart eventually. And Mrs. Fulton would not be happy about that, would she."

Just saying her name, I could tell that it registered. I could see it in his eyes.

"And why are you no threat to me?" he said.

"Because I can't touch you," I said. "You didn't kill anybody. What am I going to say, arrest Lane Uttley because I think he made Julius do it? And by the way, Edwin isn't even dead? It was all a plot and Mrs. Fulton is behind it, too? How far am I going to get with that?"

I watched him as he thought it over.

"I'm not here to stop you," I said. "There's no tape recorder, no police outside waiting to break the door down. I'm not going to stand in your way."

"Then what do you want?"

"I want you to tell me why you did this," I said. "That's all. Why did you put me through all this?" I watched him shift the gun in his hand. I knew the man wanted to tell me how it happened. Above everything else, in his heart the man would always be a lawyer. And lawyers have to talk. Especially about how smart they are.

"Because you were the right man for the job," he said. "But you have to understand. It wasn't my idea."

"Tell me how it worked," I said. "Tell me from the beginning. You owe me that much."

"It all starts with Edwin's gambling problem," he said. "That much you probably know. What you don't know is how *big* his problem is. He was into those guys for a good half a million."

"That's not that much," I said. "Not for a Fulton."

"That was just the current total," he said. "He had lots of other big debts in the past. He paid them all. He was draining money out of the Fulton Foundation. His mother found out. She threatened to cut him off if he didn't stop gambling. He tried to stop, but he couldn't. She put the squeeze on him, cut off a lot of the money. He fell behind on the debt, started betting even more, trying to win it back. The bookmakers, they started to lean on him a little bit. They wanted their juice every week, just maintenance on the debt. They're all connected, of course. It's all one big network."

"Of course," I said. "So why kill two bookmakers? They're just the frontmen. The debt would just get picked up by someone else."

"That's what I tried to tell Mrs. Fulton. I told her it would be like that Hydra monster, you know, the one that Hercules had to kill? You cut off one head and two more grow back? But she was adamant. I think part of it was she didn't want to pay those guys any more money. They were calling the house, making threats. They found out her private number and starting calling *her*. I think that's what did it. She wanted them dead. And Mrs. Fulton gets what she wants."

"So hire a hit man," I said. "Like any other rich person would."

"No. She didn't want that. She said if we hired somebody, then *that* person would have an angle on her. He'd blackmail her. That's the way she saw people. Everyone wanted a piece of her. All the things she's been through, who can blame her? So she wanted a way to get rid of the bookmakers. Get Edwin away from gambling, if that was possible. And she wanted it to be clean. No loose ends."

"Did Edwin know about all this?"

"Not at first," he said. "She left it up to me. I had Prudell working for me, and he had this other guy, Raymond Julius. This guy was psychotic. He came to me a few times on the side, told me he wanted to be my private investigator. Said he'd do a lot better job than Prudell. Said he'd be willing to do *anything* that had to be done.

That got me thinking. So I started asking him questions. What kind of things would you do? Would you do the tough things? The real dirty work? He said the dirtier the better. He told me about all these guns he had, all of them unlicensed. I asked him why he didn't have permits, and he just started going off on the fed, the international plot to make a one-world government and to take everyone's guns away, you know, all the psycho gun-nut conspiracy horseshit. So I tried leading him on a little bit, just to see how he would react. I told him I might be involved with an underground movement that was trying to fight the international conspiracy, and that we might need someone to do some important secret work for us."

"You've got to be kidding me," I said.

"I know it all sounds crazy. But this guy ate it up. I told Mrs. Fulton about this. That it might be a possible avenue to explore. She jumped all over the idea. She wanted it done as soon as possible. Have Julius kill the two bookmakers, then have someone kill Julius. Problem was, she wanted *me* to kill Julius. But I just . . . I couldn't do it. So she said, have Prudell do it. But do it carefully, with no loose ends. Don't let Prudell know what's happening. Make it look like Julius is coming after him or something, so he *has* to kill him. But that was no good, either. I wouldn't trust Prudell to kill a gopher with a shovel."

"So that's where I come in?"

"Mrs. Fulton knew about you. Edwin was always talking about you. She wanted details, so I told her everything I knew. You being a policeman, getting shot. She was particularly interested in that part. She wanted to know how it happened. She wanted me to find the news clippings. So I did. She read them all, and she told me that you would be perfect because you knew what fear felt like. That was the one thing you can always count on, she said. She knew from her own experience. The fear never leaves you."

"So you did have this planned out from the beginning," I said. "Before you even hired me. Before you even asked me if I wanted to become a private investigator."

"Yes," he said. He must have sensed the anger in my voice. He jiggled the gun in his hand as if to remind me that it was still pointed at me. "But remember, none of this was my idea."

"That's right," I said. "You were just the helpless pawn in this game. So what happens next? You get Julius to kill Tony Bing and I get to come see it? What was that for?"

"Mrs. Fulton insisted on that. She said you needed to see it. Your fear needed to be fed. She has this really strange fascination with fear, Alex. I'm sure you've noticed it."

"We had a nice conversation about fear, yes."

"I told Julius that Bing's bookmaking operation was just a small part of the network. The Mafia, the federal government, the European Common Market, it was all tied together. And even though Tony Bing didn't seem like much in the big picture, we had to start somewhere. You know, everyone fights their battles where they can find them, all over the country. Send a message to the network. I told him we needed to make it dramatic. Lots of blood. Something that they would never forget. Of course, that was really for you, Alex. All that blood."

"So how did Edwin figure into all this?"

"Edwin was supposed to see Bing that night. The five grand he had, that was just the weekly juice to keep him off his back. He went to the motel and then he called you. Simple as that."

"So he knew what was going on."

"He knew that you were going to help him solve his problem, that's all. And that nothing would happen to you, in the end. I don't know if he really knew about the disappearance idea yet. I think he honestly believed that killing the two bookmakers would solve his problem. Or if he didn't know, at least he was trying to make himself believe it."

"And then Julius kills the other bookmaker a couple days later."

"He did. And I gotta tell you, this guy really got into it. I was worried he'd start killing people on his own, just because he loved it so much."

"The voice on the phone," I said. "That was you?"

"Yes," he said. "Nobody can recognize a whisper." He dropped into a low raspy growl, the same sound I had heard on the phone. "Alex, do you know who this is?"

"And you wrote the notes," I said.

"Naturally," he said. "I used an old typewriter I found at a yard sale. Wrote the notes on them, and the diary. I had a key to Julius's apartment. I told him it was all part of being in the underground. I needed access to his house in case he was captured."

"So the two bookmakers are dead," I said. "And of course that doesn't solve your problem."

"Of course not," he said. "Just like I told her. There were other men ready to pick up the debt. And they were even worse. Dorney's body wasn't even cold yet, they were already calling Edwin. So I'm thinking this has all been a waste of time so far. But Mrs. Fulton was *happy*. I swear to God, that woman was reborn all of a sudden. And then I figured it out. That whole thing with the kidnapping, when she was a girl, this was like her way of working that out. The fear of bad men or just men in general, whatever. That's why she had to be here. It wasn't just because she's a control freak, she had to be here so she could be close to it. She wanted to be close to *you*, Alex. She wanted you right in the house. Originally, we were going to have Julius come to the house so you could kill him there."

"But then the police got in the way, right?"

"Yes. We didn't figure on them making you stay at your cabin with a cop waiting outside. And then later, when Maven thought you might be involved in the killings, we *really* didn't want that to happen. You've got to believe me on that one, Alex."

"Your concern for me is downright touching."

"No, really. It didn't do *anybody* any good. I was starting to lose my mind there for a couple days. I've got Julius calling me up every hour, wanting to know who he can kill next. I've got Mrs. Fulton calling me up, wanting to know when we can get Edwin out of town and then get Julius killed. And Edwin, he wasn't too happy about his little disappearing act. He tried to back out of it. If his mother hadn't been here to keep him in line, I don't think we would have pulled it off."

"I suppose he's very far away from here by now," I said.

"I don't even know where he is," he said. "It's like in that witness relocation program. You get a new identity. Plastic surgery, maybe. All it takes is a lot of money. Mrs. Fulton said it felt good to be able to disinherit him without even having to die."

"So with Edwin gone and the cop not outside my door every night anymore, you finally had your chance to end it, right? What did you do, tell Julius that I was part of the conspiracy, too?"

"Yes," he said. "Although this time, all we wanted to do was scare you. I told him to take the silencer off, make a lot of noise, really shake you up. You see, I had found out that you were actually spying on me. And on Julius, as well. We had to scare you so it would get back to Brussels."

"Brussels?" I said. "In Belgium?"

"Yeah, that's where the headquarters is. Didn't you know that? Ask any gun nut. The international conspiracy all reports to the secret main office in Brussels."

"I didn't know that," I said. "I just thought they made waffles."

"Some of the stuff these guys believe, I tell ya, it's amazing. Anyway, I told him I had a plan for how we could really scare you. All he had to do was put on a blond wig and pretend he was some guy named Rose who shot you before. Somebody who should still be in prison."

"And how did you make him believe my gun wasn't real?"

"That was easy. You've been afraid of guns ever since you got shot. You can't even touch one anymore. Which really got him going, you being one of the people who want to take his guns away, and you're not man enough to even touch one yourself. So you carry a fake, just in case you have to bluff somebody."

I almost laughed. "You set him up. He didn't have a chance."

"I guess not," he said. "It all worked out like I had planned. I mean, just like Mrs. Fulton had planned. It was self-defense. You're home free. No loose ends."

"And you were right behind him," I said. "You proba- bly went right to his house, planted the typewriter and the news clippings and the fake diary you wrote with that whole story about him stalking me and becoming Rose somehow. And then you followed him to my cabin. As soon as it was over, you showed up. With your gun. And if things hadn't gone right, you would have had to use that gun, am I right?"

He looked away for an instant and then back at me. "Mrs. Fulton told me I would have to kill somebody if it didn't work out right. If he accidentally killed you, I would have had to kill him. And if you were both alive, then I would have had to kill him and maybe you, too, depend- ing on how it happened. I was trying to think of a way I could just kill him, Alex. You know, drive up, shoot him right away, like I thought you were in danger. I didn't want to kill you. I *know* I wouldn't have done it. You have to believe that."

I sat there thinking about it. There was a long silence. His gun was still aimed at my chest. There was a sudden pop from the fireplace.

Finally, Uttley cleared his throat. "How did you figure it out?"

"The diary," I said. "It was all wrong. This guy is supposed to be *obsessed* with me. You'd think he'd be writing pages about me every day. And if he really contacted Rose, there would be lots of details about that. When and where and how. You glossed right over that. But I guess that makes sense. You knew they could check it. They'd find out that he never really talked to him. But so what? They'd just figure he made it up. I was starting to think that myself. Even though there was stuff in those notes that only Rose and I knew. Or so I thought. When I saw him today, he started talking about how he said some things he shouldn't have. I thought he was just talking about me and Franklin. But now I'm thinking, he must have said some of the same damned things to his defense attorney. I'm sure you had no problem finding out who that was. And I'm sure you had no problem finding him and pretending to be someone else and making up some story about why you wanted to know what he said. What was it? Were you a journalist? Another defense attorney working on a similar case?"

"You're close," he said. "I was an editor for one of the law reviews. All I had to do was get him talking. You know how lawyers are."

"And of course the fact that you didn't say anything on the telephone that one night. You knew it was being recorded. And that business in the note about knowing the policeman was there. It all makes sense now when I look back on it."

"I suppose it does," he said.

"And when I was out looking for Edwin," I said. "You insisted on helping me, remember? When I was ready to quit, you made me keep driving. I didn't realize it at the time, but you were leading me right to that boat. You knew that somebody had to find it before the rain washed his blood away. What did he have to do, anyway? Cut his finger?"

"No, he had a whole pint of it in a bag. Rich people like to store up their own blood, you know, in case they ever need a transfusion. They don't like to use common blood."

"So what's in this for you, Uttley? Why did you do all this? No, let me guess. You'll be working down in Grosse Point now, right? Some nice job at the Fulton Foundation?"

"Something like that," he said. "No more chasing ambulances in this charming little frozen wasteland."

"And I get to live with all these wonderful memories, right? Two weeks of terror and then I kill somebody?"

"You get more than that, Alex. You do deserve some compensation, after all."

"What, are you going to pay me?"

"No," he said. "You get Sylvia."

"What are you talking about?"

"Come on, Alex. We all know what was going on. Just think, now she's not married anymore. Edwin is dead. She's all yours."

"I suppose you're right," I said. "All right, then. I guess I'll let you finish your packing." I stood up. The gun barrel followed. "I wish you'd put that gun away. It's starting to get on my nerves."

"You're just going to walk out?"

"What else can I do? Like I said, I can't touch you. I know what happened, but I can't prove any of it. So I might as well just leave."

He seemed at a loss for words. I guess there's a first time for everything. "Okay then," he finally said. "I guess this is good-bye."

"No, not really," I said. "You'll be seeing me again."

"That's not a good idea," he said. "As you can see, Mrs. Fulton has a way of making things happen. If she found out that you knew any of this, she would start thinking of you as another loose end. And you know how much she hates loose ends."

"Yes," I said. "Which is exactly why you can never tell her about our little chat here. Because then *you'd* be a loose end, too. In fact, I'm not so sure you aren't already." I let him think about that one for a while. "In the meantime, I'm going to just sit back and wait a while. See how I feel about what's happened to me. Maybe I'll just let it go. Or maybe I'll get more and more upset. Maybe I'll get so upset I have to come find you one day. No matter what the cost, no matter what Mrs. Fulton can do to me. Maybe one day you'll open your front door and I'll be standing there."

He leveled the gun at me.

"You know what it feels like when somebody shoots you, Lane? When a piece of metal tears right through your body? It's nothing like what you'd imagine. It doesn't even hurt that much at first. If I were to shoot you the same way that Rose shot me, you'd be lying there on the ground, wondering what had happened."

He was holding the gun with both hands.

"Until you saw your own blood," I said. "Then you'd know."

His hands were shaking.

I walked out of the room. "Good-bye, Lane," I said as I left. "Have a nice vacation."

I DROVE BACK to my cabin. I found the bottle in the back of the medicine cabinet. I emptied all the pills into the toilet and then I flushed it.

The fear was gone. I had finally gotten rid of it. Not by destroying it, but by giving it away to someone else.

I splashed cold water on my face and looked in the mirror. What do I do now?

Maybe I should go back to Sylvia. Tonight. Right now. See if maybe we *can* start over, after all. But I won't tell her what happened. Let her keep believing that Edwin is dead.

Or hell, maybe I'll tell her everything. Edwin is still alive somewhere. They played us both for fools. What would that do to her? Maybe we'd *both* go after them. Sylvia Fulton hot on your trail. Talk about fear.

I didn't know what to do. I looked at my watch. It was just past midnight. I still had time to stop in at the Glasgow. See if the regular gang was there, see if they still knew how to play poker. Have a couple cold Canadians, think about it. There's no rush, after all. It's going to be a long winter.

If you're really a private investigator, I said to the mirror, then you should be able to find them. Let Edwin think he really has made a new life for himself, wherever he is. Let Mrs. Fulton think she won her little game. Let Uttley have a long winter of restless nights. Let him dream about blood.

And then in the springtime, when the world is new again and the hunters start coming back to the cabins, that's when you'll start tracking them down one by one.

Mark it on the calendar, right next to the hunting seasons for rabbit and pheasant and grouse. Make a new category for rich people and their lawyers, with a bag limit of three.

Two minutes. That's how long it took me to realize I had
made a big mistake.

The blue team was good. They were big. They were
fast. They knew how to play hockey. From the moment
the puck was dropped to the ice, they controlled the
game. They moved the puck back and forth between
them like a pinball, across the blue line, into the corner,
back to the point. Once they were in the zone they settled
down, took their time with it, waited for the best opportu-
nity. They were like five sharks circling their prey. When
the shot came it was nothing more than a dark blur. The
center moved across the center of the goal mouth,
untouched, taking the puck and with one smooth motion
turning it home with a sudden flick of the wrist. It hit the
back of the net before the goalie even knew it was coming. Right between his legs. Or as they say on television,
right through the five hole.

It was going to be a long night for the goalie on the red
team. Which I wouldn't have minded so much if that
goalie hadn't been a certain 48-year-old idiot who let
himself get talked into it.

"It's a thirty and over league," Vinnie had said.
"Every Thursday night. No checking, no slapshots. They

call it 'slow puck.' You know, like 'slow pitch' softball? 'Slow puck' hockey, you get it?"

"I get it," I said.

"It's a lot of fun, Alex. You'll love it." Vinnie was my Indian friend. Vinnie LeBlanc, an Ojibway, a member of the Bay Mills tribe, with a little bit of French Canadian in him, a little bit of Italian, a little bit of God knows what else, like most of the Indians around here. You couldn't see much Indian blood in him, just a little in the face, around the eyes and cheekbones. He didn't have that Indian air about him, that slow and careful way of speaking. He looked you right in the eye when he spoke to you, unlike most of his tribe members who still think it's rude to do that.

Vinnie was a walking contradiction. He was an Ojibway and proud of it. But he didn't live on the reservation anymore. He didn't insist that you call him a Native American. He never drank. Not one drop, ever. He could put on a suit and pass for a downstate businessman. Or he could track a deer through the woods like he knew the inside of that animal's mind.

He had found me at the Glasgow Inn, sitting by the fireplace. I should have known something was up when he bought me a beer.

"I don't think so, Vinnie. I haven't been on skates in thirty years."

"How much you gotta skate?" he said. "You'll be in goal. C'mon, Alex, we really need ya."

"What happened to your regular goalie?"

"Ah, he has to give it a rest for a couple weeks," Vinnie said. "He sort of took one in the neck."

"I thought you said it was slow puck!"

"It was a fluke thing, Alex. It caught him right under the mask."

"Forget it, Vinnie. I'm not playing goalie."

"You were a catcher, right?" he said. "In double-A?"

"I played one year in triple-A," I said. "But so what?"

"It's the same thing. You wear pads. You wear a mask. You just catch a puck instead of a baseball."

"It's not the same thing."

"Alex, the Red Sky Raiders need you. You can't let us down."

I almost spit out my beer. "Red Sky Raiders? Are you kidding me?"

"It's a great name," he said.

"Sounds like a kamikaze squadron."

Red Sky was Vinnie's Ojibway nickname. During hunting season, he did a lot of guide work, taking downstaters into the woods. He liked to use his nickname then, playing up the Indian thing. After all, he once told me, who are you going to hire to be your guide, a guy named Red Sky or a guy named Vinnie?

"Alex, Alex." He shook his head and looked into the fire.

Here it comes, I thought.

"It's just a fun little hockey league. Something to look forward to on a Thursday night. You know, instead of sitting around looking at the snow and going fucking insane."

"I thought you Indians were at peace with the seasons."

He gave me a look. "I got eight guys on my team. They're going to be very disappointed. We'll have to forfeit the game. All because a former professional athlete is afraid to put on some pads and play goal for us. You gonna just sit here on your butt all winter? Don't you ever get the urge to do anything, Alex? To actually use your body again?"

"You're breaking my heart, Vinnie. You really are."

"You can use Bradley's stuff. It's all new. Mask, blocker, glove, skates. What size do you wear?"

"Eleven," I said.

"Perfect."

I didn't have much chance after that. Vinnie had been there when I needed him, taking care of the cabins while I was out making a fool of myself pretending to be a private investigator. So I certainly owed him one. And he was right, I was tired of sitting around all winter. How bad could it be, right? Put on the pads and the mask, play some goal. It might even be fun.

It was fun all right. The referee took the puck out of my goal and skated it back to center ice for another face off. I barely had time to take a drink of water from my bottle when they were back in my zone again, moving the puck back and forth, looking for another shot. The blue center was skating around in front of my goal like he owned it. I had to keep peeking around him to follow the puck.

"Get this guy out of here," I said to anyone who would hear me. "Don't let him just stand here."

A long shot came from the blue line. I knocked the puck down, but before I could dive on it, the blue center knocked it into the net. Three minutes into the game, and I had given up two goals. The center did a little dance, waved his stick in the air, his teammates jumping all over him like they just won the Stanley Cup.

Vinnie skated by. "Hang in there, Alex," he said. "We'll try to give you a little more help."

I grabbed the front of his red jersey. "Vinnie, for God's sake, will you hit that guy or something? He's camped out right in front of me."

"There's no checking, remember? Alex, we're just playing for fun here."

"I'm not having any fun," I said. "You don't have to take his head off, just . . . . give him a little bump."

The blue center was skating around in wide circles

now, bobbing his head. He was chanting to himself, something like "Oh yeah baby oh yeah oh yeah oh baby oh yeah."

I knew the type. It doesn't matter what sport you play, you always run into guys like this. In baseball, it was usually a first baseman or an outfielder. They came up to the plate with that swagger in their step. I'd ask them how they're doing as they're digging in, just because that's what you do in baseball, but they'd ignore me. First pitch is a strike, they look back at the umpire with that look. How dare you call a strike on me. I'd throw the ball back to the pitcher and then give him the sign for a high hard one. Guys like that need the fear of God put in them every once in a while, something to remind them that they're human just like the rest of us. If not a bolt of lightning then at least a good 90-mile-per-hour fastball under their chin.

It was reassuring to see that hockey players had to deal with these guys, too. Vinnie smiled at me, took off a glove and adjusted his helmet strap. "Maybe just one little bump," he said.

I knew they played three ten-minute periods in this league, a concession to age and to the fact that most teams only had nine or ten players. So I only had 27 more minutes to go. I slapped my stick on the ice. Go Red Sky Raiders.

Vinnie's men finally woke up and started playing some hockey. While the puck was in the opposite zone, I stood all alone in front of my goal, looking around at the Big Bear Arena. It was brand new, built by the Sault tribe with money from the casino. There was a second rink on the other side, locker rooms in the middle, a restaurant on the upper deck. The stands were mostly empty, just some women watching us. None of them looked like they were on our side. I pulled the mask away from my face, wiped away the sweat. The catcher's gear I wore a million years ago, the chest protector and the shin pads, that was nothing compared to these goalie pads. It felt like I had a mattress tied to each leg.

The game started to get a little "chippy," as the hockey announcers like to say. The elbows were coming up in the corners, the sticks were hitting other sticks, maybe even a leg or two. There was only one referee, a little old guy skating around with a whistle in his hand, never daring to blow it. He was probably retired from a civil service job, never got in anybody's way his whole life and wasn't going to start now.

I finally stopped a couple shots. It wasn't like catching a baseball at all, I realized. A pitch in the dirt, you become a human wall. The glove goes down between your legs. You don't even try to catch it. You let it bounce off you, you throw the mask off, and then you pick it up. A hockey goalie can be more aggressive, move out of the net, cut off the angle.

"Att'sa way, Alex," Vinnie said. He was breathing hard. He bounced his stick off my pads. "Now you're getting it."

Towards the end of the first period, there was a loose puck in front of the net. I dove on it. The blue center came at me hard, stopping right in front of me. He cut his skates into the ice, sending a full spray right into my face. The old shower trick. I had seen it on television a thousand times, now I got to experience it in person.

As I got up I stuck my stick into the hollow behind his knee. He turned around and cross-checked me. Two hands on his stick and wham, right across my shoulders.

I looked into his eyes. A cold blue. Pupils dilated, as wide as pennies. My God, I thought, this guy is either stone crazy or high. Or both.

The referee skated between us. "Easy does it, boys," he said. "None of that."

"Hey ref," I said. "That metal thing in your hand, when you blow in it, it makes the little pea vibrate and a loud sound comes out. You should try it. And then you can send this clown to the penalty box for two minutes."

"Let's just play some hockey, boys," he said, skating off with the puck.

The center kept looking at me. Those crazy eyes. I took my mask off. "You got a problem?"

He smiled when he saw my face. "Sorry, didn't realize you were an old man. I'll try to take it easy on you."

When the first period was over, we all got to sit on the bench and wipe our faces off for a few minutes. Nobody said anything. We could hear the other team on their bench, laughing, yelling at each other. Just a little too loud, I thought. A little too happy. Then they started making these noises. It sounded like . . . That stupid chant you hear them do down in Atlanta at the Braves' games. The Indian war chant.

Vinnie stood up and looked at them over the glass partition. Then he looked at us. Eight faces, all Bay Mills Ojibway. And one old white man. Nobody said a word. They didn't have to.

Here it comes, I thought. I've seen this look before. I've never met an Ojibway who wasn't a gentle person at heart, who didn't have a fuse about three miles long. But when you finally gave that fuse enough time to burn, watch out. You see it in the casinos every couple months. Some drunken white man makes a scene, starts yelling at the pit boss about how the no-good Indian dealer is cheating him. Doesn't even realize that the pit boss is a member of the tribe himself. If he pushes it far enough he goes right through a window.

I felt a little looser in the second half, watching my

Red Sky Raiders take it to the blue team. Vinnie was right about one thing—it felt good to use my body again. For something other than cutting wood or shoveling snow, anyway. If this was a mistake, it certainly wasn't a big one. It wouldn't rank up there with the other major mistakes of my life. Like getting married when I was twenty-three years old, just out of baseball, not sure what I was going to do with my life. Not a good reason to get married.

Or letting myself get talked into becoming a private eye. And everything that happened after that.

Or Sylvia. Letting myself fall in love with her. Yes, I'll say it. The puck is in the other end. I'm skating back and forth in front of my net, wondering why I'm thinking of these things. But yes, I'll say it. I loved her. "I've been hiding up here," she told me. "I've been hiding from the world. I think you are, too, whether you admit it or not." And then she left. Just like that. "I hope I've touched your life." The last thing she said to me. What a melodramatic college-girl thing to say. I hope I've touched your life.

Yeah, Sylvia. You touched my life. You touched my life the same way a tornado touches a trailer park.

The puck coming this way. The blue center behind it. The sound of his skates in the empty arena. Snick snick snick snick.

Funny how things come into your mind at a time like this. It used to happen in baseball. I'd be settling under a pop fly and I'd think of something else in my life with a sudden clarity like it was the first time I'd ever thought of it.

Like my biggest mistake of all. Rose's apartment in Detroit. Aluminum foil on the walls. My partner and I frozen with fear, watching the gun in his hand.

Snick snick snick snick.

Sylvia. I am in her bed and she is looking down at me. We have just finished making love in the bed she shares every night with her husband. He is my friend, but I don't care. She owns me.

The skater is fast. He is the best player I will ever play against. He looks up at me. A peek over his shoulder. The other players are far behind. Time slows down. It's something every athlete knows, an unspoken understanding between us. It's just him and me.

I didn't pull my gun in time. I waited too long. I am shot and my partner is shot and we are both on the ground. There is so much blood. It all comes back to me. Not as urgently as it once did. I don't dream about it much anymore. I don't need the pills to make it through the nights. But it still comes back. I am lying on the floor and my partner is next to me.

I come out of the net to cut off the angle. He shoots. No! It's a fake. He pulls the puck back. I can feel myself falling backwards. He's going to skate right around me and slip the puck into the open net. Unless I can knock the puck away. My only chance. I jab at it with my stick as I fall.

I hit the puck and my stick goes between his legs. He trips and slides face first into the boards. Then he is up, his gloves thrown to the ice. I take my gloves off, my mask. He throws a punch at me and misses. I grab him by the jersey and we dance the hockey fight dance. You can't find any leverage to throw a good punch when you're on skates. You just hold on and try to pull the other guy's shirt over his head. It's a funny thing to watch when you're not one of the guys dancing.

The man's eyes were wide with bloodlust and whatever the hell chemicals he was flying on. "Take it easy," I said. "I'm sorry."

"The fuck you're sorry," he said. Spit and sweat hitting

me in the face. All around us the other players in the same dance, every man picking his own partner according to how much they really felt like fighting. The old referee was skating around us, blowing his whistle. I guess he finally remembered how it works.

"I didn't mean to trip you," I said. "Just calm down."

"Fucking Indians," he said.

"I'm not an Indian," I said.

"Yeah, fuck that," he said. "I know, you're a Native fucking American."

I started laughing. I couldn't help it.

"What's so funny?" he said "Did I say something funny?"

"You always get high when you play hockey?" I said.

"The fuck you talking about."

"You're higher than the space shuttle," I said. "If I were still a cop I'd have to arrest you. Skating while impaired."

He gave me a good push and skated away. The dance was over. "Fucking Indians," he said.

We finished the game. Vinnie scored once in that period. Another of his teammates scored in the third period to tie the game at 2-2. I made a couple nice saves to keep us tied.

In the last minute of the game, my new friend the blue center had an open shot at me. He wound up and launched a rocket. No slapshots, my ass. I got a glove on it, knocked it just high enough to hit the crossbar with a loud ringing sound that reverberated through the entire arena.

The game ended. There would be no overtime. The next game was ready to start, as soon as they got us out of there and gave the Zamboni a chance to take a quick run over the ice.

He stared at me, breathing hard.

I look back on that moment now, the two of us looking at each other on the ice. I wonder what I would have done if I had known what would happen in the next few days. I probably would have hit him in the face with my hockey stick. Or broken off the end and jabbed him in the neck. But of course, I had no way of knowing. At that moment, he was just another hotshot asshole hockey player, and I was the old man who just took away his third goal.

"No hat trick today," I said to him. "Looks like the Cowboys and Indians have to settle for a tie."

THE NIGHT WAS cold. It had to be below zero. My wet hair froze to my head the moment I stepped outside. Across the street the Kewadin Casino was shining proudly. It was a big building and it was decorated with giant triangles that were supposed to remind you of Indian teepees. It was almost midnight on a frozen Thursday night but I could see that the parking lot was full.

The Antlers was not far away, just over on the east side of Sault Ste. Marie, overlooking the St. Mary's River. As soon as you walk in the place, you see deer heads and bear heads and stuffed coyotes, birds, just about any animal you can think of. I usually don't spend much time there, but Vinnie was buying that night so what the hell. It was the least I could do, even if it *was* American beer.

"Here's to our new goalie," he said, raising a glass of Pepsi. We had pushed a couple tables together in the back of the place. His eight teammates were all there, all quietly working on their second beers.

"Stop right there," I said. "You said this was a one-night gig, remember?"

"Yeah, but you were great, Alex. You gotta keep playing. Do you realize that those guys had a perfect record before tonight? We just tied them!"

If his teammates shared his enthusiasm, they didn't show it. I looked at each of them, one by one. A couple you'd know were Indians the moment you saw them. The rest were like Vinnie—a lot of mixed blood. Maybe you'd see it in the cheekbones. Or the dark, careful eyes.

They were all drinking. Most if not all would get drunk that night. More than one would get to a state well past drunk. I knew it bothered Vinnie. "I feel guilty sometimes," he once told me, "living off the reservation. A lot of my tribe, they think I abandoned them. When I was growing up, I could go down the street and walk in any house I wanted to. Just walk right in. Open the refrigerator, make a sandwich. Go turn the TV on. Everybody was my family. I really miss that, Alex. But I just couldn't take it anymore. It was too much, you know? Too much family. And somebody always in trouble. Somebody in jail. Somebody passed out drunk. I just had to get out of there."

He lives in Paradise, right down the road from me. He's my closest neighbor, maybe my closest friend next to Jackie. He deals blackjack at the Bay Mills Casino when he isn't doint his Red Sky hunting guide thing. "You know the difference between a Indian blackjack dealer and a white blackjack dealer?" he once asked me. "This is going to sound like a stereotype, but it's true. The white blackjack dealer never gambles. Those guys in Vegas? They see a thousand people playing blackjack all night long, maybe fifty of them walk away big winners, right? You think those dealers are gonna cash their paychecks and play blackjack with it? I've got a couple cousins who lose every dime, every week, guaranteed. They cash their check, maybe they buy some food and beer, then they go right to the casino and lose the rest of it. Every fucking week, Alex. You know what they tell me? You want to hear what they say? They tell me that there's no word in Ojibway for "savings." You know, as in life-savings. A nest egg. The only word that comes close is this negative word, you know, like hoarding. Keeping something to yourself. Which they wouldn't have even known if they hadn't taken a course in Ojibway at the Community College. But now that's supposed to convince me it's okay to always be broke. It's like they're saying that they're real Ojibway and I'm not. I'm just tired of it."

Vinnie sat at the table, staring at a moose head on the wall. Nobody said anything. Just a quiet frozen winter night at the Antlers.

Until the blue team showed up.

They busted into the place with a lot of noise and a gust of arctic air that rattled the glasses on our table. "Goddamn," one of them said, "will ya look at this place?"

They pushed a few tables together at the other end of the room. There were nine men and nine women. Most of them had leather bomber jackets on. Even with the fur collars, they couldn't be warm enough.

My new buddy the center went up to the bar, told the man to start the pitchers coming. He had one of those hockey haircuts, cut close on the sides and long in the back.

"So who the hell is that guy?" I finally said.

"Who, the center?"

"Yeah, Mister Personality."

"That's Lonnie Bruckman. Some piece of work, eh?"

"He always play high?"

Vinnie laughed. "You noticed, huh?"

"Hard not to."

"Guy can skate, though, can't he? I think he played for one of the farm teams somewhere. Most of those guys on his team are ringers. Old teammates from Canada. He brings in a new guy every week."

Bruckman took a couple pitchers back to the tables. When he came back for more, he spotted us. Our lucky night.

"Hey, it's the Indians!" he said. As he came and stood over us, I got a good look at him without the hockey gear on. Whatever he was on, he had just taken another dip, probably in the car on the way over here. Coke or speed, maybe both. "Nice game, boys," he said. "Can I bring a couple pitchers over?"

Nobody said anything.

He looked at Vinnie's glass. "What ya got there, LeBlanc? Rum and coke? Lemme buy you one."

"It's just Pepsi," Vinnie said.

"You're kidding me," Bruckman said. "An Indian that doesn't drink?"

He laughed like it was the funniest thing he'd heard in two weeks.

"We're all set here," Vinnie said. "Thanks just the same."

"Hey old man," he said to me, "that was a nice save you made on me. You took away my hat trick, you know that?"

"Yeah, I know," I said. "Sorry about that."

"I'll get you next time."

"Won't be a next time," I said. "I was just filling in tonight."

"You gotta play again," he said. "You're good. Believe me, I know. I played in the Juniors, on the Soo Canada team for a couple years, same team Gretzky played on before he went up. I would'a gone up myself if I wasn't an American."

Here it comes, I thought. There's always an excuse. All the guys I played ball with, and most of them never went to the major leagues, of course. Maybe one in a hundred guys who starts out in the rookie leagues ever makes it. The other ninety-nine, they all have a story. Coach never gave me a chance. Hurt my knee. Didn't get enough at-bats. It's never just, "I just wasn't quite good enough."

This American thing, though, that was a new one, because of course you're only going to hear that one from a hockey player. I should have let it go. Just nodded at the guy, smiled, let him stand there making a jackass of himself, laughed at him later. But I couldn't help it.

"That's a shame," I said. "They should really let Americans play in the NHL. It's just not fair. Ain't that right, Vinnie?"

"It's gotta be a conspiracy," Vinnie said.

"How many Americans are there?" I said. "I bet we could count them on one hand. Let's see . . . John Le-Clair, Brian Leetch, Chris Chelios . . ."

"Doug Weight," Vinnie said. "Mike Modano, Tony Amonte."

"Keith Tkachuk," I said. "Pat LaFontaine, Adam Deadmarsh."

"Jeremy Roenick, Gary Suter."

"Shawn McEachern, Joel Otto."

"Bryan Berard, is he American?"

"I believe so."

"Derian Hatcher, Kevin Hatcher. Are they brothers?"

"I don't think so," I said. "But they're both American."

"Mike Richter in goal," Vinnie said.

"And John Vanbiesbrouck."

"All right already," Bruckman said. "You guys are real comedians. I didn't know Indians could be so funny."

"We forgot Brett Hull!" Vinnie said.

Bruckman grabbed Vinnie's shoulder. "I said all right already." His smile was gone.

"Get your hand off me," Vinnie said.

"You're making fun of me and I don't fucking appreciate it," he said.

"Last guy who made fun of me lost most of his teeth."

The whole place got quiet. His teammates were all looking at us, as well as the men at the bar. There were maybe a dozen of them. They had all been watching the Red Wings game on the television. The bartender had a sick look on his face. He probably had a nice streak going. Seven nights in a row without a drunken brawl.

"Bruckman," I said. I looked him in the eyes. "Walk away."

He held my eyes for a long moment. He was sizing me up, calculating his chances. I could only hope the chemicals racing around in his brain didn't make him decide something stupid, because I sure as hell didn't want to have to fight him without skates and pads on.

"You were lucky," he finally said. "I should have had the hat trick. You never even saw that puck."

"Whatever you say, Bruckman. Just walk away."

"Look at you guys," he said. "You Indians are so pathetic. I don't know why they ever let you have those casinos."

The bartender showed up with a baseball bat. "You guys gonna knock this shit off or am I going to call the police?"

"Don't bother," Bruckman said. "We're leaving. Too many drunken Indians in this place."

He gave me one last look before he went back to his table. I didn't feel like telling him I was really a white man just like him.

When they had all put their leather jackets back on, knocked over a few chairs, muttered a few more obscenities, and then left without paying for their beer, the place got quiet again. Vinnie just sat there looking at the door. His friends all sat there looking at the table or at the floor.

I tried to think of something to say to break the spell, but nothing came to me.

"You know what bothers me the most?" Vinnie finally said.

"What's that?" I said.

"Those women that were with them? One of them, I think I recognize her. I think she's somebody I grew up with. On the reservation."

Be sure to read all the books by
Les Roberts
featuring Cleveland private eye
Milan Jacovich

THE CLEVELAND CONNECTION

Who hated an old man—a veteran of World War II—enough to kill him? When an old Serbian immigrant is murdered, Milan Jacovich must follow the old blood ties that lead to a world of hidden violence, family secrets—and old hatreds that die hard.

_____ 96218-5 $5.99 U.S./ $7.99 Can.

COLLISION BEND

When a television reporter is found strangled in her own home, Milan Jacovich's ex-girlfriend asks him to clear her current love as the chief murder suspect. But as Jacovich goes behind the scenes to uncover all the scandal and intrigue of big-city television, he comes closer to making the evening news—as a murder victim.

_____ 96399-8 $5.99 U.S./$7.99 Can.

Perched at the foot of Montana's Crazy Mountains, Blue Deer is a small town boasting an uneasy mix of longtime residents and hotshots from both coasts looking to possess their own piece of the Big Sky. Local sheriff Jules Clement manages the town's tensions fairly well...until someone blasts a hole in screenwriter George Blackwater's office window — and in George himself.

As more of the town's prominent citizens start turning up dead, the pressure on Jules keeps rising. It starts to look like this rookie sheriff may not survive the next election...if he lives to see it.

THE EDGE OF THE CRAZIES

JAMIE HARRISON

THE EDGE OF THE CRAZIES
Jamie Harrison
_____ 95942-7 $5.99 U.S./$7.99 CAN.

Under a wide Montana sky he plays the fiddle and dreams of the Red River. Gabriel Du Pré is a mixed-blood French-Indian cattle-brand inspector. Sometimes he doubles as a deputy. Sometimes he even uncovers murder. Like now.

A cowboy has found the wreck of a plane that had been missing for 30 years. Du Pré sees that one of the sun-bleached skulls, the one with the bullet hole, doesn't belong. He wants to avoid the matter, but a rich man's demons, another murder, and Du Pré's own past keep pulling him back—to a truth he can bury, but cannot kill.

COYOTE
W ▲I▼N▲D

PETER BOWEN